The True
Ancient Aliens

The
True
Ancient Aliens

Finding a new Planet to Live on

Johnson D. Karam

Printed in the United States of America
ISBN 978-1-952182-16-7 (sc)
ISBN 978-1-952182-17-4 (e)

Biography

2020 | 08 | 20

Johnson Karam Books

Table of Contents

PREFACE

Some 11,000 years ago, astronauts escaping from the devastation of their world, came to planet Earth in search for survival and a better life. They all arrived in different points in the Earth, some even landing in the oceans.

The group's central command landed in Mesopotamia, particularly in one location called Assur, where eventually, their initial settlement expanded into a powerful nation.

Short on manpower, they employed genetics to fashion primitive workers—they called them homo sapiens. They also created the Great Flood, a deluge that had swept catastrophically over the entire Earth, which for them, required a fresh start. By doing these, they were perceived as gods by the real inhabitants of the planet, granted civilization and taught humankind to worship. They were called the "Gods of Heaven". People looked up to them as living in the heavens just as the Biblical God urged Abraham to do.

It was during their first Earth landing, they brought along with them the knowledge of astronomy and celestial mathematics. It is now wonder that the earliest ancient sculptures and drawings showed symbols of constellations and planets. Whenever gods were represented or invoked, their symbol was utilized as a graphic form of shorthand through its invocation of the divine. It was clear and the message was evident: man was no longer alone. These symbols connected earthlings with the astronauts, Earth with the heavens, and humankind with the universe.

What had taken place here on Earth, especially events since the beginning of human history, allowed us to learn from Biblical clay tablets, ancient myths, and archaeological discoveries.

The big question is this: what had preceded those events on Earth, and what had taken place on the astronauts' own planet, Tiamat, that precipitated the journey through space to Mother Earth; the need for a new life or a new planet in order to survive? What emotions, rivalries, beliefs, morals (or lack thereof), had motivated the principal players in this celestial space saga?

What were the relationships that caused mounting tension on their origin planet and on Earth among the old and the young, between those who had come from Tiamat and those born on this planet? And to what extent were these happenings determined by destiny—one whose recorded past events could hold a key to the future?

What if one of the major players were an eyewitness, one who could distinguish between fate and destiny and who has recorded for posterity the how and where and when and why of it all—of the first things and, perhaps, the last things?

Foremost among the key players was the very leader who had actually commanded the Biblical tales of Creation: of Adam and Eve in the Garden of Eden, of the Deluge, and of the Tower of Babel (built in Babylon), all based on texts written down a millennium earlier in Mesopotamia, especially by those who came down from the sky - the Anunnaki. He who has clearly stated that he obtained his knowledge of many past events from a time before civilizations began, even before mankind came to be—from the writings of the Anunnaki ("those who from heavens to earth came")—to the 'gods' of antiquity.

ADAM AND EVE

As the result of a century and half of archaeological discoveries in the ruins of ancient civilizations, especially in the Near East, a great number of early texts have been found. These finds have also revealed the extent of missing texts— the so-called 'lost books'—which are either mentioned in the discovered texts, which are known to have existed because they were catalogued in royal or temple libraries (but today are in the hands of Europeans, particularly in England, France, and Germany.)

Sometimes the 'secrets of the gods' were partially revealed in epic tales, such as the Epic of Gilgamesh, that disclosed the mass perishing in the Deluge, or in a text titled Atra Hasis, which speaks of mines that led to the creation of primitive workers: earthlings.

From time to time, leaders of the astronauts authored compositions themselves, sometimes dictating the text to a chosen scribe, like the Erra Epos, in which one of two blames his adversary. Sometimes the 'god' acted as his own "Thoth" (the Egyptian god of knowledge), in which case the 'god' hid secrets in a subterranean chamber.

Many other books have survived over the millennia in the Assyrian, Arameans, Slavonic, Syrian, and Ethiopian languages, as well as in others.

The readers of this book (and I hope there will be many) will not appreciate its value nor fully understand this amazing heritage, nor be proud of the glory of their ancient ancestors, or come to realize the extent of their present degradation, without at least knowing something—no matter how minimal—of the resplendent past, the stock from whom they emerged, and the land in the universe where their notable forefathers once occupied.

The past has always been fascinating, with all of its blood, vainglory, delight, honour, and splendour. Even so, sometimes there is a spirit of pride that possesses a being and carries one off to feelings of celestial bliss.

I had read so many ancient Assyrian historical books, but when I stood on the banks of the Tigris and the Euphrates rivers in 2002, right before the U.S. and Iraqi war, I found it difficult to believe that these two rivers once watered Sumaria, Akkad, and Assyria, and nourished the Hanging Gardens, was built by Assyrian King Sennacherib in nineven for his wife.

One finds it hard to believe that today's Kuyunjek (ancient Nineveh), with its palmy days under Ashurbanibal, held 400,000 people, and that all of the western Orient came to pay tribute to its great king. In fact, this capital was once the mistress of the ancient world, producing giants among pygmies, such as Shalmanezer, Tiglath-Pilezer I, Ashurbanipal II, Sargon, Sennacherib, Esarhaddn I, and many more, among them an illustrious queen - Shamiram.

Intrigued by its history, I very often feel great pride in the name "Assyria," once the most dominant nation in the East. However, I wondered where that nation actually originated from. A glance at the Assyrian nation and her history would take us back, perhaps to 5000 B.C. or even further.

More so, I have always been fascinated by the universe. In my younger years, during the summers, we slept on the roof. I used to wake up at 2:00 in the morning and stare at the heavens, the stars. Simply by looking deep into the universe, I became an eyewitness to its evolution, and though that perhaps, I would be able to reconstruct its history. Since then, I believed in the existence of life beyond the Earth. To further expand my knowledge, I read many historical and astronomical books. I studied them in detail, and I was able to come up with my own conclusion that life really did exist somewhere in the vast cosmos, millennia ago.

But astronomers seemed to believe it is unlikely to find advanced extra-terrestrial life within the confines of our solar system. Instead, they postulate that to find intelligent life, we have to look further afield, beyond the sun's vicinity.

Ever since Charles Darwin shocked the scholars and theologians of his time with the evidence of evolution, life on Earth has been traced through man and the primates, mammals, and invertebrates, and backward through ever-lower life forms to the point billions of years ago at which life is presumed to have begun. But having reached these beginnings, and having contemplated the probabilities of life beyond our galaxy, scholars have become uneasy about life on Earth somehow, as though it does not belong here.

In the North eastern part of Iraq, archaeologists have found evidence of Earthly man's remains, people who were part of the semi-arc of civilization. After an extensive research, evidence points out that human culture has shown not a progression but regression.

Starting from a particular standard, the following generations showed not more but less advanced standards of civilized life, and from about 27,000 B.C. to 11,000 B.C. the regressing and dwindling population reached the point of an almost complete absence of habitation.

For reasons assumed to have been climatic, man was almost completely gone from the entire area for some 16,000 years. Then on circa 11,000 B.C., the "thinking man" reappeared with new vigor and on an inexplicably higher cultural level.

How was it that after thousands and even millions of years of painfully slow human development, everything suddenly and abruptly changed? In a one-two-three punch, circa 11,000 B.C. to 7400 B.C. to 3600 B.C., something seems to have transformed the primitive nomadic hunter/gatherers into farmers and pottery-makers, into engineers, mathematicians, astronomers, metallurgists, merchants, musicians, authors, librarians, and builders of cities.

This question has been well-stated by historians and archaeologists. The Assyrians, the people through whom this high civilization so suddenly came into being, had a ready answer. It was summed up by one of the tens of thousands of uncovered ancient Assyrian inscriptions:

Whatever seems beautiful, we made it by the grace of the God Ashur.

It was as if an unseen coach, watching the faltering human game, dispatched to the field a fresh and better-trained team to take over from the exhausted one.

Was life, then, imported to Earth from elsewhere? We now know where civilization began and how it developed. The unanswered question is this—how did civilization come about? Most scholars admit in frustration that by all extant data, man should still be without civilization.

There is absolutely no obvious reason we should be any more civilized than the primitive tribes of the Amazon jungles or those in the inaccessible parts of New Guinea. The abrupt change in the course of human events that accrued around circa 11,000 B.C. in the Near East (and some 2,000 years later in Europe), has led scholars to describe that at that time, it signalled an end to the old stone age (the Palaeolithic) and the beginning of a new cultural era - the middle stone age (the Mesolithic).

From an overall point of view, it would be more appropriate to call that era not the middle stone age but rather the Age of Domestication. In the span of 6500 years—it simply happened overnight, compared with the endless eons of life's beginnings, that man became a farmer, and wild plants and animals were domesticated. A new age clearly has begun.

Our scholars call it the new stone age (the Neolithic) but the term is totally inadequate, for the main change that had taken place circa 7500 B.C. was the appearance of pottery.

The obvious question then is this; did we and our Mediterranean ancestors really acquire this advanced civilization on our own? Though our scholars cannot explain the appearance of Homo sapiens and the civilization of the Cro-Magnon man, there is no doubt regarding this civilization's origin: it was in the land between two rivers, Tigris and Euphrates, the land the Assyrians called Bet-Nahrain.

On the other hand, the Old Testament has filled my life and mind from childhood, when its seeds were planted nearly sixty years ago. I was totally unaware then of the raging "Evolution versus Biblical Old Testament" debates. But as a schoolboy studying Genesis in the original Assyrian language, I created quite a lot of arguments of my own. One day, while we were reading from the Bible about the time when God resolved to destroy mankind through the Great Flood, with the "the sons of deities" who married the daughters of man were upon the Earth. The Assyrian and Sumerian original name for these "the sons of deities" was "Anunnaki" (in Hebrew, the term "Nefilim"). My teacher explained that it meant "giant," but I objected. Did it not literally mean "those who were cast down" (who had descended to Earth)? I was reprimanded of course, and I was told by the teacher to believe and accept the traditional interpretation (which was always his belief and interpretation, not mine!)

Since I have learned different languages: Assyrian, Arabic, English, and Armenian, and studied history and archaeology of the ancient Near East, especially Sumeria and Assyria, the word "Anunnaki" (Hebrew term "Nefilim") became an obsession for me.

Archeological finds and the deciphering of Sumerian, Assyrian, Babylonian, Hittite, Canaanite, and other ancient texts and epic tales increasingly confirmed the accuracy of biblical references to the kingdoms, cities, palaces, temples, kings, rulers, artifacts, planets, and customs of antiquity. Is it not high time, therefore, to accept the word of these same ancients defining the "Anunnaki" as visitors to the Earth from the heavens or other planets?

The writings of the ancient Near East, which include profuse and detailed astronomical texts, clearly speak of a planet from which these astronauts or 'gods' had come from. However, when scholars 150 years ago converted these texts into intelligible form and translated the ancient lists of celestial bodies, our visitors were not yet aware of Pluto (only discovered in 1930). How then could they be expected to accept the evidence of yet one more member of our solar system?

But now that we too, like the ancients, are aware of the planets beyond Saturn, why not accept the ancient evidence of a planet call Tiamat (the "lost planet")?

As we ventured into space, a fresh look and an acceptance of the truth held in ancient scriptures is more than timely. Now that astronauts have landed on the moon and unmanned spacecraft have explored other planets, it is no longer impossible to believe that a civilization on another planet, more advanced than ours, was capable of coming and living in our planet sometime in the past.

Indeed, a number of popular writers have speculated that ancient Assyrian and Babylonian artefacts—such as the Assyrian colossal lions about 20 feet high and carved from limestone, the War Battering-Ram; the Gate of Ishtar of Babylon (one of the seven wonders of the world); the Pyramids of Egypt, the numerous giant stone sculptures, and many other memorials—must have been built and fashioned by advanced visitors from another planet. Surely primitive man could not have possessed on his own the required progressive type of engineering knowledge and technology. How was it, for example, that a civilization of Assyrians seemed to blossom so suddenly nearly 6,750 years ago, without a precursor? Most writers do not have an inkling as to where, such ancient intelligent humans have originated and these intriguing questions remained as unanswered speculations.

It has taken me many years of research—of going back and forth to the ancient sources and studying astronomical books, ancient Assyrian tablets (and accepting them literally), to re-create in my own mind a continuous and plausible scenario of prehistoric events. I now seek to provide the reader with a narrative, providing answers to the specific questions of when, how, why, and where we all come from.

The evidence I present here consists primarily of Assyrian and Sumerian ancient texts, plus my understanding of the solar system. Looking at the planet Tiamat, I have sought to decipher a sophisticated cosmogony which explains, perhaps as well as modern scientific theories do, how the solar system was formed, where the lost planet was located in our solar system, where it is now, and what happened to it after all these years. After much closer scrutiny, these invaders have journeyed through space, looking for another system to inhabit. Through this, they have catastrophically invaded our solar orbit, with Earth and other parts of the solar system being brought into existence as a result.

To answer these questions, it makes sense to start here. Humans have always looked up in wonder at the night sky -- filled with thousands of sparkling lights in countless patterns—it has been a source of inspiration and curiosity for millennia.

OUR SOLAR SYSTEM BEFORE & AFTER

Our solar system is situated in the Orion arm of a spiral galaxy known as the Milky Way. Located around 25,000-28,000 light-years from the galactic center, the solar system has been on a circular orbit around that center over a period of 220-250 million years. Our Sun and its family are heading in the direction of the constellation Hercules.

In our local neighbourhood, the solar system is embedded in a region called the Local Interstellar Cloud, itself part of a larger volume known as the Local Bubble—a 300-light year wide void in surrounding space.

So this leads us to the question: how do astronomer's define a planet? Until recently, the answer was obvious—a planet was really a large body that goes around the Sun. Most people live today have grown up with the certain knowledge that our solar system has nine planets: Mercury, Venus, Earth, Mars, Jupiter, Saturn, Uranus, Neptune, and Pluto—and generations remember their order. It was long believed that our solar system consisted of only nine planets, but we know now this was not the case 11,000 years ago.

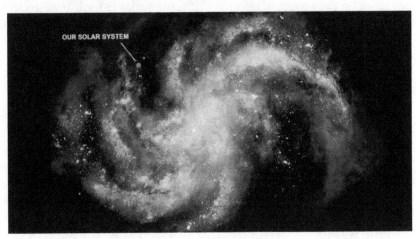

FIG 1

Let us briefly examine new theories of how the solar system was formed over millions of years. Many theories of the origin and its formation have been advanced over the years, but the one that is currently central, and which I perceive is the strongest evidence, is called the "Nebular Hypothesis." It was proposed independently by two famous scientists, Immanuel Kant and Pierre-Simon La Place. In this scenario, everything in the solar system originated in a huge interstellar cloud, or nebula, of gas, known as a molecular cloud.

This cloud is comprised of material ejected into space during the death throes of earlier generations of stars. It contains not only large amounts of hydrogen and helium, the most abundant elements in the universe, but heavier elements as well, produced by the earlier stellar generation.

Slowly, local regions within this cloud began to collapse on themselves, perhaps triggered by a shockwave from a nearby supernova (exploding star), and they began to spin as they did so. One such region was destined to become our solar system. It is referred-to as the per-solar system nebula. Gradually, as it contracted and began to spin faster, held together by its own over-all gravity and magnetic fields, it began to flatten out into a huge spinning disk of gas, thousands of times wider then our solar system is now. As it continued to contract, most of the materials gravitated (literally) into the center of the Nebula. Becoming hotter and under increasing pressure, this central portion would become the proto-sun.

FIG 2

As the rest of the material whirled around in the disk, the gas molecules combined to form particles called "dust grains." Gradually, over millions of years, the spinning disk of materials become "clumpy." Small clumps struck together to form larger clumps, and larger and still larger, until eventually some of them grew large enough to become planets.

The inner parts of the disk became too hot for ices to form. or gases to liquefy, so the only materials able to remain solid were those with points, i.e., rocky substances and metals; Consequently, the inner planets: Mercury, Venus,

Earth and its moon, and Tiamat and its moon (Mars) are rocky worlds.

Further out, the temperatures were cooler, so ices were able to form the gas planets. Jupiter and Saturn became the dominant bullies in the middle reaches of the solar system, with Uranus and Neptune further out still and somewhat smaller.

FIG 3

Jupiter's massive bulk gave it a large gravitational in hence, preventing any other rocky planet from coalescing further in toward the sun, in the region known today as the asteroid belt.

By this time, nuclear fusion had begun in the infant sun's core, and it began to release copious amounts of energy. A super-solar wind began to blow though the solar system, sweeping it clean of the remaining gases and preventing any more major planets from forming.

Although this whole scenario was worked out on a theoretical basis, it is no longer all speculation—strong evidence has been found that indicates this very process is occurring right now around many infant stars elsewhere in our galaxy.

The two scientists wrote theories about "Solar System Formation." These were written within the last 50 years. But without considering how many planets existed at the time of the solar system's creation, they are expressing only one theory of how planets are created in the universe.

In relation to all that, an Akkadian seal from the third millennium B.C., now at the Vorderasiatische Abseiling of the State Museum in East Berlin (catalogued VA/243), departs from the usual manner of depiction in showing the solar system as it was known to the Assyrians when they were on the planet Tiamat: a system consisting of eleven celestial bodies (not planets).

FIG 4

We usually show our solar system schematically as a line of planets stretching away from the sun in ever-increasing distances. But if we depicted the planets not in a line but one after the other in a circle: the closest, Mercury first, then Venus, then Earth, and so on), the result would look something like Fig. 5. (All drawings are schematic and not to scale; planetary orbits in the drawings that follow are circular rather than elliptical for ease of presentation.)

FIG 5

If we now take a second look at an enlargement of the solar system as depicted on cylinder seal VA/243, we shall see that the 'dots' encircling the stars are actually globes, whose sizes and other aspects conform to that of the solar system depicted in Figure 6 & 8: small Mercury is followed by a larger Venus, and Earth, the same size as Venus, is accompanied by a small moon orbiting Earth in a counter-clockwise direction. Mars is shown correctly as smaller than Earth but larger than Earth's moon or Mercury.

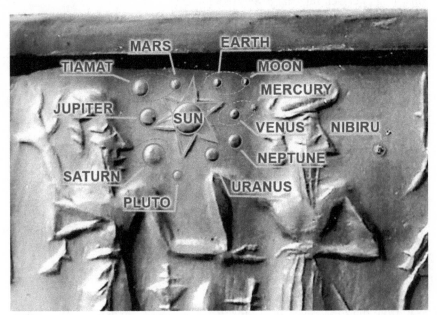

FIG 6

The ancient Assyrian depiction also shows a planet unknown to us—considerably larger than Earth, yet smaller than Jupiter and Saturn, which clearly follow it. Farther on, another pair perfectly matches our Uranus and Neptune. Finally, the smallest of them all, Pluto, is also there, but not where we put it now (after Neptune); instead, it appears between Saturn and Uranus.

The 6,500-year-old depiction, however, also insists that there was—or has been—another major planet between Mars and Jupiter. It is, as we shall show, the "lost planet," the planet of the Anunnaki. But this unknown planet as shown in Figure 7 between Mars and Jupiter, actually was called planet Tiamat by ancient Assyrians, and Mars was the moon of planet Tiamat, similar to our moon and the Earth.

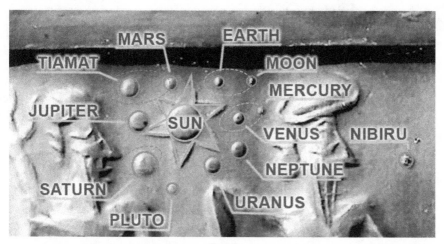

FIG 7

Mars is not much greater in size than our moon; because of its unusual characteristics, it has been suggested that this 'misfit' might have started its celestial life as a satellite that somehow escaped its master (Tiamat) and went into orbit around the sun on its own when a big calamity occurred (11,000-years ago when the planet Marduk, or Niburu, crashed into the planet Tiamat). Another fact: the ancient Assyrian cylinder pictured in Figure 4 did not show and did not mention the "asteroid belt" which now exists between the inner planets and the outer planets (see Figure 5), so at the time the seal was made by the Assyrian astronomers (Chaldean), the planet order was: Sun, Mercury, Venus, Earth and its moon, Mars, Jupiter, Saturn, Uranus, Neptune, and Pluto (see Figures 5). This is another proof that the cylinder which was made 6,500 years ago shows that ancient Assyria had complete knowledge that their ancestors had come from another planet, and this confirms the ancient familiarity with a celestial and solar system.

FIG 8

The hot topics in modem astronomy raise some even bigger questions—and indeed, they are among the biggest we can possibly ask. They are also among the most embarrassing, since astronomers have had to admit that they don't know what our solar system consists of, even after reading all of the Assyrians' historical facts about intelligent human having landing on Earth.

For a long time, it was assumed that the planet Tiamat did not exist, and astronomers around the world did not know about it, even after all of the historical proofs the ancient Assyrians and Sumerians of 6,500 years ago documented on tablets that were found in the Assurbanipal library in Nineveh 170 years ago by astronomers from various countries: Britain, France, Germany, Israel, and Iraq. The truth is that for the past 170 years, representatives of these countries, especially European museums, have been holding these valuable tablets far from the eyes of Astrologists, historians, and scholars.

I wonder why. Major damage to the Assurbanipal Library occurred in May of 612 B.C., when Medes and Babylonians laid siege to Nineveh. Three months later, the city fell. The Babylonian army consisted of thousands of Israelite prisoners of war. When they returned, the Israelite army looted the library and took thousands of tablets back to their homeland. At that time the Jewish people used to speak and read the Assyrian language and were familiar with Assyrian cuneiform inscriptions.

Nebuchadnezzar, the Babylonian king, defeated the Israelites at Carchemish in 605 BC, after which Judea became a vassal state of Babylon. Nebuchadnezzar crushed a revolt in 597, and deported many Jews (also called "Judeans" or "Israelites") to Babylonia.

A second revolt later resulted in the sack of Jerusalem and the removal of its entire population to Babylonia, where they stayed until a time when the Persians let them return to Judea (Israel). During their return to the land of Israel, the Israelite army looted the royal libraries of Sennacherib and Assurbanipal. This was their second looting, and because they knew exactly what valuable historical information the Assyrians had documented on their tablets, they took more than 1,000 tablets away with them.

Some Jewish scholars subsequently started to rewrite the Old Testament, altering the meticulously documented past history for their present benefit. In doing so, they cast the Jewish people as "God's People." It is the handiwork of these revisionist scribes that has influenced the world to view Assyria with hatred.

The Assyrian empires, particularly the third one, had a profound and lasting impact on the Near East. Before Assyrian hegemony would come to an end, the Assyrians would bring the highest civilization to the then-known world.

From the Caspian to Cyprus, and from Anatolia to Egypt, Assyrian imperial expansion would bring nomadic and barbaric communities into the Assyrian sphere, and would bestow the gift of civilization upon them.

Fig 9

Although today we are far removed from that time, some of our most basic and fundamental devices of daily survival, to which we have become so accustomed that we cannot conceive of life without then1, were originated in Assyria.

One cannot imagine leaving his home without locking the door; it is in Assyria were locks and keys were first used. One cannot survive in this world without knowing the time; it is in Assyria that the sexagesimal system (based on the number "60") of keeping time was developed. One cannot imagine driving without paved roads; it is in Assyria where paved roads were first used. And the list goes on, including the first postal system, the first use of iron, the first magnifying glasses, the first libraries, the first plumbing and flush toilets, the first electric batteries, the first guitars, the first aqueducts, the first arch, and on and on.

But it is not only things that originated from Assyria, it is also ideas—ideas that would shape the world to come. It is these ideas, for example, of imperial administration, of dividing the land into territories managed by local governors who reported to a central authority, at first the king of Assyria. This fundamental model of administration has survived to this day, as can be seen in America's federal-state system.

It is in this place where the mythological foundations of the Old and New Testament was found. It is here that the story of the Great Flood originates, 2000 years before the Old Testament was written. It is here that the first epic was written, the Epic of Gilgamesh, with its universal and timeless theme of the struggle and purpose of humanity. It is here that civilization itself was developed and handed down to future generations.

It is here that the first steps in the cultural *unification* of the Middle East were taken, by bringing the numerous diverse groups in the vast area from Iran to Egypt under Assyrian rule, breaking down ethnic and national barriers and paving the way for a cultural unification that facilitated the subsequent spread of Hellenism, Judaism, Christianity, and Islam.

The origin of Chief Joseph's Assyrian Tablet

And the first nation that travelled around the world to US territory and South America. and the first nation that had contact with US and South American tribes. In 1877 the respected leader of the Nez Perce tribe surrendered to the US Government. At his surrender, Chief Thunder Rolling Down the Mountain (known by his Christian name Joseph), presented General Nelson Appleton Miles with a pendant, a 1- inch square clay tablet with writings unrecognizable to General Miles. The writing, which was translated by Dr. Robert D. Biggs, Assyriology Professor at the University of Chicago, turned out to be a sales receipt dating back to 2042 B.C. in Assyria. It read: Nalu received 1 lamb from Abbashaga on the 11th day of the month of the festival of AN, in the year Enmahgalanna was installed as high priestess of Nanna"

Chief Joseph said the tablet had been passed down his family for many generations. So far they found 3 Assyrian tablets one and Georgia and another one in Oklahoma.

The Story of Chief Joseph's tablet leaves us with a mystery. How did the ancient Assyrian Artifact make it to the western Hemisphere? The Scholars are still scratching their heads in search of an explanation.

Assyrian History is long and magnificent. It lasted 3000 years. The nation was ruled by about fifty kings who were great in the history of mankind. I will not go into the many kings' stories here. If you wish to read Assyrian history in greater detail, I would recommend "Mesopotamia the Mighty King," and "Ancient Iraq." These books can be found in any library in the United States.

The purpose of this book is to open your eyes to an astonishing theory: where did the original Assyrians come from? Did these remarkable people really come from another planet?

HORMUZD RASSAM

ASSYRIAN EXPLORER (1835)

Hormuzd Rassam (1826-1910), A renowned Assyrian explorer, was born at Mosul in 1826. He was the youngest of the eight children of Anton Rassam (archdeacon in the Assyrian Church of the East) and his wife, Theresa, daughter of Ishaak Halabee of Aleppo, Syria. Christian, an elder brother of Hormuzd, married Matilda, sister of George Percy Badger, and became the first English Consul at Mosul.

As an infant, Hormuzd narrowly escaped death by the plague. During his childhood, he learned to write and speak Assyrian, the native language of the Christians, and Arabic, the language of the country. Mrs. Badger, his brother's mother-in-law, helped him with the study of English.

Growing up, he served as an acolyte in the Roman Catholic Church of St. Miskinta. There was even a plan to send him to Rome to study the Catholic faith; however, it did not come to fruition. Therefore, this led him to his doubts about the Roman doctrine.

When he was twenty years old, with his brother Christian's permission, he was hired by the British archaeologist Austin Henry Layard as a paymaster at a nearby dig site. Layard, who was in Mosul for his first expedition (1845-1847), was impressed by the hard-working Rassam and took him under his wing. They would remain friends for life. The mentor provided an opportunity for Rassam to travel to England and study at Oxford (Magdalen College), where he stayed for 18 months before accompanying Layard on his second expedition to

Iraq (1849-1851). It was then Layard begun his political career, whilst Rassam continued the field work (1852-1854) at Nimrud and Kuyunjik, where he made a number of important and independent discoveries, including clay tablets that would later be deciphered by George Smith as the *Epic of Gilgamesh*, the world's oldest-known example of written literature.

Hormuzd won Layard's fullest confidence, and when the latter went to Baghdad to arrange for the transport of the antiquities to England, Hormuzd was left in charge, and all the accounts of the excavations passed through his hand. His services, however, were unpaid. After the discovery at Nirnroud of the palaces of Assur-nasirapli, Shalmaneser II, Tiglath-Pileser IV, Sennacherib, and Esarhaddon, work was pursued from May 1847 with equal success at Kouyunjik (Nineveh).

Rassam's stay at Oxford was short though. While Charles Marriot was preparing him for matriculation, Layard recalled him to Assyria to assist in excavations at the expense of the trustees of the British Museum. He subsequently presented to Magdalen College a sculptured slab from Nineveh. Because of this, Rassam now had a fixed salary, with an allowance for traveling.

Arriving late in 1849, he pushed on vigorously with the work at Kouyunjik, and the excavations at Nimroud were re-opened. Rassam accompanied his patron to the ruins in Babylonia and returned to England in 1851, when Layard brought back his discoveries.

The next year, the trustees of the British Museum sent Rassam out alone— Layard's health compelling his withdrawal. He worked at Nimrod, Kouyunjik, under the direction of the British Museum and Sir Henry Rawlinson, the British ambassador in Baghdad, and tried again uncovering the mounds representing Assur, the old capital of Assyria, now called Qala'a-Shergat. Here, he found many antiquities, a lot of them of considerable importance. His greatest discovery on this occasion was the palace of Sddur-baniapli at Kouyunjik—the North Palace—with a beautiful series of bas reliefs, including the celebrated hunting scenes. Among the numerous tablets were some supplying accounts of the Creation and Flood legends. A few of the slabs found in this edifice are now in The Louvre, Paris, but most of them are in the British Museum basement.

Returning to England, during a year's leave of absence, Rassam married Anne Eliza, the daughter of Captain Spencer Cosby price, formerly of the 77th Highlanders. Resigning his appointment at Aden, he travelled widely in the United Kingdom and the Near East. He then settled first at Twickenham and afterwards at Isleworth. In 1877, he was again employed by the British government in Asiatic Turkey, where he inquired into the condition of the Christian communities and sects in Asia Minor, Armenia, and Kurdistan. He revisited his native town of Mosul in November, 1877, afterward giving a detailed account of his observations of the journey in his *Asshur and the Land of Nimrod*, (1897, Cincinnati and New York).

Meanwhile, in 1876, with the help of Layard, then British ambassador to Turkey, Rassam had obtained a *firman* from the Turkish government, on behalf of the trustees of the British Museum, for the continuation of the excavations in Assyria and Babylonia.

He at once organized the work of exploration, and every year from 1876 until the end of 1882, he carried on excavations, not only at Kouyunjik (Nineveh) and Nimroud (Calah) but also at Balawat.

In Babylonia, the sites explored included the ruins of Babylon, Tel-Ibrahim (Cuthah), Dailem, and Abu-Habbah (Sippar). Among the more important finds were the bronze gates of the Assyrian king Shalmaneser II (Balawat), the beautiful Sungod-stone, the cylinder of Nabonidus, giving its date for the early Babylonian kings Sargon of Agade and his son NaramSin, and a valuable mace-head inscribed with the name of king Sargon.

The inscriptions included additions to the Creation and Flood legends, the first tablet of a bilingual series prefaced by a new and important version of the Creation story in Sumerian and Semitic Babylonian, and numerous other documents; the fragments, large and small, amounted, it was estimated, to close to 100,000 pieces, though many of these were small and consequently of little value.

Among the imperfect documents was the cylinder of Cyrus the Great, in which he refers to the capture of Babylon. Rassam's important discoveries attracted world-wide attention, and the Royal Academy of Sciences at Turin awarded him the Braza Prize of 12,000 for the four years 1879-1882. His discovery of the site of the city Sippara was especially noted as grounds for the award. An allegation that Rassam's kinsmen had withheld from the British Museum the best of Rassam's finds was successfully refuted in 1893, in an action at law in which Rassam was awarded 50L. damages for libel.

After 1882, Rassam lived mainly at Brighton, writing an Assyro-Babylonian exploration on the Christian sects of the Near East, or on current religious controversy in England. Like most Oriental Christians, he was a man of strong religious convictions, and, having adopted evangelical views, became a bitter foe of the High Church movement. He was fellow of the Royal Geographical Society, the Society of Biblical Archaeology, and the Victoria Institute.

An autobiography which he compiled before his death remains in manuscript.

He died at his residence at Hove, Brighton, on September 16, 1910, and was buried in the cemetery there. He was survived by his wife, Anne Eliza, daughter of Captain Spender Cosby Price, formerly of the 77th Highlanders, whom he married on June 8, 1869, and with whom he had a son and six daughters. The son, Anthony Hormuzd, born on December 31,1883, joined the British army and became captain in the New Zealand staff corps at Wellington.

This is a biography of Hormuzd Rassam and his family. But this is not the complete story as I knew it. I knew of a secret discovery never told nor mentioned, neither in his diaries nor in the book that he published.

Rassam was a dedicated British subject who worked all of his life for the British government. He was honest and trustworthy, and he often put his life in danger— all for the British government. He succeeded in communicating with the frontier.

This is the story of his discovery. In a military expedition, he was dispatched to India by Sir Robert Hope to help with the release of a British captive. He was sent back to Mosul in 1852 and was soon hard at work, making various discoveries including the white Obelisk of Ashurbanipal I (1049-1031 B.C.) in the southern part of the Kuyunjik mound. But his eyes are being drawn to the northern part of the mound, where he suspected there might be another palace.

Under a rather loose agreement, this part of the mound was a French preserve. Because of this, he retreated to the expedient of digging at night.

It seems that he had some inkling of what was to be found in this area, but he had been prevented from working there openly, since it was in the part of the mound which Rawlinson had handed over to the French. Archaeologist/expediter Place had not taken advantage of the offer, and, anyway, he thought that Rawlinson had not been entitled to make it. It was an embarrassing situation, and so he decided that his only hope was to work secretly, by moonlight.

On March, 1852, at 10 pm., the night was very cool, the moon was full and bright. Rassam was in his tent at the field office, and under the kerosene light, worked very hard on the last night's discoveries. Under that same full moon, Rassam and his 12-member Assyrian crew were working beneath the North Palace of Ashurbanipal. Everyone on the crew were local Assyrian Christians and for that, he trusted them. They were his long-time employees who spoke the language very well and were fluent in Turkish.

His two supervisors, Mr. Dawood and Mr. Yousif, were very experienced and knowledgeable about the ruined areas of Nimroud in Babylonia, located in the south of Baghdad. They have worked under his supervision in all excavations for the past eight years.

On the third night, when news of the clandestine operations had already reached Mosul, Rassam anticipated that he might be interrupted by the Turkish police at any moment. They used to visit the dig site not for security purposes but to take bribes, though Mosul's governor, Ali-Riza-Pasha, had given the British Consulate full permission to excavate in the area.

At around 9:00 p.m., his workmen found one of their trenches in the middle of a paved stone road. The supervisor then alerted Rassam, who was at his office at that time, and asked him to come to the excavation site immediately. He was a bit surprised of the news and since he was busy, he asked the supervisor to keep on excavating and follow the paved road.

Rassam knew, and he told his crew, that this road would take them to the palace basement. He had had his eye on this hill for a long time. He also advised the supervisors and crew to work hard and keep a low profile. "Do not talk with anyone, not even with your friends.", he told them.

"The French excavation group are working very close to us during daytime. They have been wanting to get news about our excavation. So today, I decided to have a guard stay inside my tent in the morning. No one is to come close to our excavation area, anyway."

"Please, Dawood, Yousif," Rassam continued, "let me know if you find anything else. I will be in my tent."

With a newfound vigour, the workmen continued digging. After excavating about 20 to 30 feet, the road suddenly started sloping downward to a minimum slope of 10 to 20 percent. The tunnel was becoming much deeper and darker as well.

The crew started to worry about dirt and rocks falling on their heads since they had no protection. Dawood then asked Yousif to bring out more lights and instructed the crew to be more careful and avoid the falling rocks.

As they worked, the soil grew harder and harder to break. They needed specialized working tools, however, the lack of equipment did not deter them from completing their task. They continued to dig then cleared away the loose soil to make sure they were following the paved road. After 50 feet of digging, the road suddenly became flat. One of the crew hit the blade of his axe on a solid object. He immediately screamed, "Dawood, Yousif, come! I found a wall! It looks like this is the end of the excavation and the end of the tunnel!"

The two supervisors came running to see what had been found and alas— it was a wall!

"I think it is the foundation of the palace," Yousif said. They all huddled to take a closer look, and one by one they started cleaning the wall's surface carefully with their bare hands.

"Please bring the light closer, I cannot see," Dawood called out.

"There are features on the wall and a lot of writings. I wonder what this is! Dawood, please ask your staff to bring hand brooms or hand brushes, and bring the light closer. I would like to clean the wall because there are a lot of features and pictures here!", exclaimed Yousif.

Someone brought the requested materials and each one of the crew helped with the clearing, concentrating their efforts on the area just in front of the wall. After seeing what was revealed before them, Dawood realized he should get Rassam right away. "Go now and call Rassam!" he cried. "This is not a wall—it is a giant gate!"

Yousif and two workers then ran with their kerosene lights to get Rassam. A few minutes later, Rassam and Yousif came back. The remaining supervisor and his crew worked very hard to expose a large area of the surface that was 15 feet high and 15 feet wide before Rassam's arrival.

Upon arriving, Rassam asked Dawood: "What did you find, sir?"

"We found a big gate with a lock! Come see, and be careful!" Dawood's voice was shaking as he described what they recently found.

"Yes, it's such a great discovery!", echoed Rassam in agreement. He then asked one of his crew to go and bring a hammer immediately. Every nerve ending in his system was buzzing with excitement and he cannot wait to see what this gate would open to.

He proceeded to scrutinize the gate and found out it was really large and made of solid, cedar wood. On its surface, there were carvings of ancient figures and an Assyrian cuneiform inscription. He put both hands on the gate and kept saying, "I knew it! I knew it!". He was beaming inside and kept saying like he was chanting "I finally found it!" Rassam had been looking for this treasure ever since he had started working with Layard.

As he was waiting for word about the hammer, he discovered a curse written in cuneiform at the top of the gate. It warned newcomers with this inscription:

Whomever opens this gate or breaks this seal, his spirit will not receive
[kispo] funerary with other spirits. It is taboo
and great gods of the underworld will impose on his corpse and spirit
restlessness for all eternity.

Rassam read the curse, but because he had seen many curses while working with Layard, he did not mention it to his workers. Meanwhile, Yousif had noticed it and felt uneasy. He asked, "Is there any curse when we open the gate?"

"Yousif," Rassam replied, "we must be really careful and vigilant when we get inside."

While waiting for Dawood to bring the hammer, Rassam instructed Yousif to bring the light closer as he was trying to read the inscriptions on the gate. He felt confused seeing them as much older inscriptions. He tried to decipher the figures but they were different from what he is used to; these hieroglyphs depicting an ancient, unknown science that showed astronomical units and a flying machine with an astronaut seated inside.

It was then he realized that what was behind the gate must be something strange, old, and exciting!

Although a bit confused yet excited, he accepted the hammer from Yousif, who just came back with it, then he stared at the lock for a moment and asked everyone to pray in Assyrian before they broke the lock. Then he grabbed the lock with his hand and asked everyone to move back, with the exception of Dawood and Yousif. The rest of the crew felt uneasy; however, Rassam said, "Let's open this gate, Yousif. Please break the lock now with the hammer."

The lock was made of bronze material. It was in very poor condition, rusted due to thousands of years covered up with soil. Then Yousif took the hammer and hit the lock, and it immediately broke and fell into piece. At that moment, the crew moved back a few steps, awareness and fear showing in their faces.

"Do not be afraid," Rassam reassured them.

"Abraham," he instructed, "go to the tent and bring back the sketch book and pencils—hurry, please!" Abraham was the member of the crew gifted in drafting site sketches, and he is essential to this expedition since they had no camera with them.

Rassam then asked the crew to start cleaning around the gate and to move the soil and rock fragments away from it. He felt every excitement in his bones, and considered about not opening the gate until daybreak. But he thought the morning would be too late because by then, the French crew would take credit and claim the discovery for themselves. So he decided to open the gate now, and he thought to himself "it's now or never."

Abraham arrived a few minutes after and started sketching the gate while the rest of the crew was cleaning the site. At half an hour after midnight, they decided to push the gate together to open it, but it did not budge. Rassam then ordered Dawood to bring back four heavy steel rods. However, Yousif volunteered to go and get it instead, so he ran and brought back four steel rods as requested.

Rassam then asked the crew to come together to help. They all gathered around and together, inserted the steel rods into the bottom of the gate then pushed it together. Slowly, the gate began to open. The crew then stepped back because they all were scared, except, of course, for Rassam, Dawood, and Yousif.

When the gate was opened, they saw another wall, about 20 feet away from where they stood. It was scrawled with depictions of kings, gods, angels, and stars, with rows and rows of cuneiform.

Rassam stepped inside the chamber and looked around. It was dark and he did not have an idea which part of the building it was - whether it was a basement of the north palace of Ashurbanipal, or the royal tombs of Ashurbanipal and his family. He thought of this since the road they had excavated sloped below the palace floor. At any rate, he was not exactly sure where the paved road would take them, but he believed that they were under the palace.

He was actually worried, that he quite admitted to himself. He was hesitant to go further deeper into the chamber. Aside from the foul smell that enveloped the space, he could not bear to lose their exploration opportunity to the French archaeology group that he believed would come in the morning.

Finally, he made a decision to go in, bringing with him three torches which he asked from his companions.

"We will enter slowly and I will tell you exactly what to do, and you will both follow my instructions," he told them. "I know it is very dark but we have to do it tonight. We'll need three more people to help us when we go inside, and they must follow us with light torches."

Turning to Dawood, he asked: "Who do you recommend?"

"Well, Abraham is young and aggressive. Adel is a hard worker, and Robert is both young and hard working. I think they will do." Dawood replied. "Excellent! Now prepare fire torches and bring kerosene light. Put it on the ground, then tell the three workers to come here. I would like all of you to listen and listen well, you hear." Rassam told his men.

"I do not know what's inside this chamber, but I believe we might find some artefacts or it's possible that it could be empty. However, I will not let this chance pass and we have to investigate it now. We might come face to face to some obstacles, like traps or possibly curses, but we have to do it tonight, so I want you all to be vigilant and follow my command. Do you understand?"

"Yes, sir," said the workers.

"Now Dawood, start to prepare new torches. Three of us will move slowly towards the gate, and we will observe inside the threshold of the gate. Then we will move inside carefully, and the rest of you will wait until I ask you to come in." he told his men.

Rassam led the crew inside, with Dawood and Yousif on his heels. They stopped at the gate and looked down a dark hallway. He looked around to make sure everything was going well. Facing front, he looked at a wall that was covered with Assyrian inscriptions and two protective genies carrying a deer, possibly guardians of this chamber. Looking down at his feet, he noticed that the floor was made of stone about two feet by two feet in size, and covered with dust.

He was a bit dismayed with what he was seeing yet he proceeded to walk down the hallway. When they had gone five feet from the gate or threshold, a piece of the floor began to slide downward at very high speed.

"It's a trap!" he yelled. "Run!" Everyone struggled to escape, each running in a different direction. Rassam ran towards the hallway. Dawood hung at the edge of the wall, but managed to throw his torch to his master. On the other hand, Yousif fell into a 15-foot deep hole.

Chaos erupted inside the chamber. Everyone was screaming for help; however, the crew outside could not help! It was impossible because the hole was large and deep!

Rassam immediately rushed in, put his torch down, and tried to pull Yousif up. He then told one of the crew to bring a rope so they can use it save Yousif.

Rassam yelled to him, "How are you feeling? Are you hurt?"

Yousif answered, "I'm okay. Just get me out of here, please!"

"Someone's already getting the rope and once we have it, we'll use it to pull you out, okay?" Rassam said, "We'll it's here now. Listen, I'll throw this to you then tie the rope around your waist, and when you are ready, they'll pull you up, okay?"

"Yes."

The crew lowered the rope to Yousif, and they slowly pulled him out. Yousif was in shock yet still appeared to be in high spirits.

"You okay, Yousif?" Rassam asked. "Do you want to get some fresh air?"

"Yes, just let me rest for a few minutes," responded Yousif While Yousif was resting, Rassam instructed the crew, "Go to my tent. There are a few 2" by 6" wooden boards there we can make a walkway with, across the hall. We can use them to cross over it. Please bring them immediately!" Adel and Abraham, you along to help the crew. Make sure to bring three or four boards 12-feet long." Within a few minutes they had brought the materials, and the crew started to construct a pathway, or bridge. Yousif, Adel, and Abraham then crossed over the bridge to join Rassam. When they were all inside, Rassam started to observe the main entrance of the room.

In the corner of the room facing the main gate was a large stone table heavily-laden with golden artefacts. On both side of this table were two bronze statues of gin (guardians), placed there to guard the artefacts in this room. The walls were covered with astronomical texts and textures, all of it written in special cuneiform script.

This was one of the world's geological wonders. Rassam was in heaven! He could not believe his eyes and the beauty of this room. But he kept on reading and looking at the inscriptions in detail, especially the astronomical features he had never seen before in all his years of experience.

This is not like other palaces, this building is completely different from others.

"Yousif, Dawood, please bring the light closer."

Rassam was trying to read the inscriptions on the wall, but he could not read them because this was chronologically a much older inscription, and he tried to understand the astronomical figures, but they were inexplicable to him. He had never seen anything like it, and it did not seem logical.

While moving around the room, Rassam looked to the left and to the right, swinging his light. Following him were Dawood and Yousif. To the left was a long hallway. He could see steps there, heading downward. Rassam then went to the right, where he could see other steps going downward.

Rassam and his two assistants decided to head down the left hallway. Inside the hallway it was very dark, and the smell of the chamber grew even worse as they walked further from the gate. It was even becoming difficult to breathe. Rassam asked Dawood to stay at the top of the stairs and asked Yousif to go down the stairs with him.

When all of them had reached the top of the stairs, Rassam noticed another warning curse. It was written on the ground in cuneiform writing, in only two lines.

Rassam yelled at Yousif to stop. "There's another curse on the ground! It is right under your feet!"

Yousif cried out, "Oh no, not again!"

Dawood, who was a few steps behind asked, "What happened now?"

Rassam said, "Dawood, we found another curse at the top of the stairs. Please come close to us with the light. I need to read it. I need more light!"

And call Adel and Abraham to come inside to help.

Dawood yelled, "Adel, Abraham! Rassam wants you inside now!"

When Dawood came close and saw the stairs, he yelled, "Oh my God, the stairs look deep and dark!"

He asked Rassam, "How are we going down? This looks like a deep, dark water-well with no bottom!"

Rassam answered, "Dawood, quiet! You are scaring yourself. We have a job to do here. Let me first read the curse. Then we'll decide how we are going down."

Again he started to read the curse. He had difficulty understanding the meaning of it. After he had tried again and again, he finally yelled, "I got it!

It says,

> *God Assur will punish those who attempt to go down.*
> *These stairs go to the underworld.*
> *You will never come back.*

Yousef cried out, "Rassam, what are we going to do? It says the stairs go to the underworld! I do not want to die!"

Dawood said, "Rassam, Yousif is right! I do not mind going down, but down *where?*"

Rassam replied, "We *are* going down, understand? I do not want to hear any complaints. I depend on you two. You have to understand that whenever there is a curse, there is treasure!"

He asked Dawood to stay five steps behind him and Yousif, and then the rest would follow them. He told Adel and Abraham, "We are going down. You must follow and stay 15 steps behind us. We need a lot of light. The stairs are very dark and very steep."

Hormuzd Rassam was a very courageous person, and he was young. But although he was quite experienced in archaeological work, he had never before been so terrified. On his expeditions, he had explored many sites in Mesopotamia. But none of the sites had put so much pressure on him: only this one. From the beginning of this expedition, he had experienced doubts and mistrust, always feeling hesitant to move or to act fast. He had a very experienced and good crew who were neither frightened nor demoralised but followed his directions during more difficult situations as well as easier ones.

But from the very beginning, when they had opened the main gate and he had noticed extraordinary artifacts on the walls and gates, he had recognized that he was entering an alien, unexplored territory—and then the curses! He had never thought that curses could be so technologically advanced! It seemed that his conscience had been bothering him from the start of this odyssey because he knew they were doing something very advanced and feared that they might encounter something unforeseen in the chamber.

And he took a deep breath and slowly started climbing down, step by step. Again the walls along the stairway were engraved with astronomical archaeological features and relief sculptures. After going down twenty steps, Rassam asked Dawood to come down and stand in their place, "...but before you come, ask Abraham, Adel, and Robert to take your place. We need more light! We have more than twenty more steps to go to get to the bottom of the chamber."

"Yes, sir," Dawood replied. Then Dawood asked the crew to come in and to be careful of the trap.

Abraham said,

"Yes, Dawood, we already covered the trap: we installed a walkway over it."

"Very good," Rassam replied. "Please, Adel and Abraham, stay close so you can come down behind me. Please just watch your step!"

On the way down, Rassam was surprised at the height of the stairway. The steps were forty-five degrees steep, one step horizontal and one step vertical, making it resemble the Ziggurat of Nanna or the stairs of the White Temple in the Sanctuary of Ana in Urkuk that made going down very difficult and dangerous, especially at night, when they could not even see what was under their feet.

A good aspect of all this was that the stairway was ten feet wide.

The ornamentation on both sides of the walls amazed Rassam. He noticed that the description on the walls were more about astronomy than the usual depictions of war scenes or kings killing lions. These sculptures were about stars, planets, and the universe, and some had a direct resemblance to gods of divine power and symbols of Assur and many other gods, but at the bottom of the stacks were Assyrian cuneiform scripts.

Rassam knew that he had found a new discovery.

Rassam started slowly climbing down the stairs. He knew that where there is a curse, there is a problem. Dawood and Yousif were following ten steps behind him, in case he stepped on the curse's effect. [punished only but] "Please, watch your step!" he exclaimed.

They slowly continued to move twenty-five steps further down. Rassam still could not see the bottom of the staircase, because the thickness of the webs draping the stairway was creating still more problems. The torches burning the thick webs draped all down the stairway were depositing clouds of tiny particles in the air, along with the smoke that was already there.

That was one reason Rassam could not see the bottom of the stairway. He instructed Dawood, "Call Adel and Abrahim closer so that we can see better. I am having a hard time seeing to the end of the stairway. It's dark and smoky. Dawood told both to come down close to them on the stairway, very slowly, step by step.

Rassam was about thirty-five steps further down but still could not see the end of the stairway tunnel. He was running out of patience while at the same time trying to calmly tolerate the delay. He began to complain to Yousif and Dawood about how deep this chamber was and asking when they were ever going to get to the bottom. At that moment, when they all were talking to one another and not being careful, Yousif suddenly stepped on a loose tile on a stair, triggering a firing mechanism inside the stairway, and with a loud noise, the stairs suddenly hydraulically flattened out.

This created a slide, and the crew slid the rest of the way down to the bottom of the stairs and onto a flat area 10 feet wide by 15 feet long. It happened so fast that they did not know what was happening. They were yelling and screaming all the way down to the bottom.

Rassam was the first one to land, then Dawood and Yousif, and finally Abrahim and Adel, crashing over each other with their torches still in their hands. Luckily, none of them got hurt, except for the scratches all over their bodies. They were terrified while they were sliding, but the moment they arrived on the flat area, they immediately struggled and scrambled to get up. Because he had been ahead of them, Rassam was under everyone else. At any rate, after yelling and screaming some more, they all got up, finding themselves on a flat floor in front of a brick wall, in an area of 3 meters by 4 meters.

Up at the top, Robert could hear their screaming during the entire ordeal. He ran to the edge to see what had happened to his boss and all of the others.

When he got to the edge of the stairway, he could see them all at the bottom trying to organize themselves and yelled down, "Are you okay? Where are the stairs?" He was surprised by the stairway's absence when he looked down. "What happened to the stairs?"

Rassam called out, "We are all fine! We do not know what happened to the stairs! Someone stepped on the track. It is the 'curse,' quote-unquote. I hope the stairs will come back. Otherwise we have to find another way up."

Robert called back, "Do you want me to look for a rope that we can use to pull you out?"

"Wait, we will let you know later. We're all looking for a solution. Do you understand?"

Robert responded, "Yes, yes, I hear you! I will stay here if you need me."

In his entire career, Rassam had never felt so agitated or disturbed. He was really frightened during the slide down, not knowing when or where he was going to land. It could have been worse, though.

Somehow Rassam managed to keep himself cool and calm. He was worried about the curse, but more worried about the group. So far, the crew had not said anything. They were all totally speechless.

Yousif then admitted, "I thought we were going to die! It took so long to get to the bottom!"

Dawood said, "Yes, it was very scary! I thought we would never stop!"

Adel said, "We were very lucky we did not catch fire, with those five torches! But we landed safely over each other!

Rassam said, "I'm glad we're all fine! This was an extraordinary experience that I did not expect to happen, but we are here now. Let us see what is behind this brick wall!" Abrahim said, "Rassam, there is not a door here! We are trapped! What are we going to do? With no stairs, we cannot go up!"

Rassam said, "I know, Abrahim, I can see we're trapped, but I believe there is something behind this brick wall. We have to demolish this wall!"

"Yes, it is sad how we are trapped with no equipment," responded Abrahim. "How are we going to demolish it?"

Rassam was hesitant to move fast. He knew he was trapped with no exit and no stairs. He decided to call up to Robert.

"Robert," he yelled from the bottom, "Send us some tools and equipment! Hammers, chisels, and sharp-edgeed hand tools. We have a brick wall here, and we need to demolish it!"

"Okay, Rassam, we have heavy tools. Do you want me to slide them to you? I'm afraid you will get hurt. Or, do you want me to tie them together with a rope and send that down to you?"

Rassam replied, yelling, "Yes, please tie them with a rope and send the bundle slowly down to us. Do it fast, please!"

Robert said, "Okay, sir!" He instructed two crew members to go and get the tools and the long rope from Rassam's office and bring them to him. In a few minutes, they brought back the rope and tools. Then they tied them into bundle and slid them down to Rassam, who called, "Good, Robert, I got everything! A good job!"

The crew started demolishing the wall. They made a small hole in the wall, 12 inches by 12 inches. Rassam asked the crew to stop then, and pushed his torch inside the hole to see what was behind the wall.

Suddenly Rassam yelled, "Oh, my God!" Instantly the crew ran to the hall to see, and each of them took turns cramming his head into the small hole.

"Guys! Take it easy!" Rassam said, "Let me tell you what I see inside.

"Two meters away from the wall, there is a giant door made out of some kind of metal, iron or gold, I cannot see which. It is not very clear. There are a lot of spider webs between the door and the wall.

"Okay, boys," he continued, "let's bring the wall down!"

Dawood admitted he was anxious about this step. "Yes," he said, "we will break through the wall, but then what? How are we going to get out of this hole? Where? Can you tell me where?"

Rassam answered Dawood, "Do not worry! We will find a way to get out. You have many workers waiting to pull us up. Please, just relax, okay?"

Despite their fears, the crew worked hard, and in a half an hour, they had knocked the entire wall down. Rassam asked them to clear the area of debris on the side, away from the main entrance. He was excited, looking at the gate. He could not tear his eyes away from this giant gate! The gate was made of gold, but the ancient inscription on the golden gate had never been seen before. On the gate were two pieces of solid gold. The gate had no visible lock of any kind.

Above the gate was a relief image of the god Asher. On each side of the gate was a golden statue of a protective spirit genie with the head of a bird, looking toward the gate. To the right and to the left were continuations of the relief carved alongside the staircase, indicating impressions of stars, planets, and galaxies. Included there were flying machines similar to those on the other relief.

"Yousif," said Rassam, "I would like the webs cleared out from the space: please do a good job of it. I would love to find out if the gate is really made of gold. It does look shiny. And how are we going to open this giant golden gate that is 10 feet wide and 15 feet high?

The crew worked very hard to clean the thickly draped webs away until the gate looked very shiny and new. Once they saw this, they all started looking for ways to open the gate. They started pushing.

Pushing together, they tried many times to move it, but to no avail.

They did not know what to do. Rassam started becoming uncomfortable. Because the gate did not have a keyhole, he had been looking all over the surface panels and on the abutting walls to find a mechanical button that would open it. After a half hour of searching and surveying both on and around it, suddenly Yousif, impatient with the situation, was so angry that he hit the bottom of the gate with his right foot in rage. The smell of the chamber was very unpleasant, and it made everyone furious.

At the same instant that Yousif's foot hit the bottom of the gate, a piercing sound, high vibration, and strong oscillation occurred. The stairway started to shake, and suddenly the gate started to slowly open inward, stopping at three-quarters open. The gate had not opened completely, but all of the noise and vibration abruptly stopped. A higher vibration followed throughout, with loud noises. The stairs started to reappear, and everything became normal again, as it had been when they had arrived. Adel and Abraham were so frightened that they did not know where to run, and at the top of the stairs, Robert was yelling and screaming. He did not know what was happening below, but when the gate opened, a strong wind and an unpleasant smell of ancient basement came through and wafted up to the top level. They started congratulating each other because the doors of the gate were opened.

Rassam called out, "Robert, we opened the gate!" Robert said, "Yes, I could hear the noise and vibration! I thought something had happened to you all!"

Then Rassam looked around. His eyes lighting on Yousif, he said, "Yousif, good job! What did you do when you hit your foot?"

Yousif said, "I just hit it at the bottom of the gate because I was so mad and sick that we've been trapped in this dark hole for an hour!"

Dawood added, "I think the gates opening trigger is at the bottom there.

"You can see two inch strips on both sides of each door. No one believed that the bottom of the doors held an opening trigger for this giant gate!

Adel whispered emotionally, "I thought we were going to die in this chamber! I'm so happy now. I'm glad we're all fine now!"

"While we are here, let us see what is behind this beautiful gate," Rassam urged. "I hope it's something good, that we will find something really good after all of this agony!"

Dawood exclaimed, "And what about the stairs? How are we going to go up? What are we going to do without stairs?"

Rassam responded, "Just take it easy, Dawood, we will find a way to get us up the stairs. I'll ask Robert to look for a long, strong rope. We have some crew up there who would love to pull us up." Okay, Robert," he called out, "Please go to my office. There's a long rope there. Bring it here and make it ready to pull us out when we need you to. Do you understand?" Robert called back, "Yes, sir!"

Rassam was considering how to move in the chamber. He was hesitant to move inside and waited a few minutes. He noticed that the gate was only partially open, but he did not want to wait because it was getting late.

He suddenly seriously decided to move on and continue the research. He asked Adel and Abrahim to push the pair of doors in the gate all the way open and asked Yousif and Dawood to follow him inside the chamber and to stay very close on either side of him. Using all of the torches, Adel and Abrahim each headed for one side of the gate.

Adel and Abrahim started pushing the gate, in order to fully open it. At the same instant the gate had completely opened, a loud screeching noise filled the basement, and, again, a bad smell followed the noise. It was unpleasant and extremely intense; then a loud rolling noise started. The noise grew even louder, and then there was a clanging, and a rolling noise filled the stairway.

For a few minutes they were all so terrified they did not know where to run, standing silent and transfixed until the rolling and the noises had completely stopped. Suddenly, unexpectedly, the stairs automatically came back into their properly-angled form.

"The stairs are back!" they yelled, and after that, all were cheerful and happy. Rassam said, "I think we found a trick about the stairs. When you open both sides of the gate, the bottom of stairs will come back."

Robert addressed them, calling down, "Are you okay?"

"The stairs are back!" Rassam yelled.

"Then I think you do not need the rope!" Robert yelled back.

"We are fine, and no, we do not need the rope, but, please, you and Janan stay at the top. We might need you downstairs!

"Okay," said Robert.

Yousif commented to Rassam, "These people are so advanced in technology and science! How can they do all of this?"

Dawood said, "Yes, Rassam, how can they do this? This is not a small project!"

Rassam responded, "I believe these people are not from this planet. They are very intelligent; I can see that from all of these artifacts on the walls! Who knows what is inside this chamber?

"Let us try to go in. Now that we have the stairs back, we have no basis for worry about it; we can escape at any moment we face trouble, with no worries."

Rassam wanted to explore further inside the chamber. He poked his head inside while the gate was fully opened. He could see along the wall on one side. It was very dark. But he not see anything on the other side of the chamber. He estimated that this room must be 60 meters by 60 meters by 20 meters.

They started walking along the wall, from left to right. There were a lot of objects on the ground to the right just beyond the gate: objects such as special cuneiform tablets never seen before. They were made with a special material, written upon with gold writing. It was all well-preserved and nicely organized, placed on wooden racks. Statues of kings and queens plated with gold also appeared there.

Then the wall suddenly curved inside, opening up into a big room.

They kept following the curved wall and finding more advanced equipment. It surprised Rassam to unexpectedly find new equipment they had never before seen, equipment such as television screen receivers, a hand telephone, computers, hand tablets both small and large, and very small electronics.

. . . and much more astronomical equipment. Then they came upon an astronaut's helmet and uniform, each one brown in color. Suddenly, Rassam noticed in a pile far across the room, a massive collection of equipment such as he had never before seen, and he could not believe his eyes: equipment such as gauges, watches, color televisions—and a massive golden box. Rassam had been very quiet until now because he didn't know what all of this machinery and equipment was for. But when he saw the golden box, he did know that something important must be hidden inside.

"You should go and see what is inside that gold box, Rassam."

"I cannot, it's too far away. Yousif, Dawood, would you go?

"No? You scared yourselves. Why are you afraid? Dawood, would you go?"

"I would go together, all of us together. Please, let us go together!"

It seems Rassam was scared as well, frightened to get too close to the box. But he went. It looked very heavy. Rassam lifted the cover. Inside were three very old books with special covers, together with many golden objects, some large, others miniature consisting of groups of trinkets, strips of gold foil, and tiny beads and colourful shells sealed into a cupboard. The collection had been elaborately hidden within the golden box, particularly the three books.

"You should read these, Rassam! This box is very heavy: it's 1.5 meters (59") long and half a meter (4") wide. We cannot lift it, and we need help!"

Dawood: He is right! There are no handles.

Rassam: Okay, let us keep the cover open. We have a lot to see here. We will come back later. I need those three books!

Yousif: Rassam, did you see the equipment there that we passed?

Rassam: I have no clue what it is. It looks like they are people who came from a different planet! They are not from here.

Dawood: What planet?

Rassam: I do not know where they came from! All of this equipment, it's not made in our world!

God only knows where they came from! That would be so awesome! Do you think these people are Assyrians?

Dawood: We are in the basement of Assurbanipal Palace, and we are in Nineveh, the Assyrian capital, so, yes, yes they are. What do you think they are? Turks! Why ask such a stupid question? You know they are all along the wall, all the objects, miniature ivory plaques, elaborately-carved ivory containers, and many extraordinary relief sculptures.

Rassam, Yousif and Dawood were very quiet the entire time they were concentrating on the treasures they had discovered, especially Rassam, who was wondering to whom this wealth belonged and why it had been hidden in this deep basement. Many questions poured into his mind with no answers. He was concentrating so intensely that he never even looked into the rest of the basement, where an enormous trove of treasure was stacked under the walls, all the way from where he was too close to the entrance gate.

Suddenly Rassam remember that Adel and Abrahim are at the gate.

"So please call them inside to join us, because we are very far inside."

Yousif turned to call Adel and Abrahim and ask them to join the crew further inside. "Adel! Rassam wants you to come join us, with Abrahim!"

Yousif yelled loudly. "Yes, both of you, and please tell Adnan to come down to stay at the gate. We need him immediately! Adnan, come down! And ask him please to be very careful when coming down. You must stay on one side of the stairs so you avoid stepping on the curse (the trigger), otherwise you will slide all the way down, and you may hurt yourself. Call Adnan to take your place. Just do not forget to light the torch!

"I will come down, and I will take care with the stairs, but first let me call Adnan to take my place."

"I said not to come down and to stay at the top of the stairs!"

Very carefully, Adel started to go down. He was very frightened because it was his first time, and it was very dark, and everything was covered in spider webs in the stairway.

Adel and Robert had warned him not to go inside until he had arrived down at the gate. He arrived at the gate without any problem. Adel and Abrahim slowly moved forward to join the group, bringing their torches, to join the group.

When they finally arrived close to the center, the basement looked much brighter, and they could easily see their way because now there were five torches.

"What is that big object and that human figure standing in the middle of this large basement?" Adel suddenly called out, "Rassam, Yousif, Dawood, have you seen this large object and human figure in the middle behind you?"

Rassam was still so busy looking at all of the exciting treasures before him that he never took the time to see behind him. He had kept Yousif and Dawood busy as well. All along, he had thought this basement he had found was a storage room for the king's and queen's treasures. It had never occurred to him that that he would find a large object.

Rassam: What did you say? What did you see?" with a loud a large object where Rassam asked.

Adel: "Look behind you, at the center of this basement!"

When they all turned to see what Adel saw, they first saw a human figure seven feet tall standing under a three-legged, very large object. The human and the object were about 30 feet away, looking very real under the five-torch lighting. Suddenly they thought they saw that human object moving toward them!

Rassam yelled, "Oh my God!" and all of them ran toward the gate, yelling and screaming and pushing one another so they fell on the ground with their torches. Rassam turned back to help Dawood and grabbed his hand to take him to the gate. Luckily, they could find the gate's location because Janan was already at the gate with the torch. When they got to the gate, some started going up the stairs. Others just stopped at the gate waiting for Rassam and Dawood to arrive. Then Yousif started to follow the others who were heading up the stairs.

Suddenly Rassam yelled, "Stop! All of you! Where are you going?"

Yes," said Abrahim, "they are on the stairs and they are scared to death and shaking, yelling, and screaming, trying to run away!"

Rassam said to Yousif, "Tell them to come down! We are not leaving yet!"

An instant before Yousif had a chance to ask the workers to come down, one of the workers stepped on the trigger.

Suddenly the stairs again flattened, and all of the crew slid down to the gate. Luckily, again no one was hurt, but who's had slid and hit Yousif very hard, and he fell on the ground.

Rassam said, "Oh good, you're all here. Why are you running away? The human object could be one of the Assyrian king statues."

Rassam was trying to calm them down, particularly himself. He was scared too, but tried to show his crew that he was not scared. He tried to look at the large circular object, and especially the human figure, from behind the gate, but it was impossible because it was very dark from where he was standing. He asked Yousif and Dawood to go inside to see if the human figure was moving or not.

Dawood answered,

"Rassam I do not think we can see from here. We are 20 meters (65.5 feet) away from the human figure, and you're right, it could be the king statue.

Yousif said, "Rassam, Dawood is right, let us all let us all enter together and get close to see the human statue and the big circular object with three legs.

Rassam responded, "You're right, we have to get close to the object or statue to examine it, to find out what type of machine it is and whose statue it is."

Rassam decided to get serious. He called all of them to stay close behind him and to follow him very closely to find out if these objects were worth being frightened of. This has been closed for the last 1000 years.

"I do not know why we are scared. Anyway, it was I who was hired to excavate for the British Museum. I have work to do. So I decided to find out about these strange objects in the middle of the basement, whatever it takes."

After talking to his crew, Rassam grew more courageous. He directed everyone to be ready to move very slowly behind him and to be vigilant, and please keep your torches high so we can see better! Rassam: Yousif, Adel, Abrahim, do you feel okay to go inside?"

Abrahim; immediately said

"Yes, sir, I would like to come with you. I am not afraid."

Adele said, "I would love to follow you, so I have no problem."

"Dawood, how about you?".

Dawood answered with a frightened face and voice, "I will if you do."

Yousif; immediately before Rassam asked him

"I will come too, if all of us go together."

Rassam said, "I am glad you are all committed to follow me, but I need you now to stay at the gate with your torch high so that we can see the location of the sky just in case we face another emergency. As you can see, it's very dark here, and we're expecting to get further way to investigate the rest of this basement before the sun comes. Please call Robert to stay at the top of the stairs with the light once we go inside.

Rassam pushed the gate open and walked inside toward the machine, and all four followed. Rassam was very close. When they came nearer, they could see a large circular object, and underneath that large object was a human figure, a robot. It was a very strange figure without eyes or mouth, and no ears. He was seven feet tall, very scary, and made of metal. They try to stay away from the human the robot, they kept looking at the robot, no matter what they were doing.

All of them were worried and scared. They were grouped together behind some old [almost touching him] they were all quiet. They did not know that Rassam was scared, too. Suddenly Rassam could not keep quiet.

"What is this human statue standing in the middle of this chamber under this large three-legged machine? He is very ugly. He does not look like any Assyrian king; "Yousif said it looks like he is made of metal." Like other statues that we have seen in the other building, Rassam. said No eyes, no mouth, big legs and big shoes! I wonder what they use it for. Dawood said, "probably, it's a statue but never finished. Look at this large circular machine, Rassam!"

"Yes, I did," Rassam replied, "I can see it it's very beautiful and large. It's sitting on those three legs. I cannot see the rest of the object. We are too far away. We need to go closer."

Looking at the large circular object in the middle of the chamber, trying to study it from far away, hesitant to move closer as he promised his crew, but the crew knew that Rassam was scared and was buying time.

The time was 1:30 a.m. Only a few hours before morning, so Rassam had no choice but to start the expedition now or leave it for another day. Delaying it would create problems. Finally, Rassam decided to go closer.

What was this strange object in the middle of the chamber? He wanted the crew to be ready to move slowly behind him, but if they had to go closer or go under the circular object, they would have to bypass the robot.

Rassam decided to go to the right. [behind one of the left the wheel of their strange object hey] from the ugly robot before they moved. Rassam asked that Dawood, Yousif Abrahim and Adel follow him, "but please do not touch any part of this object"

Closer and closer they moved, very carefully, under the bottom of the object. The object was huge. It was made of very shiny material. They could see their torches reflected in the bottom of the object. This huge object was sitting on three legs, which were its landing gear. Each of the three legs was connected to the body, the fuselage, of this giant object, this flying machine. Its landing gear was touching the ground with four large rubber wheels. Each wheel was five feet in diameter. So there were three landing gears, with a total of 12 rubber wheels.

In time, the crew somehow became more relaxed and less tense. Rassam and his crew carefully observed and studied the bottom of this huge object, this flying machine, but they could not find any opening except where the landing gear met the fuselage.

The machine was about three meters (10 feet) high off the ground, and it was very dark for climbing up to see the top of the machine. They did not have a ladder.

Rassam's intention was to find an opening or entrance he could look inside of to explore the identity of this huge object.

The only thing they found was a name and serial number written with large words and in black colour in Assyrian classic script, the old Assyrian language.

Rassam said, "Dawood, I know I can read it, but I cannot understand the meaning of it. It's a very old dialect." Yousif, it is probably the name of the machine.

Rassam said, "It may be. I will try to find out the meaning later. On the other side, facing the Assyrian, there was another kind of writing and an Assyrian cuneiform inscription.

"Abraham, did you bring pencil and paper with you when I asked you to?"

Abrahim answered, "Yes, I did."

Rassam said, "Can you copy both writings so that I can read what you copy later? Give your torch to Adel before you write.

They did not see an entrance to this huge object. They could not see above the object; they could see only the bottom because the machine was too high and too big, and the bottom was completely sealed.

And then, while walking underneath to see the other end of this huge object, Rassam noticed two large tubes for exhaust, and on the opposite of one other, connected to the circular object. Rassam projected that these two tubes on each side of the object could be the engines.

He continued looking and imagining for a few minutes, moving from one side to the other side. He was amazed at these two engine tubes. Dawood asked him, "What are you looking at, Rassam?" Rassam answered, "Do you see these two tubes? They could be engines!" Yousif asked, "What is engine? What engine? Is that the big object?"

Dawood said, "You believe these two tubes can push this big object from where they came from?"

Rassam answered, "I think that is what it does." He made them all believe him. "Rassam has studied in London. He knows better than the crew," Yousif said. These engines are a different colour from the body, but the body is shiny."

"I think they are different materials," Rassam said. At that time he was standing close to one of the wheels, and intentionally wanted to feel the shiny material that supported and held the wheels together. Rassam reached over to touch the shiny material with his hand, touching it. Suddenly, at the same instant, this huge machine instantly came alive, and all of the lights came on both inside and outside of the machine! A hydraulic ladder came down automatically in two places, one in front and second one at the back, under the body of the object.

At the same instant, the computers on the machine started to welcome the new guests. They were programmed and started making noises from inside the machine. The moment this happened, the basement chamber became bright from the machine's outside lights. than The robot started moving closer to the entrance stairs, preparing to guard the machine's entrance. His eyes came alive. He opened his eyes a few times, and bright light reflected from both eyes. The robot turned and looked all around. When he spotted Rassam and his crew, he studied them all for a few seconds. They were all frozen in one spot. Then the robot shut his eyes again and relaxed at the foot of the stairs.

At the same instant, Rassam and his crew grew so terrified that they all broke and ran once again again toward the stairway entrance. where Janan understanding, some of the crew started yelling and screaming as if it were the end of the world.

Dawood and Yousif collided while escaping, falling to the ground and losing their torches. The chamber was fully lit now. They could see every detail of the spaceship's exterior and the chamber with all of its treasure inside. Some of them stood behind the gate at the foot of the stairs, while others tried to climb the stairs. Looking in from behind the gate, Rassam could see close-up and noticed that the robot started to move a few feet left and then right. It repeated this motion a few times, then it stopped and faced one of the spaceship's ladders. Rassam saw a strange light burst from the robot's eyes, a red reflection being radiated through both eyes, after which it moved its head about 80 degrees twice, seeming to check the chamber. Suddenly the robot stood still in front of the ladder.

While Rassam was occupied looking at the robot, his crew members were gradually climbing up the stairs. He called out to them, "Dawood, Yousif, Abrahim, Adel, where are you going? Come down now, there's nothing to be scared of—do not be frightened! It is so beautiful! Everything I'm looking at, the machine, it's huge! It's huge—you can see all of the treasures in the large chamber because it's so bright! You can see the other side of the chamber, the gold statues, the artefacts on the walls all painted and gold, the wall inscriptions!

"And the bas-relief of the universe, and our solar system! Because it is so bright, you can see the whole room. You can see all of the statues along the walls of the chamber, the wall inscriptions and the alabaster relief of the universe and the solar system!

"It showed the Sun, Mercury, Venus, Earth, Moon, Tiamat, Mars, Jupiter, Saturn, and all the other planets. It even showed our place in the galaxy! There was gold and other treasures, but the most beautiful was the flying object! You can see the light inside and outside; you can see the windows up and down, the blinking lights around the object, the two ladders, one in the front and the other in the back, and the lights on the ladder looking up!" You could see clearly. two large engines above the machine, the site was amazing and powerful. He could not believe his eyes and was more committed than ever to finding out about the object, especially when the ladders opened by themselves without his having to look for them.

He told the others to get ready to go in right away. «Without our torches we must move as soon as possible, because I believe the lights may go off, and it will become hard to investigate the object with our torches.

Dawood said, "Yes, um, do you think it is safe to go in?"

Rassam assured him, "Yes, I do not see anything. I do not know why you were so frightened! Yousif, Abrahim, and Adel, you can join us as well. We will go in together this time. I want Yousif and Abraham to come with me to see inside the object." Rassam was very excited to see inside this huge machine. Now he was not scared. With all of the spaceship's light lit, it looked like it was daylight.

The crew began talking among themselves. Some wanted to follow Rassam while others were hesitant due to their extreme fear. None had ever seen an alien spaceship.

"Silence!" cried Rassam. "Thank you. I assure you there is no one inside this object. If there were, he would be dead by now, and I do not believe that any human can live in this place for thousands of years. It is impossible! Those who attended with me can vouch for the enthusiasm and excitement that will last all your life! Of course, you are free to follow whatever strategy you see fit. Just be aware that this experience will not come again in your lifetime! This is your last chance. Should you fail to see it, it will be your loss. We have time for one more question before we move inside to explore the object. Anyone have something to ask?"

No one opened his mouth. They were all ready to move inside with Rassam, who immediately walked from the staircase to the ladder of the giant object. Yousif and Abrahim followed Rassam, but Dawood and Adel went off to investigate the artefacts and sculptures scattered along the walls of the chamber. Seeing them go, Rassam instructed them, "Do not touch any object!"

They reached the ladder okay. The robot started moving a few feet left and then right, facing the ladder to the spaceship entrance. They could see that the robot opened its eyes a few times and red beams were radiating from its eyes.

Rassam, Yousif, and Abrahim arrived at the ladder of the machine. Rassam suddenly noticed five gates at the other side of the chamber, each with a god Assur emblem on its top, visible because the emblems were painted in gold. Rassam immediately called everyone together to go to those five gates. When they ran to see what Rassam had found, they discovered that each door was decorated differently from the others. The doors were 5' wide by 10' high and covered with copper plates engraved with Assyrian cuneiform writing and a face of a man and a woman, but the faces did not look like those of a king and queen.

"Let us open one of the doors and see what is inside!" Rassam said, "I am trying to read the names, but it's hard. I think it is a coffin of a husband and his wife, a burial place."

Yousif cried out, "There is not a handle on the door! How are we going to open it and get inside, Rassam?" He tried one door; the door did not move. He tried the second, and the third—none of the doors would move. [date or solid doors] Then all of them tried to push, but it was no use. Suddenly Abrahim notices the 2" by 2" by 2" square bottoms between each door. Abrahim said, "Yes, and please this time push the square between the doors." Good thinking!" Rassam said. He touched the bottom of the door, and it opened immediately. A bad smell came from the room. They all perceived it instantly. The room was about 8' wide by 20' long in the front.

On one side there was a pile of women's golden jewellery, and on the wall were hanging two astronaut costumes, one for a man and the other for a woman. There were astronaut's helmets, gloves, and boots, and many other objects. In back of all this, they found two coffins, well preserved and organized.

Rassam said, "I told you this could be a tomb. Yousif asked "Whose tomb is it, some Assyrian king and queen?" Rassam replied, "No I think it is the pilot's, the person licensed to direct or to fly this ship."

Dawood asked, "What is this uniform hanging on the wall?"

"Maybe they have to wear it before they fly," responded Rassam. "I have no clue. It looks that way, because there are two uniforms, one for the pilot and the second for his wife, Adel asked why there were five doors.

"The rest must be tombs, too," Rassam said. "There must have been more than five astronauts when the ship arrived from a different planet! Let us open next one, Yousif, if you push the bottom...."

Yousif said, "No way, sir! It smells very bad!" Abrahim... said. "So I will open it. you stay behind."

"Okay, I'll push the bottom. The door opened slowly, and again a bad smell hit their noses. The tomb looked exactly like the first one, well organized, and had some uniforms on the wall and different types of gold jewellery. "Next time, okay?" Rassam said, "Let us close both doors and go inside the ship. We will investigate these five tombs later, if we have time. Let us move to the ship. Yousif and Abrahim, come with me. Dawood said, "I'll look around."

Rassam reminded him, "Do not touch any object, please"

They had to pass by the robot. When they approached the robot, it checked them by opening its eyes for a second. Rassam, Yousif, and Abrahim arrived at the ladder to the machine. Rassam was more worried now. He could hear a lot of noises coming from inside the object, like someone talking. It was the computer programming itself. He grabbed the rail of the ladder-stairs and went up just one step, stretching his head upward to see if there was anyone inside. He could not see anything, but he was more confident now that no living human was inside this machine.

Slowly, step by step, he climbed to the top. There were a minimum of 20 steps. Rassam could hear voices coming from inside, the computer talking. It was welcoming them by greeting the passengers. This happened when they put their feet on the stairs, but he did not know that or recognize any of the words, since it was the ancient Assyrian language.

Carefully climbing, he finally arrived on the first floor. Yousif and Abrahim followed very closely and very frightened, but the same time paying careful attention to all of the details and the movements of Rassam, who entered the first floor of the machine and immediately saw another staircase going up to the second floor. Rassam grabbed Yousif's hand and pulled him up. Then Abrahim followed.

They were in a very large room that looked like an eating area. There were chairs and tables. The room was filled with cabinets, all made of a silver-white light metallic element like aluminium. Flat TV screens sat above some of the cabinets. On a few other cabinets were LED-blinking red and yellow lights. The space looked as though it could hold about 50 people.

Awestruck, Rassam and the crew walked around. They were amazed and speechless. They could not believe what they had discovered! While walking through the floor space, suddenly two sliding doors opened automatically and unexpectedly. They were scared again, but there were lights on in the new space. It was an empty, large room that looked like the machine's cargo bay.

Rassam kept moving toward the stairs to the second floor. Very slowly and very carefully, step by step, he climbed up another 20 steps to get to the second floor.

He looked over the second floor everywhere before calling to Yousif and Abrahim to say, "It's fine to come up!"

They reassembled on the second floor. What they saw was unimaginable! It was a very large room, and in the middle of the room, there was 60 specially-designed chairs. On each chair was an astronaut's helmet, with a name on top of the helmet. There were colourful blinking lights on each chair, blinking repeatedly on all of chairs, looking like Christmas tree lights.

All around were cabinets with glass doors, and inside of them white space suits were hanging. Embroidered on the left side with an Assyrian god symbol of Assur in a circle. [and on the right hand and embroidered with Assyrian seals and on the bottom of the seal. there were numbers of the astronauts, the same numbers as on those chairs.

Two large screens in the chamber displayed a landing site. One showed the Tigris and Euphrates rivers in blue, from south to north. The landing was in the Nineveh area.

The second screen showed the pattern of travel from the planet Tiamat up to the Earth, with all of the planets circling [the orbital access the travel pattern] between Tiamat and Earth shown on the screen and coloured dash lines with arrows and distances and X and Y coordinates in the ancient Assyrian alphabet.

There were many other pieces of equipment for exercise: treadmill machines with computer screens attached. Between the chairs was a wide walkway. There were 30 seats on the right side and 30 seats on the left side.

Rassam's crew walked between the seats. Behind the seating compartment, there were other steps going up to the third floor, where the computer sound became stronger and other noises with the computer reading, comparing, and programming itself somehow.

All together, they went up the stairs. Rassam looked into the room. He called out, "God, what *is* this?"

The space was smaller. It was the ship's command center. 15 screens, some small, others big, sat all over the room. The ship's console was divided into four main areas. The central view screen, the control viewing area for the major displays, the auxiliary view screen for viewing ship status and sensor information, the control panel for executing commands through an array of buttons, and the text window where all of the text messages were displayed, this four area an array of bottom described in detail below and in detail below, an additional area above the main screen, displaying the coordinates in space.

The first screen displayed the ship's horizontal position; the second displayed the vertical position. In front of the command control console, there were five seats for the captain, pilot, engineer, navigator, science officer, and communications officer.

At the command center there was an exhilarating feeling, with communications equipment and another three seats for electrical engineers.

«It must be the ship›s command center, Rassam said. He could see the visual screens of all sizes; they were blinking. Many instruments and other gadgets were on the main console. At the head of the stairs was a 42» gate to prevent people from directly entering the main command center without the captain›s permission.

The door of the gate was unlocked; they pushed the door and it opened. Rassam entered than Yousif and Adel followed. Once they were in the command center, they suddenly triggered a warning system, and the computer started to send out warnings in the ancient Assyrian language asking intruders to leave the restricted area, and all the screens in the room were blinking the same warning.

Rassam ignored the red light alert and loud noises of the sirens. He refused to take notice, because there was no place to run. He went inside the command center anyway, but Yousif and Abrahim started going down the stairs They were trying to run away.

The noise and red lights scared them to death; they had never heard this kind of noise before.

Rassam did not want to stay there alone. He yelled at them, asking, "Where are you going? Just wait! It only annoys—it will go away! But outside the ship, inside the basement, the noise was much louder than inside. It scared Dawood, and Adel especially the red light signal, the chamber became red and white. So

Dawood and Adel ran immediately to the machine ladder. where was Rassam, Yousif and Abrahim climbed up, went up a few steps, and started yelling, calling for the rest. They repeated their names many times in very loud voices, but no one could hear them because of the loud siren making so much noise.

Up in the control center, Rassam went very close to the ship's console where he could see the control panel and an array of buttons. One of those buttons was blinking with a red light. Reaching it he pushed it down with his hand. All of a sudden the blaring warning siren stopped completely.

Everyone relaxed. Now they could hear the faint voices of Dawood and Adel.

Rassam asked Yousif if he would go down and bring them up.

"No, sir, I cannot go alone—but I can go together with Abrahim." Rassam responded, "Go together and bring them up! But do not leave me alone for long."

Said Rassam, Yousef started yelling to Dawood and Adel immediately after leaving the control room, "We are coming down to bring you up! Stay where you are!" Abrahim and Yousif happily went down to bring them up so stay where you are. Yousif and Abraham happily went down to bring them up so that Dawood and Adel could see the command control center of this great, giant machine.

Rassam knew that they would really appreciate it, but was worried that it took them more than fifteen minutes to come up, even though he was busy with the main ship's console control panel auxiliary view screen and large main view screen. He was extremely surprised about the technology of this giant machine. He suddenly heard the crew coming up. He could hear their voices. He felt very happy and relieved when they finally came up to the main control room and saw the control panel and all the screens.

Surprised, Adel cried, "Rassam, what is this?"

Rassam explained to them all, "It seems to me that this is the heavenly abode of the Gods I have been studying! The screens show that they travelled here from a different planet. See, the screen shows that they came from this planet to Earth, thousands of miles, you can see that it is all written here on the screen in Assyrian, and on the third screen they show the map of two rivers and the Gulf of Arabia. They came down from south to north and landed. Clearly, where they landed was in this exact location of Nineveh!

Rassam knew about the solar system better than all the rest of the crew because he had travelled to England and studied at Oxford. He was very happy to explain the path of the ship's travel to his crew, as shown on the screen, but the crew were silent the entire time because they did not understand what was being explained.

"Rassam, when we were down below we could see a lot of amazing ancient artefacts, stone sculptures, gold statues, and many other exciting artefacts in the chamber." Dawood said.

"I would love to see them," replied Rassam, "once we are finished here, we will go down to see the other side of the chamber, which I have not seen.

While deeply immersed in their conversation, they started to hear disturbing noises on the control room speakers in the Turkish language. It seemed that these ancient Assyrians were so advanced in computer and electronic technology that they had installed a surveillance system all over the chamber holding the ship, to reveal anyone entering or trying to steal from the chamber.

Unexpectedly, one of the security screens in the central panel where Rassam and Dawood and Yousif were came alive automatically came alive. It showed two Turkish officers with guns forcing themselves through the gate. At the main gate, they started arguing with the outside crew and looking for their supervisor, Rassam.

Having no choice, the outside crew told them that Rassam was in the basement. So the two officers pushed away the crew at the gate and got inside. Adnan was at the top of the stairs with a torch when he heard the argument and came to see what was happening. Suddenly he met them at the main entrance. One of the officers shouted in Turkish,

"I have a gun on you, Christian thieves! Give me your torch!" When Adnan refused to give up his torch, the officer pushed him into the wall set his rifle and pointing it at Adnan's chest, cursed him in Turkish.

Adnan did not want to fight with him, so he gave his torch to the Turk. When the officer got the torch, he loudly said, "Hey, dirty Christian, where is your supervisor?" Adnan answered, "He is downstairs, in the basement."

The officer asked in the Turkish language, "How many people are in the basement?" Adnan answered, "I do not know." The second officer said, "I hope you are not lying! If you are, you will be punished! I will be back."

"Why should I lie to you?" asked Adnan, with a shaky voice.

The officers looked at Adnan in a dirty way, as though they knew he were lying, and then they walked to the edge of the stairs to go down.

They had not known the stairway was so steep. One of the officers told his comrade, "This is deep! Do you want to go down?

The second officer said, "Yes."

"When you see how much gold there is down in this basement, you will be surprised!"

"Fine, let us go down there. Just be careful," his comrade said.

Rassam and the crew in the control room sat there in shock, watching and hearing what was on the screen—all of the commotion at the main gate between the two Turkish officers and the members of their crew. Especially when the officer pulled a gun on Adnan.

Rassam was immediately aware of a very big problem—these two officers should not be here!

"Dawood, Adel! Go down, get the three books we found in the gold box, and keep them with you. Yousif and I will come down in a few minutes. Abrahim, you go down with them, too. Please, Dawood, do not fight or urge? with the officers, understood?"

Dawood, Adel, and Ibrahim immediately ran from the control room and rushed downstairs. But when they had nearly reached ground level, they saw the robot standing beside the flying machine stairway and realized they would need to pass close by it. Slowing down, they moved very cautiously while passing the towering robot. Each of them noticed it was looking at him—there was a bright light in each of its eyes.

Coming alive whenever the lights of the flying machine would appear, it seemed the robot had been programmed to maintain a close watch on the basement, especially the flying machine and all of the collected treasure. It even knew the difference between foreigners and Assyrians. The robot now recognized each of the crew members. When they had climbed up the staircase before, it had known they all were Assyrians.

Without any problem, the men slowly and cautiously moved past the robot.

Once out of its range, Dawood, along with Adele and Ibrahim, immediately sprinted across the chamber to the large golden box and, working together, they carefully lifted the three heavy books from the box made of gold where they had nested, unread, for eons.

They closed the cover of the box. With ornately decorated book covers, the books were very heavy. Dawood, Adel, and Abrahim stayed where they were until Rassam and Yousif came down to join them.

Standing at the top of the stairway, the two Turkish officers were apparently trying to come down to the basement. They could see the light at the bottom of the stairs, but they did not know about the curse. Unfortunately for them, one of the officers stepped on the trigger. The stairs automatically flattened out, and both officers slid all the way down to the flat area near the second gate. Their guns and torches scattered all over the ground, and they were hurt, with back pain. It took them a few minutes to realize what had happened to them. The officers had survived the ordeal, but they were very angry and would love to kill all of the men in the basement.

Both officers were suspicious of Adnan, thinking he had triggered it from above the stairs. On the TV screen, Rassam and Yousif saw the entire slide by the Turkish officers down the stairway. Rassam knew the officers were furious and told Yousif, "It is time to get down from the spaceship. These two officers will give us a lot of problems. They have no right to be in here!"

Rassam was very angry. He wanted to see more of this great machine! He was very excited, too excited, about all of the technology. Leaning on the control panel while he was talking, Rassam unknowingly came into contact with one of the control panel buttons, and suddenly the main console shut off.

All of the TV screens on the ship started blinking large numbers, beginning at 60 minutes and descending second by second in Cuneiform numbers. With a soft noise, the computer started counting down every 10 minutes. When the chronometer was indicating almost sixty minutes, the computer noise grew very loud.

Rassam declared, "Yousif, let's leave here immediately!" Fearing that the ship might shut off the lights and lock all the doors, they both started running from the control room, pushing each other down the staircases, but when they got to the last stairway, they found an excuse to stop and then move forward very slowly. "The robot is watching us!"

Yousif went first, and when he passed the robot, its eyes lit up. When Rassam went by, the robot's eyes again lit up.

Rassam: "I do not know what this robot is doing!"

Yousef: "I think it is counting, or it has recognized us. That would save some time for us." He continued,

"We are all here, we got all the books."

Rassam: "Good job! Come over here with the books."

Dawood: "What happened to those Turkish officers?" Rassam reported that he saw them sliding down the stairs. "They must be hurt!"

Suddenly the two officers burst into the basement chamber from behind the gate, pointing their rifles at the crew and loudly cursing them in Turkish. The pair circled the flying machine, moving closer and closer to Rassam and yelling, "Allah Akbar! Allah Akbar!"

The robot opened and closed its red eyes three times and prepared to kill the two Turkish officers, who mumbled to each other in Turkish and then laughed, amused by the robot's actions. One officer turned to the crew and bellowed, "You are stealing Turkish government property! Who is the leader of the thieves?"

Rassam, upset, responded, "I am! I am *not* a thief, and do not call me one!

We have permission from Ali Riza Pasha, the governor of Mosel. *You* are the thieves!"

Officer number two moved forward with his rifle and stuck the barrel hard in Rassam's chest while screaming, "You dirty Christians, *you* are the thieves!"

"Do *not* call us thieves, understand?" said Rassam, "Take your gun off my chest!"

He pushed the barrel away with his right hand and wrist, telling them, "You had better leave now, before I report you to the governor! We have a permit from British government!

Officer number one responded, "Go? What British? This is Turkey! This property belongs to us! You have no right to steal! You will be executed!"

Officer number two added, "What is in the hands of these men, these three things? Put them on the ground, he yelled, pointing the gun at Dawood, then at Adel and Abrahim. Rassam was extremely angry, but he did not want to aggravate the situation.

"Yes," he instructed the crew, "put the books back in the box." in the Assyrian language. Dawood, Adel, and Abrahim headed back to where the gold box was.

One of the officers, presuming it was a box of gold, ran and tried to rip the book away from Dawood.

At that very moment, the robot, aiming its high-beam eye lasers all the way from where it stood, killed both officers. In one second, the officers fell to the ground, dead.

When this happened, the crew froze, and there was total silence in the chamber for a few minutes. Then Rassam broke the silence by saying, "Is that all?" He turned and looked at the robot. Deep inside his heart, he wanted to thank it.

He moved closer to the fallen officers. They had both been burned. Smoke could be seen rising from their bodies. Dawood lifted the book he had carried from the ground, and all of them, terrified, started running toward the gate.

When they arrived at the gate, they found that the stairs were still flattened.

Rassam asked Yousif to open both sides of the gate. "Wait a few minutes," he predicted, "and the stairs will come back."

The flying machine's 1-hour timer was reaching its final count. The lights in the basement started to blink, while the computer's audio indicator grew louder and louder. After waiting 5 minutes, they heard a rolling sound begin in the stairway.

Little by little, the stairs moved back into normal alignment. "Stay against the wall as you go, and watch your step," Rassam directed his men. "And most importantly, watch the books! I do not want any damage to come to these books."

They all started climbing up. Rassam went last. At the top of the stairs, Adnan was waiting for them with a torch. He was very happy to see them all alive.

Rassam waited several minutes at the top of the stairs, peering down to see if the lights had gone off completely in the chamber and to find out whether the computer would stop when the lights went off.

The two Turkish officers lay dead in the chamber. Five members of his crew had seen the unexpected killing. Even more surprisingly: Why had the robot killed the two Turkish officers but none of the Assyrians?

Adnan asked Rassam, "Sir, where are the two officers?"

Rassam responded, "They are downstairs looking for gold."

"Then why are we clearing out and closing the chamber while they are still inside?"

Rassam answered, "Never mind, I will tell you later, okay? Just do what I tell you. Come on."

Adnan left the main gate last. Rassam turned and faced the gate for a few moments, then directed the crew to close the main gate and cover it completely so it looked the way it had before.

While the rest of the crew was working hard to cover up the tunnel, Rassam called Yousif to his office to offer him a deal.

It was about 4:00 a.m. The crew worked non-stop until 6:30 in the morning to restore the previous appearance of the area. Rassam asked everyone to keep the expedition completely secret.

"Just deny that you have ever seen them in this area."

Rassam further instructed his assistants, "Would you please be sure the tunnel is fully restored to look as it did? After that, you can send the crew back home, but I want you to come back here so we can take these three books to Mosel. I have a horse that will do, and you should each have a donkey to come to work every day from Mosel to the site. That is a 20-minute ride. Dawood and Yousif, came back in 20 minutes."

Rassam was in his tent waiting to load the three books and their equipment on the horse and two donkeys. When they had packed up, they had one of the three heavy books wrapped and packed on the horse and one each secured out of sight on each donkey. Everything was fine.

It was 7:30 in the morning. They were preparing to move out when suddenly, three Turkish officers arrived at the site on horseback, demanding to see the permit to work in Nineveh.

They asked Rassam why the horses and donkeys were so heavily loaded. He handed the officers the letter and permit from the governor of Mosel and told them, "We work only at night, so we need many torches and a lot of equipment. We have 10 workers. We cannot leave our equipment here because the Arab thieves will steal it, so we have to take it with us every day. It is very hard for us, but we must do it."

The Turkish officer handed over the letter and permit and seriously asked Rassam, "You're sure you are not hiding any jewellery?"

"No, sir, the British consulate always reports to the governor of Mosel, Pasha al Risa, anything we find. But I do wish to thank you for your protection, and I would like to give you 10LR gift to buy something for your children."

Rassam walked over to the officer and gave him 10LR in coins, thanking him again for his protection from the Arab thieves. He told the officer in Turkish, "Working at night is very hard for the crew. We need to go home." The officer took the 10 LR and they rode away without thanking Rassam. They had no respect for Christians.

He did not believe Rassam and was suspicious of him. He knew Rassam was hiding something, otherwise he would not have bribed him. The Turkish officer ordered his policemen, "Follow them, but don't let them see you. Just watch them and let me know where they are going."

The officer mounted his horse and departed, leaving two policemen to follow Rassam and five members of his crew.

Rassam was anxious to reach the British consulate and get the three books to a safe place, and to report to his brother what they had found in the basement of Ashurbanipal as fast as they could. With the horse and two donkeys carrying three large books, they could not move fast enough. They had to walk about 20 kilometres (c.12.5 miles) on a dirt road from Nineveh to Mosul.

It was a very long walk. Rassam did not know that two Turkish policemen were following them. They all were discussing the discovery made the night before. All were in shock, emotionally disturbed; it was something they could not explain, especially the space machine and all of the jewellery, ornaments, and sculptures, and the screens inside the machine. It seemed like a dream. But the robot's murder of those two Turkish officers tempered their excitement.

Rassam said, "I'm sure no one will believe us about what we discovered last night! I do not know how I can explain it to my brother. It's inexplicable. You have to see it to believe it!

Rassam, do not give these books to the English people!" pleaded Dawood. Rassam told him, "I promise I will keep them in a safe place, but I want you to promise that you will not talk to anyone, not even your family, about these discoveries. These books can get us into a lot of trouble!"

"Not only me, but all of you and your families! You have to understand that whatever we find in Nineveh belongs to the Turkish government, and how it's their country. The British and French are paying a lot of money to the Turkish government of Mosel. That is the main reason why Britain and France have special permission to excavate Assyrian antiquities. Otherwise, they would be kicked off these projects," Rassam explained.

"I know it's very hard for you to realize our situation and understand it, but this treasure does not belong to the Assyrian people anymore. This was our country for the last four thousand years, but now you must accept the reality that it belongs to the Turkish government. They have all of the rights to do whatever they want.

"The Muslim governments do not care about or respect the Assyrian artefacts and might want to destroy it all.

"We are just lucky that the British and French are willing to spend thousands of Pounds to take them to Europe. Otherwise, the Muslim government will leave it in the ground for another thousand years to come, and they will build mosques or make it a Muslim cemetery on top of all the hills where they find Assyrian kings' palaces. Or they'll turn the hills into a Muslim graveyard just to prevent excavation by anyone except themselves! Then they will loot all the jewellery and leave the history to be destroyed, and in time they will eradicate the Assyrian history here and annihilate it completely!

Yousif asked, "What are we going to do with these three books? And what about the two officers?"

"We are going to the British consulate," responded Rassam, "where my brother is Vice Counsel. That is the safest place to keep these three books, and later on, we will try to find some Assyrians who can read ancient Assyrian or can read Aramaic, a dialect that served as the international language of the Middle East from about the 4th century B.C. to the 7th century A.D.

"As you know, Assyrian has used the Aramaic language. Assyrians used two languages throughout its history, ancient Assyrian and modern Assyrian, also called neo-Assyrian. The Arameans would eventually see their language, Aramaic, supplant ancient Assyrian because of the technological breakthrough in writing. Aramaic was made the second language of the Assyrian Empire in 752 B.C.," Rassam explained.

"I just wonder what type of language or dialect these books are written in," he continued, "it looks like the Neo-Assyrian alphabet, but why are these books in the chamber? How did they get in the golden box, and what is that big machine doing in that chamber? Where do they come from?

"I hope these three books will eventually answer all of these questions. But now we have to find someone to read the books and explain them to us in detail.

"But about those two Turkish officers, I told you never to mention them to anyone, even your family We did not kill them. Their religion and their attitude killed them. Please, again, just forget the officers!"

Dawood commented thoughtfully, "Rassam, I believe these books are written in a very old Assyrian dialect. I do not believe any Assyrian today can read these books. Yes, it looks like the Assyrian alphabet. But how do we know its meaning? It could be different from our language."

Abrahim said, "Rassam, there is a very old Assyrian Eastern church in the old section of Mosel. The priest is very old and knowledgeable in religious rites. He has a lot of old Assyrian religious books. I know him. I live in the same area. He lives next to the church in a small house, himself and his wife. I can take you to him."

"Abrahim is right," said Yousif. "I know this priest as well, and you can meet him first. Do not forget, Rassam, the first ancient Assyrian bible was a manuscript in the Assyrian language between 1400 and 1600 years ago. There are many copies that I know exist in the Assyrian monasteries in south Turkey, Syria, north Iraq, and Urmia in Iran. They are written on leather by the hands of Assyrian priests."

Rassam said, "I agree. Very well. Let us first arrive safely at the consulate. I believe that there are Turkish officers following us. Then, after we and the books are safe, we will take one book to the priest. Yousif, you know the easy way to the church."

"Yes, sir," said Yousif.

An hour later, about 8:30 in the morning, they arrived at the consulate in Mosul. The walls facing the street were about 15 feet high, covered with cement and off-white in colour. The door-keeper opened the large wooden gate of the consulate. The gate was 6 feet wide with two openings and made of unvarnished old wood,  looking typically Arabian in design.

They all got into the consulate safely, with the three books, the horse, and the two donkeys.

Christian Rassam, the British Vice Counsel, came forward when they entered, closing the gate to the two policemen at the end of the block.

When all of the guests have entered and are within a courtyard, it is an Arabian custom to close the gate. As the doorkeeper started shutting the two gate doors, he suddenly saw two policemen sitting on horses a half block away and staring at the British Consulate. Because the gatekeeper sensed that they were either watching or following Rassam and his crew, he called out, "Rassam, Rassam, come and see! There are two policemen following you!" [zero over there]

Rassam ran to the gate. Peering through a slender opening between the two doors, he saw the two policemen wait in silence for a few minutes and then leave.

He was very angry, very upset. He now realized the Turkish officers had not believed him and had sent Turkish policeman to follow him. But at that very moment, he was not too worried, since he was already safely inside the British Consulate with his discovery.

Christian Rassam, the British Vice Council, emerged from his office and greeted his brother Hormuzd Rassam. [were some routes are some in] and the rest of the crew. He had never met the crew before.

Christian Rassam was 45 years-old, 6 feet tall and well-built. He looked like a European. Very polite, respectful, and well-educated, he had studied in London, married an English woman, Matilda—sister of George Percy Badger—and had become the first English Consul in Mosel.

After Christian had finished introducing himself to the crew, he asked the doorkeeper to bring cold water and hot tea to all of them and invited them to sit under a tree in the consulate courtyard, a large oak tree that grew in the middle. Beneath the tree were wooden seats. The group gathered to sit there and rest up from their long walk.

"Hormouz," Christian asked, "Why are you here? And what are this horse and two donkeys doing here in the British Consulate courtyard? What happened? Did you have problems with Turkish officers?"

Rassam replied, smiling, "No, Christian, we are fine. It is a long walk, all night long, from Nineveh, and we have been working very hard. But I would like to speak with you alone in your office about last night's discovery."

The two brothers walked into Christian's office while the crew waited in the courtyard. Before they disappeared into the office, Hormouz Rassam asked the crew to pull the books from their packs and bring them inside immediately.

Once behind closed doors, the archaeologist Rassam explained to his brother, the consul Rassam, what he and his crew had found under the royal palace: the treasure, the statues, the gold jewellery, and, most importantly, the flying machine (UFO). Consul Rassam was totally shocked and completely speechless.

Hormouz then told his brother, "There I have found three books written in the ancient Assyrian language. They are here with us. We have brought them inside, and I want you to keep them in a safe place.

«These books might tell us the secret of the Assyrian race and where they came from!

"Brother, you should see this chamber, this basement! I cannot begin to describe this huge machine—the lights and moving pictures (TV screens) and many other things! They are not from this world! They must come from a different planet!"

"What do you want me to do?" Christian asked Hormouz.

Hormouz answered, "I want to keep this place secret and not to tell the British authorities! I ordered the crew to close up and bury the entrance so it is now as it was before. That has been done. Later on, we will see if we can find some Assyrian who knows the ancient dialect and ask him if he will read and explain the three books to us."

Christian asked, "Where are the books? May I see them?"

Rassam answered, "Wait, they are taking them down from the horse and donkeys. I hid the books with our tools, because the Turkish officers were following us from the site to here.

The meeting with his brother lasted only 15 to 20 minutes. Then Rassam came out of his brother's office. His five crew members were waiting with the books in the shade of a huge tree in the courtyard.

"I brought them," Adel said. Adnan wanted to go home. He was tired. "But Yousif and I will stay behind to help," said Adel.

The three books were brought into Christian Rassam's office.

Christian said, "Oh my God, these are the books! They are so beautiful, large and thick, with so many pages! [it is very in cheek with the gold cover and go to] Assyrian title. I am astonished, overwhelmed, that these are our ancestors' treasures from the ancient history of the Assyrians. We need to keep them for us!"

Rassam said, "Christian, these are the only treasures we could manage to take out of that basement chamber. There is much more down there."

Christian said, «I will keep these books here in the consulate. I have a very safe place. And as the Vice Consul, I am immune of from the Turkish government.

Rassam thanked his brother profusely. "Yousif and Dawood are waiting. We are going to take one book and go to see the old priest in the Assyrian Eastern Church. He may be able to read these books. It is walking distance from here.

He wrapped one of the books in a rag. "I am with you," said Christian. Yousif and Dawood left the consulate, walking to the church. Mosel was a very dangerous city, especially for Christians, but fortunately, no incident arose on their way.

Rassam did not want to lose any of the books, but he was very worried about the one he carried. After 20 minutes walking in the old Assyrian neighbourhood on the very narrow streets of Mosel—some were 2.5 mm wide, made of bricks, and always wet in the middle of the street. On both sides of the street were very old two-story houses, probably built over 100 years before. It was a very depressed neighbourhood, but it was very safe also, because only Assyrians, Chaldeans, and Armenians lived in this neighbourhood.

They arrived at the Assyrian church at 11:30am on Friday. The church gate was locked. They knocked at the gate a few times. Yousif said, "They must be in the house." Rassam asked, "Where is the priest's house?" Yousif pointed, "There, next to the church."

The door of the house was very small and narrow. Rassam knocked at the door. The wife of the priest opened the door. In the Assyrian language, she welcomed

Rassam, Dawood, and Yousif. Rassam greeted her and asked if the priest were home. She said, "Ye, he is preparing to go to a wedding."

She was very polite. "Oh, the wedding is on the outskirts of Mosel. Some friend will take him, he has a horse and carriage. But please, come inside, he has another hour."

Rassam was young and tall, a tall man, and he had to lower his head to go through the door and down two steps to get to the small yard. They all went down.   Then she took them into the living room.

The priest's wife's name was Nanaja, but they called her Nonno. She was 65 years old. The priest's name was Rabi Yokhana. Nonno said in a soft voice, "Rabi, you have Assyrian guests. Please come."

The priest came out of his study and shook hands with all of the guests. He then asked them, "How can I help you? He was about 75 years old and had lived in Mosel all of his life. He was very familiar with Mosel and with Assyrian history.

Rassam said in the Assyrian language, [you to do some self and his helpers your sis and I would him and] "I came here to ask you a favour of you. I have heard that you can read the ancient Assyrian language. I found an old book that I want you to look at and see if you can read it for us. Rassam took the book out of the rag covering it and handed it to the priest.

The moment he looked at the book, his eyes opened wide. He said.

"I have never seen such a beautiful book! Where did you find this book? Yes, I can read it! It is in an ancient language, the pure Assyrian language. Assyrian philosophers 1500 years ago wrote a few ancient versions of the Bible. They are all written in something very close to this dialect."

Rassam said, «Rabi, what is the title of this book?

The priest said the title reads, *History of Planet Tiamat.*

Rassam said, "What is planet Tiamat? There was another planet besides Earth?"

The priest said, "Yes, Mr. Rassam, I've heard many stories about a planetary collision 15,000 years ago. If you have ever read the Assyrian *Epic of Creation*, it starts with the words "Enuma Elish" or, in modern Assyrian, "Eman Jo Shmya.""

The planet Tiamat was inhabited by a very advanced civilization, among them was an Assyrian race, but an unfortunate collision between planet Tiamat and a second planet called Niburu occurred. In the *Epic of Creation*, this planet was three times bigger than Tiamat.

It suddenly appeared in our solar system, and it became visible two years before the collision. It missed all of the planets except planet Tiamat. The inhabitants of the planet Tiamat tried to escape. Only a few hundred successfully made it to this Earth, and those we call the Anunnaki.

Rassam asked, "How did the Anunnaki come to this Earth?

"I do not know, but I am willing to read this book and let you know how they came here. Can I keep this book, Mr. Rassam, for a few days? Because there are a lot of words that I do not know the meaning of. I need to study it a few times so that I can follow the sentences and can understand it.

Rassam answered, "Rabi Yokhanah, I would love to leave this book with you, but not today. You have a wedding to attend. I will come some other day when you're not busy, but overall, I would like to thank you and your wife for your hospitality.

"I just want to ask you a small favour: please, can we keep this meeting secret? If you do not mind, keep it secret between us. Do not tell anyone until we finish reading what is written in this book about this planet you call Tiamat."

The priest replied, "I am old enough to know to keep my ancestors' history secret. You are welcome anytime. My house is your house."

Rassam said, "Thank you. I will see you very soon."

While preparing again to leave the church house, Rassam wrapped the book in the same rag that he brought it in with. The priest came outside with them into their small yard at the house's gate.

The priest told Rassam, "My niece is getting married tomorrow, Saturday. I have my nephew, my sister's son, picking me and my wife up with a horse and carriage to take us to Telkaf, an Assyrian village.

It is only a few kilometres north of Nineveh and about 30 minutes from Mosel. I am inviting you and your friends to my niece's wedding. I would love for you to come and meet my family, and to bring this book with you so that we can read it together in a safe place. There are no Turkish officers in our village, and no one will bother us.

Rassam answered, "Rabi Yokhanah, thank you for inviting me and my friends to your niece's wedding. I would love to meet your family. I know the village and I'd love to come, but how long will you stay in the village?

The priest replied, "Myself and my wife will stay two days, Saturday and Sunday, and will come back on Monday. It will be good opportunity for us to try to read this book without any interference. We have a big house there, and you are welcome to come to stay with us."

The priest had his eye on the book. He was very anxious and eager to find out where this book came from. He needed to read it to understand the content and story behind this treasure book. The priest did not know that there are another two more books. He would go crazy if he found out.

Rassam said, "I would love to attend the wedding ceremony of your niece, and I promise to bring this book with me. I do not know if Dawood and Yousif would want to come"

With a soft voice and with all his heart, the priest asked both Dawood and Yousif to come to the wedding with Rassam. «I promise you will enjoy the village wedding.

Dawood said, "I would love to attend your niece's wedding."

Yousif added, Rabi, "With pleasure, yes. I thought you would never ask. I love village weddings!" Rabi repeated, again with a soft voice and a smile on his face, "You will not be sorry! You will meet all of my friends and family, and you will have fun."

Rassam said, Rabi, thank you again. I am glad to meet you, and I'd love to meet the rest of your family, especially the bride and groom. Tomorrow morning, we will rent a carriage for the three of us, and I hope to see you in the village."

Rassam, Dawood, and Yousif left the church house, and the priest closed the door of the courtyard. Rassam asked Dawood and Yousif to be ready at 10:00am at his house to go to the wedding. It was already 12:30pm on Friday. Rassam, Dawood, and Yousif were very tired. They had not slept all night. Rassam had the book covered and ready, and all of them went back to their residences.

On Saturday morning at exactly 10:00am, Yousif and Dawood arrived at Rassam's residence. When he opened the door, he noted that Dawood and Yousif were ready for the wedding, well-dressed and ready for dancing.

Dawood said, «Good morning, Rassam, are you ready for some dancing?

"Come inside and meet my mother and father. You never met my parents?"

Rassam introduced his parents to Yousif and Dawood, who were very happy to meet them. [rest time with having breakfast his mother offered to bring her to their guests. It is an Assyrian custom to offer tea or cold drinks to those entertained at the house.

"You both are so well-dressed for the wedding," said Rassam to Dawood and Yousif. Now you are forcing me to dress, too. I have no choice."

Rassam was about 20 years old when he started working with Austin Henry Leyard. Now 24 years old, he was tall and handsome. But Yousif and Dawood were each 35 years old, and unmarried as yet. [when they finish 30] They were all dressed well and ready to go to the wedding.

Rassam asked Dawood, "Where can we rent a horse and carriage that will take us to the village?"

Yousif said, "I know there is a place in downtown, close to the bazaar. They have a carriage garage that rent horses with carriages."

Rassam said, "Well, I am ready. Let us walk to the bazaar."

Yousif reminded Rassam, "Don't forget the book. That is the reason we are going!"

Rassam again wrapped the book in a clean cloth and put it in a bag so that no one could see it. He was committed to find out the origin of the book. That was the main reason he had accepted the priest and Rabi's invitation to the village wedding, even though he knew it would be tougher to carry the book 30 km out of Mosul to an Assyrian village during the Turkish occupation of Iraq.

Rassam was young, brave, and courageous, and he had a British Consulate supporting him. So he did not mind taking the book along to be read.

"It is time to move." Rassam said. Otherwise we will miss the wedding, and the priest will get upset."

Rassam, Dawood, and Yousif left the residence and walked downtown to rent a horse and carriage to take them to the village. When they arrived, they found a few carriages available, and they rented one of them with two black-colored horses that seated five including the driver, for only 15 LR one way.

They arrived at the village at 1:00pm without any difficulty, especially from the Turkish Police. The dirt road from Mosel to the village was beautiful and compelling, in reference to our changing environment. For Rassam, the journey to the village along mountain streams, rivers, and valleys was a good trip for us, they told the driver.

The driver said, "Where do you want me to drop you off?" in Turkish. Rassam said, "Please drop us off at the village church, and thank you."

They arrived in front of the church and dismounted from the carriage. Rassam gave a 15 LR tip to the driver and let him go. They walked to the church gate. The church had a small courtyard and a small garden between the gate and the door of the church. [Its wall was one and a half meters wide. to stone walkway] The church was built out of blocks of mud. It looked very old, and the door of the church was three feet wide. A sign on the top painted blue said Virgin Mary Assyrian Church of the East. Inside the church, there were 10 rows of seats on each side, one side for men and the other side for women. The church interior was very clean, and the altar was decorated with inexpensive crosses, an old Bible, a very old carpet, and Christian arts and crafts. On the walls were pictures of Jesus and Virgin Mary.

Rassam, Dawood, and Yousif slowly walked through the courtyard. From the church door, the priest and the bishop approached them.

The priest very happily said, "Welcome! I hope you had a nice trip, without any problems. I would like to introduce you to the Bishop of the Assyrian Church of the East, His Holiness, Bishop Daniel."

Bishop Daniel said, "Welcome, welcome," and happily introduced himself to the guests one by one. He was very appreciative and grateful to meet them all. "The Rabi would not stop talking nicely about you! He was anxiously awaiting your arrival."

Bishop Daniel suddenly remembered, and he began to stare at Rassam from top to bottom.

He said, "Hormouz Rassam, you are the son of Anton Rassam, the Archdeacon of the Assyrian Church of the East in Mosel, and your mother is the daughter of Mr. Ishaq Halabee of Aleppo, Syria."

Rassam answered, "Yes, Ravi Daniel, how do you know my parents?"

Bishop Daniel said, "I knew your mother and father a long time ago. We are good friends, and we are from the same church. I lived in Mosel 20 years ago, then I was transferred to this area. We have many Assyrian villages that I have to take care of. Anyway, how are your mother and father? I hope they are fine and in good health."

"Thank you," said Rassam. "My mother and father are fine. We still live in the same house in Mosel. I will let them know I met you. They will be very happy."

Bishop Daniel said, "Give my best regards to your parents. I'm too old to move from this village, and I like it here. I have all my family here, too. Otherwise I would love to see them."

The priest suddenly moved very close to Rassam and with a very soft voice, asked him, "Did you bring the book?"

Rassam said, "Yes, Rabi, I would not miss it."

Rassam was not aware that the priest had told the bishop about the book. The night before, the priest Yokhana had already told Bishop Daniel that Rassam had found an ancient Assyrian book, but he did not tell the priest where or when he had found it, and he did not let the priest see it.

"I have opened the book only for a few minutes, in my house, in Rassam's presence. The book is printed in classical Assyrian alphabet.

"It's one of the most beautiful books I have ever seen, but it's very hard to understand. It's very old. I needed more time to be familiar with its dialect. That is why I invited them to my niece's wedding," the priest told Daniel.

"Let us walk to our house," said the priest. The wedding will start very soon, all of the families are here and very impatient."

Rassam asked, "Is the groom from this village?"

The priest replied, "Yes, he is from this village. He is a very nice gentleman, and he is from a good family. We are very happy with him."

Bishop Daniel said, Rabi, your niece, Shamira, is a very lucky girl: Robert is a very nice boy. I know him and his family. I wish them a long life together, and I hope they will have many children and live happily.

Rassam said, "Rabi Daniel, can you explain to me in our common Assyrian language the Assyrian wedding customs and ancestral traditions? I am still young, but I would love to marry one day, and I would like to follow Assyrian customs."

Bishop Daniel responded, "Rassam, you are not young! You must start looking for a future wife. We have a lot of nice Assyrian girls in our village. You will see them at the wedding.

"But let me explain briefly the Assyrian wedding customs.

"In general, Assyrians favour early marriages. Less than a generation ago, it was not uncommon for a sufficiently grown-up boy, 17 to 20 years old or older, to marry a rather young girl of 12 to 15 years, though often older.

"Parents married their daughters off early because they were considered to be little future to the family. The marriageable age has been steadily rising in recent times, however. Once the parents have a girl to their liking and have agreed to seek her betrothal (*talubutha*), the father, accompanied by a few elderly relatives, calls on the girl's family to expresses interest in formally requesting the hand of their daughter.

"This traditional arrangement of marriage is called the *mashemetha*. The sun never the company is his father during this visit. As for the girl, who is always under the direct authority of her father, she remains secluded in a room of her parents' house and has no voice and choosing her mate (*tliba*). Indeed, if the boy (*yalee*) and the girl (*brata*) are not from the same village, they often do not see one another very much until the marriage ceremony itself.

"When the visitors arrive, the host reaches out to them with a decorous welcome, "Come on in" (*paqdhu*), and he ushers them into his living room where they sit on rugs.

"Greetings, questions as to the health of both families, and ceremonious preliminary remarks are exchanged. The parties then engage in mundane conversation, as though this were just an ordinary visit. Finally, the moment arrives to bring up the main reason for the visit.

"Avoiding a direct approach, the boy's father tries to please the head of the household by saying

"*Ithekh reshan khetaya w'aglathan layeh.*"

"He then continues, 'Perhaps you know the purpose of our visit. We have come to appeal to you to give your fair damsel to our son.'

"Before framing an answer, the host acts as though the purpose of the visit were a complete surprise to him. Respecting the ideals of kinship (*khizmayutha*), he puts this delicate matter exclusively in the hands of the close relatives sitting next to him.

"If they think favourably of the union, they will nod their heads, or just your suggesting and improving reply. In this case, the host inclined his head and pronounced in a very polite manner: "We are honoured to give you our daughter; but we know what a good reputation (*shimma*) your family has, and what a well-mannered young man your son is."

"The boy's father then acknowledges his gratitude by kissing the hand of the bride's father. "With these formalities completed, the guests are honoured with delicious dishes, and often with a drink of araq. Both families decide upon a day for the betrothal ceremony, commonly called the *mate that-d dhamanta* or *dewaqthad idha* (betrothal contract), which is cause for celebration.

"As a rule, the priest (*gasha*) is also invited to witness the betrothal ceremony. He performs a long and elaborate betrothal ritual, followed by a ring ceremony (*matewtha-d issaqtha*). He designates two character witnesses (*bakhtatha sowyatha*), matrons, to take the engagement ring to the bride-to-be, who is in a separate room with her close female relatives during the ritual. At this stage, the boy and girl are legally betrothed, and it is considered binding.

"The most important matter now is the amount of the betrothal money bride price (*nigda*), which the bridegroom's family will pay to the father of the bride. "The subject is brought up immediately and openly; the consent of the parties is the first condition essential for the validation of the marriage (*gewara*).

"The sum of the *nigda* is arrived at by bargaining between a number of distinguished people from both families. Generally, the social status of the groom's family determines the amount of the *nigda*. When the matter is settled to the satisfaction of both households, the boy's father will rise and kiss the hand of the bride's father to show his courteous regard and gratitude.

"afterwards, the groom's party will offer elaborate gifts (*pernitha*) for the bride, to gratify the bride's family. Usually the *pernitha* includes a silver waist belt (*kamarra* or *hayyasa*), bangle (*gulba*), gold bracelet (*shibirtha*), and gold earrings (*genashyatha*), and sometimes a nose-pendant (*khezzemtha*) or silver anklet (*khilkhala*). Also, the boy's father must make sure that both the bride's eldest brother and her mother's brother are generously remembered by giving each a gift (*diyyari* or *gurusha*).

"It is only after all of these delicate matters have been settled that the betrothal ceremony is climaxed with the traditional rice feast (*khatta-d rizza*). As a "reward for witnessing the betrothal contract," the guests and the members of the groom's party partake of this meal.

"Afterward, a party is given for the night-long entertainment of both families and their guests. The wide circle of *khulqaneh* keeps drinking *araq* and singing *rawatha* until the break of day. In the meantime, the women's retinue sings the folk songs of *lilyan*.

The wedding ceremony and its lengthy celebrations, occur soon after the betrothal.

"Rassam, this is the Assyrian custom. Did you understand it?

"Rabi, thank you," answered Rassam. "I learned a lot about Assyrian wedding customs. Thank you again."

Bishop Daniel said, "Rassam, Dawood, and Yousif, we are late. Let us go to the wedding. I must be early."

Rassam said, "OK, let us go and see the beautiful Assyrian girls, and dance until morning."

Rassam, Dawood, and Yousif did enjoy the wedding. They had not danced and imbibed like this for a long time. Dawood and Yousif met a long-time friend at the wedding, and he invited them to stay with him that night, but Rassam stayed with Rabi at his home.

It was 2:00 a.m. When Rabi and Daniel approached Rassam politely and asked him if he were willing to go to Bishop Daniel's house and try to read the book. Without any hesitation, Rassam accepted the offer. Rassam said, "Rabi, it is a very good idea, and it's a good time. I really enjoyed the wedding, I never danced so much! But I am here because of the book. With your and Bishop Daniel's knowledge of the Assyrian language, I have no doubt you will read this book and will find out where the ancient Assyrians came from."

Rassam never let the book out of his sight, He carried it with him during the wedding. It was wrapped with a white cloth and carried in a wooden shopping basket of a type famous in old-time Iraq. Most Iraqi shopping baskets were woven of date tree shrubs. Whenever he wanted to dance, he would ask Dawood or Yousif to watch it.

At first, Rassam was hesitant to let Yousif and Dawood join the meeting to listen to what was in the book, but before they left the wedding, out of respect and not to disturb these two men who had walked with him from Mosel, he decided he had to ask them when the dancing finished. So Rassam said to them, "The priest and the bishop are both tired and wish to go home. They might try to read the book. Are you two willing to come with us?"

Dawood replied, "It's OK. We found an old friend, and we will go with him and sleep at his house tonight."

Rassam said, "How about you, Yousif, do you want to come?" Yousif replied, "No, I will stay with Dawood. You go. We will see you tomorrow at the church."

Dawood and Yousif went back to their dancing, while Rassam, the priest, and Bishop Daniel left the wedding to go by foot to Daniel's home. It was 2:00 a.m. The alleys of the village were very dark. The priest said, "Bishop, I think it's too dark to be walking to your house. Wait, I will ask my nephew to give us a ride. It is too dark, but not for you Rassam, you are young. We need to see our steps: we are too old."

"You are right," said the bishop. "Rabi, I forgot my lamp! I always use the lamp at night, it's very convenient. The roads are too dark and dangerous. You have to see under your step, otherwise you can break your leg!" Rassam agreed. "I think it's a very good idea, Rabi, we may get lost in the small village and Bishop Daniel will not find his house and might take us to other peoples' houses!" The priest disagreed. "No, no. Rabi Daniel knows his way. He has been living in this village for 20 years, and the village has never changed since then."

While they waited in front of the wedding house, talking, Rabi Yokhanah's nephew brought him a lamp, and slowly they all started walking and talking, and after 10 minutes, they arrived at the bishop's house.

Bishop Daniel gave the key to Robbie to open the door. It was very hard for Daniel to open the door because it was very dark. After many attempts, they opened the main door and stepped into a small courtyard. They then walked 15 feet forward to the house door. Robbie tried to open it, but it seemed to need a smaller key. Then Rassam helped open it, and they were all happy.

"Daniel, thank you," said Rassam. "It is important we have arrived safely.

Please sit down and rest. Rabi, please, can you turn on the stove and make us some tea? I really need to drink."

Rabi asked, "Do you have enough oil inside the stove?"

Daniel answered, "Yes, just keep it very low, and fill the tea kettle. I need to drink a lot of tea. That will keep me awake all night. We have a long night ahead of us," he said happily. Mr. Rassam, I have been told that you are carrying a book in the Assyrian language and that it's a very old book. I would like to ask, where did you find the book? And before I see the book, I would like to tell you, my son, that we are all brothers. We are all Assyrians.

«We love our country, and we are the indigenous people of this country. You can see that my room is full of books, and they're very old books. Some of these books are 500 years old, so please, I do not want you to be worried. If you do not keep the book with us, then how can I read it? So, I think I've made my point. What would you like to say, Mr. Rassam?"

Rassam took the book out of the basket. Before he unwrapped it, he said, "Daniel, I would like to tell you the story of this book before I take it out. I work as an archaeologist for the trustees of the British Museum. I get paid by them, too; and my brother is Vice Council for the British government. So I have full responsibility for anything I find on the site of a palace. I will be in serious trouble if I do not report my findings.

"And secondly, there is the Turkish government, as you know, and if they find that this book is 5000 years old, they will take it from the British Museum.

"But as you said, very wisely, all Assyrians are brothers. I agree with you one hundred per cent. This book is our Assyrian ancient history. It was found in a special Assyrian place in Nineveh. We must cherish and protect it with our lives."

While Rassam was talking, he unwrapped the book and handed it to Bishop Daniel. Daniel grabbed the book first, and then Rabi Yokhana took it away from him. But then Bishop Daniel said, "Please, do not fight, you have all night and tomorrow. You have already seen it, Rabi. Why don't you go and bring us tea"? When the book was finally in Daniel's hands, he grew silent for a few minutes. Then he put the book on the table.

He was so surprised by the cover, and especially by the printed title. He had never seen a printed Assyrian book because at that time, all of the Assyrian books were written by hand. before opening the cover, while the book was on the table, he tried to lift it to kiss it. Then he got up and kissed the book three times. He knew that this book was very special and holy.

In a low voice, Bishop Daniel asked Rassam if he could open it. Rabi Yokhana was in the kitchen preparing the tea. But when he overheard that Bishop Daniel wanted to open the book, he immediately yelled, "Please, wait for me! I am coming! I am bringing the tea. Wait for me!"

Rossum said, "Yes, you can open it, Daniel, but please let us wait for Rabi. He is very anxious to see inside the book. I believe both of you will be able to read it." Rabi Yokhana, rushing in, brought three cups of tea and sugar, impatiently placed them on the table, and sat next to Bishop Daniel. "Now let us open the book!" he said. The two old spiritual and religious friends, experienced in ancient Assyrian classical literature and expert in the language, anxiously put their heads close to the ancient book to read.

It seemed like it had started a confrontation between Rabi and Daniel to see who could read the first sentence.

Rassam said, "Gentlemen, let us have the tea first. You do not have to fight over the book, and I promise we have plenty of time to read it, even if I have to stay here for a few days. I would like to understand everything about the book."

Daniel said, "I Think you are right. We need a lot of time."

Rabi said, "Yes, let us drink our tea before it gets cold."

After they had a few sips of tea, Daniel could not wait. He slowly started to open the first page. "I might be able to read it!" Daniel screamed. "I can read it! It's written in our ancient Assyrian dialect! I would love to look through the pages first!"

When he opened the cover, he found a few loose pages in the book. They had been typed and added to the book later.

They were all surprised. Daniel took the pages out and handed them to Rassam, who said, "Let us read these first. We will concentrate on the book afterward, after we read the loose pages."

He held the book in his hands for a second, as if it were the most expensive thing he had ever touched.

They saw that the loose pages had all been computerized. They were surprised in that it seemed as if the pages were new and just came out of the printer. There were no pictures on them. The only difference between these pages and the book's pages was that the lettering of the loose pages was slightly larger than the lettering in the book, which puzzled them all.

Daniel commented, "I think these pages were added to the book after they had printed it."

"I think, by looking at it in detail, you are right. They were added later on," said Rassam.

Then Rabi said, "While I was focusing on the papers and looking at them page by page, I was trying to read them."

Suddenly he asked Daniel to read the title.

Daniel responded, "I hope I am reading it right. It says, 'Diary of our Spaceship, From Our Planet to Yours. We are the Anunnakis' Rassam exclaimed, "Oh my God, is that what it says?"

Daniel responded, Yes, that is what it says; it seems that these pages were written here, after they arrived on our planet, and they just inserted those loose pages into the book."

When they read the title, they instantly became more interested in finding out the real story of these people and from where and when they had come. The reading of the documents would not be an easy task.

There were a lot of words on the loose pages with which Daniel and Rabi were not familiar. They described the writing on the page as very sophisticated, and said that whomever had written this document must have been highly educated. "This is pure Assyrian, not like our language now, that is mixed together with other languages," Daniel explained.

Both Rabi and Daniel were members of the Holy Church of the East, the oldest and first Christian religious organization in the world. They were knowledgeable in classical Assyrian literature and expert in the ancient Assyrian language, with access to the numerous Assyrian religious books in the church library. They had devoted their lives to the Holy Church of the East since they were each 12-years old, dedicating their lives to serve God.

As a matter of fact, the Assyrians were the first ones to believe in God and the son of God, Jesus Christ.

The Holy Church of the East in earlier times covered the whole eastern world, from Seleucia to the islands of Japan and Java, and present-day Indonesia and China.

Even the first Christian historian, Eusebius of Caesarea (265-339 A.D.) devoted scarcely a word in his ecclesiastical history to the Asian Christianity of Mesopotamia that had begun to develop rapidly in the second century. The reasons behind this lack of attention to the eastern Church grew out of the Middle Eastern geopolitical situation of that time.

Rassam said, "Daniel and Yokhana, please, let us concentrate on the pages, to read them and understand how and why these people visited our Earth from this other planet as they claim to have done in the title of those pages."

Even though Rassam had seen the flying machine in the basement of the palace, he still did not believe it.

He had been inside the flying machine and had seen all of the sophisticated space technology, computers, TV screens, spacesuits, and the gigantic size of the machine. But although he had seen these things with his own eyes only a few days before, still his mind could not take it in. It was like a prison to him.

He concentrated deeply for a few minutes, until Rabi asked him, "Rassam, what are you thinking about?"

Rassam answered, "I am thinking: Are we the same people that came from the different planet? Are these people our real ancestors?"

Daniel responded, "Rassam, my son, I believe you are right! I had never thought about it. I have been reading letter by letter while you were talking; it's a true story—let me start from the beginning so that you can understand. Rabi, please, you listen, too. It says …" You will understand why and how we migrated from our planet which we call "Tiamat" and landed on this new planet called Earth.

"I am the captain of this mission and main commander of the flying machine we call "spaceship." My name is Captain Anu, commander of the Assyrian Aeronautical and Space Administration of Tiamat. I was main commander when we left our planet; I had eight spaceships under my command. We could manage to safely fly only five of these spaceships.

With God Assur's blessing, all of the spaceships arrived safely on Earth with some difficulties, but some landed in different locations a few hundred miles apart. Some even landed in the ocean, but the passengers were safe, as we learned from our communication with other captains of the ships. Each spaceship was carrying only 60 people; there was a total of 300 Anunnaki that landed on Earth, and they were all from Assur state. But there were other states (countries) on the planet. Some had the same type of flying ships, given to them by the king of

Assur state. They had a successful mission like us. They only could manage to fly, I think, four from our state and five from another state.

Some of the spaceships could carry only 50 people including the captain of the ship. We do not know if they have arrived to earth because of the long distance. They only managed to fly three spaceships. The state of Egypt which is the second largest state on the planet Tiamat and all of the Assyrian state managed to fly five of the spaceships successfully. I had direct contact and communication with all of the captains when they were on the first day of the flight, but it lasted only a week. Later we lost contact with all of them because I was concentrating on our ship. And after that, we lost all communications because our satellite system on the planet collided with another planet. I will go into full detail on the planetary collision later in the document.

I know they landed on Earth, but far from our landing area in a different part of the Earth. We were very lucky that we could escape in 14 spaceships from our planet, even though we had more than 10 spaceships from my state to use in the escape. Some of those developed problems during take-off. And some of them stayed on the ground: it was too late.

Planet Tiamat was the third planet in our solar system. It was larger than earth by 1 ½ times it was one of the most scenic planets in our solar system with a stable orbit; neither to close and you're too far from the sun. Tiamat was 102,500,000 miles from the sun and the earth was 81,500,000 miles from the sun.

I say that because we have been observing the planet earth for a long time; and we have visited the planet earth, using our satellite system, and we have been investigating scientifically the astronomy of the earth; like the earth structures: the soil, the minerals, the oceans, the water, the mountains, the rivers and lakes, and life on earth.

All of the investigation was only for scientific purposes, at the beginning. But later, our planet, Tiamat, started dumping its resources for 50,000 years, especially oil, gas, gold, and most importantly, depleted uranium, which was used to produce our electrical system by converting it to nucleolus fuel.

The trip from the planet Tiamat lasted 190 Earth days. It was a very long space trip. We had anticipated the difficulty of this interplanetary travel, especially when we had to take off without any planning, in unfavourable conditions, and in the middle of the biggest disaster in the history of our solar system. This type of accident only happens in the galaxies, but it did happen, and it completely destroyed our planet and wiped out all remaining humankind on planet Tiamat. The disaster will be explained in detail later. The trip from our planet to Earth was extremely difficult, because none of the captains had flown to an unknown planet.

RASSAM'S DREAM OF PLANT TIAMAT

They were all tired from the wedding, especially Rassam. It was 2:30 am when Rabi Daniel and Rabi Youkanah finished reading a few pages of the ancient book Rassam and his crew found in the basement of the Ashurbanipal Palace. All Rassam wanted right now was a good night's sleep. His body was exhausted and ready to turn in for the night, but his mind won't let him rest. He cannot stop thinking about the spaceship and everything that comes with it. The two officers that were killed by the robot weighed heavily on his mind too. He was tossing and turning all night until sleep came at last.

He was standing in the middle of the city. A city. A city he has never been before. The streets are wide with manicured trees and lawn. It was the most beautiful city he has ever seen. The people looked very happy. They look different but happy. They are fashionably dressed especially the women. Everyone was busy here. The sidewalks are full of people going about their way. The restaurants and the boutiques are full too.

The cars looked different, they are more machines than cars. Some of them don't have drivers in them. Then he noticed the Sky Scrapers. The height and lights of the sky scrapers were nauseatingly beautiful but what was unbelievably breath taking was the flying vehicles. They were a cross between a small airplane/ helicopter and a flying car. There was organized traffic in the sky!

People were looking at him differently, as if they know he is not one of them. He saw his reflection in one the boutique windows and noticed that his clothes, his whole appearance doesn't look anything that belongs in that place. He must have stood out like a sore thumb and probably acted like a tourist from the hills, that people seem to be wary of him. Most of them tried to avoid him on the streets. He was a stranger in a much stranger place. Getting anxious by the minute not knowing where he is, Rassam thought he had to find out where he is. He spotted one gentleman that is looking at him seriously a few feet away.

"Shlama Aluka," he tried greeting him in Assyrian. The man did not seem to understand, and he just kept looking at Rassam.

"Where Am I?" he tried again.

"You are in Mat Ashur, in the planet Tiamat," the man answered.

Rassam woke up suddenly. It was just a dream, but it seemed so real. He sat up, trying to steady himself. His heart is racing fast. What was that all about? He asked himself.

He got up and rushed towards the ancient book. He quickly looked for the universal map in the book. He remembered seeing it before. He scanned the pages quickly but careful not to damage the book.

"What are you doing? It is 4am in the morning Rassam!" Rabi Daniel heard the ruckus Rassam was making from the other room. He was sleeping in the next room, so he grabbed his oil lamp to check when he started hearing the noise Rassam was making.

"Rabi Daniel, I'm sorry if I woke you. I had the most amazing dream. I was in Mat Ashur in Planet Tiamat…" Rassam started to explain but Rabi Daniel interrupted,

"Rassam, you are thinking too much. You are tired, you should go back to sleep."

"Look and see for yourself." Rabi Daniel brought his lamp closer to inspect the page Rassam was so eager to show him. He showed him the page where the Solar System is depicted at first until they found the map of Mat Ashur. Here, the story begins in the Planet Tiamat as it has been described in the ancient book Mat-Assur.

Mat-Assur sits on a massive 8,500,000 square kilometres covering both land and water. Governed by a monarchy based on religion, the government is headed and ruled by the King. The Assyrian people considers their King as a partly a divine being who is filled with divine spirit who can exercise just rulings and maintain the cosmic harmony guaranteeing his people divine blessings, prosperity and peace. The King is also the commander in chief of the military.

MAT-ASSUR CAPATAL CITY

It was Assyrian tradition that the King appoints a crown prince to help with his duties. The crowned Prince was second in lone to the throne. The King governs with the help of a Council of Ministries also called the Royal Cabinet. There were ten ministers that were part of the cabinet, each specializing in different parts of the government such as foreign affairs, education, finance and many others. Most of the royal cabinet members were related to the King's family.

The King also has other advisers and help. There were six legislative bodies called the Religious Legislative Council, whose main responsibility was to propose new laws or amend existing ones. The King appoints each religious members of the council.

The nation was divided into twelve provinces, each with a government and a governor. Each province has its own council that advises the governor and deals with the development of the province. Usually the Kings, appoint their sons or brothers as governors for the larger cities.

King Ashur-Adamu I claimed that his father favoured him for his bravery and intelligence. He soon took on more duties and responsibilities, commanding the court and nobles. King Ashur Adamu I was a great King, in fact, he is considered the greatest, most powerful king to have ever ruled Mat-Assur. During his reign, no appointments, not projects, nothing was ever done without his consent. Rich men showered him with gifts and everyone respected his decrees. His words were considered as laws. He was brave and mighty. No one ever wanted to make the King angry for his anger is tremendous. His campaigns and battles reached back to the early days of his youth. His body is covered in scars as a remembrance from all the battles he won. He was wild and cunning, and his soldiers loved him. They worshiped the ground he walked on. To his soldiers, he was like their God.

King Ashur-Adamu married a beautiful Assyrian, Queen Assurinu. They have two children, their son Assur-Tudiya and their beautiful daughter Atalia. Both are single and in the prime of their lives. Prince Assur-Tudiya was 35 years old and Princess Atalia was 29 years old. Prince Assur-Tudiya was the commander of the Assyrian Air Force and Training chief of the Astronaut Center.

Princess Atalia was beautiful. She had long black hair and light blue eyes. She was the favourite of the queen mother, helping her in her queenly functions. The princess was well educated but has yet to marry. According to Assyrian customs, royalty should marry within the family. The King has been encouraging the princess to marry one of the bachelors in the King's clan but to no avail. It might be due to the queen mother's secret advise to choose whoever she loves.

From the beginning of time, Almighty God Assur, the God of Assyria, whom transcends human comprehension. Assur was the "Sum Total of all gods" and He was the representative of the Assyrian gods on the planet Tiamat and beyond. It is interesting to see that on the planet Tiamat and even on Earth, unto the fall of the Assyrian Empire (609 B.C.), how God Assur grows in importance as the position of the city and the land became stranger. The intimate relationship between the God and especially the King as his priest represents a bond beyond religion and politics, which identifies the purpose of the god of the land. As the idea of having a god grew in importance from the beginning of human existence, he took over more of the functions which belonged to the other gods. For example, several times he took over the function of the Sun-God Shamash or Enir, father of creator, as the guardian of justice. He was the god of war and peace who gives the King the victory in battles, and made peace between the nations. He was the father of all gods, the creator and begetter. He was also praised for his mercy.

Now, after 432,000 years of human existence on the planet Tiamat, the Assyrian Kingdom, the most advanced and strongest of all nations on the planet, started to have economic and political issues with the other countries. This was because of the Sever shortage of Energy on the planet. They have exhausted all of their natural fuel and is triggered by the high population in every country; therefore, resulting to the smaller countries demanding to get their share of more energy. This is to help sustain the high growth of their people and their economies. The amount of fossil fuels available for use completely worsened each year and the only remaining energy was nuclear energy. Even half of that resource was already depleted. However, there was still pure uranium, which was abundant in the larger countries because they have advanced nuclear technology and industry. Because of this, the smaller countries would rely on the progressive nations.

Due to the energy shortage, the smaller nations met and planned to attack Assyria, which was the nuclear depot, as well as the other nations, to steal nuclear rods. Because of this, the God of Pantheon "Assur", sensed the tension between the nations. He called a special emergency meeting with all the gods in the Temple of Assur to discuss the ongoing problem and put a stop to the energy crisis. Aside from that, he wants to find a peaceful solution to the Assyrian kingdom, specially the King. The Assyrian kings were considered as 2/3 god and 1/3 human; therefore, strengthening the ties between god and king.

Normally, it was the King who usually prays to the god Assur for help; however, in this situation, the god takes matters into his own hands.

GOD ASSUR

Male and Female Deities with rank number and succession

No	Male	No	Female
60	Anu	55	Antu
50	Enlil	45	Ninlil
40	Ea/Enki	35	Ninki
30	Nanna/Sin	25	Ningal
20	Litu/Shamash	15	Inanna/Ishtar
10	Ishkar/Adad	5	Ninhuksag

The Gods' meeting was secretly scheduled to begin at midnight at the temple built and dedicated to the great god Assur. It was located in the north of Mat-Assur, at the peak of the highest mountain called Angel Tower. It was estimated to be 3000 ft or 1000 meters high. It features the Angel Falls, the planet's highest uninterrupted waterfalls; flowing from the mountaintop, all year round. It was located on the summit that was covered with a tropical forest. This was situated on the highest peak to make sure that it can only be used by the gods and the royal family and the high priests, and was also used for special sacramental occasions.

The temple was always guarded by winged, eagle-headed genies. They were really dedicated guards to the Assyrian King and the country and usually take turns to fly day and night to protect the temple.

On the other hand, the Ishtar temple was dedicated solely to the female deities. It was 50 meters wide and landscaped with the most beautiful flower trees in the middle of the avenue. Date palm trees were planted and were called the tree of life. With every palm tree planted, a statue of an Assyrian king was erected, dedicated to those who served the great Assyrian nation throughout the 432,000 years of their race's existence.

At the beginning of Mat-Assur 400,000 years ago, the Assur temple was one of the most beautiful architectural wonders in the Assyrian nation, often called as the Crystal Shrine. This was because all the doors and windows were made of pure gold; the interior walls and ceiling were covered in shiny crystals, which were all found deep in the mines—giving the interior a night sky look. The temple was not large as it could only accommodate 50-100 people, excluding the gods themselves.

The altar consists of a 12-foot diameter table and three chairs made of gold, with red velvet seat covering. Large chandeliers hung above it.

Every year during the Akitu festival (New Year), on the 9th of Nesanu (March 9th), the Assyrian king would spend his first four days in the temple. He would isolate himself from the rest of the world. However, on the fifth to the twelfth day, he would go to the Eshgil temple. On the twenty-first, the Akitu festival officially starts.

The Eshgil temple was built one kilometre away from the king's palace and is known to be the second most sacred temple in Mat-Assur. It was beautiful and large and could occupy 1000 people for ceremonies. It was designed and constructed to face the palace and was connected by the Star Avenue. The palace was on the north whilst the temple was on the south of the Star Avenue. It was also known to the temple dedicated to the male deities. It was built on 30 acres of land, surrounded with the most beautiful garden, including a place for the King's family to spend for a few hours on weekends or on special occasions. It was considered as a sanctuary and holy place for high-ranking families.

The temple has a special place for the King and his family. Behind them, the dignitaries sat—military generals and other high-ranking officers with their families. At the back are the senators and government officials and their families.

It has five gates. The main gate facing Star Avenue was 20 feet high and 15 feet wide, and was made of gold. The main gate was dedicated to the 430 famous Assyrian kings. The kings' faces and names were engraved on the golden main gate on an 8 ½" x 11" space, and the date they served the country. The other four gates were on both sides of the temple, facing the garden. They were made with special wood.

On weekends, the royal family, administrators, cabinet ministers would gather at the temple to play and pay respects to the God Assur, the main God of the Pantheon. The temple served as a safe sanctuary for the royal family because it was protected 24 hours by 60 winged genies.

The genies are in full control of the 30-acre site. They do not talk but they have special powers that can freeze humans on the spot.

MAN *FIGURE AND* EAGLE *FIGURE*

At midnight, the meeting was scheduled by the god Assur. All twelve gods started appearing one by one at the Crystal Shrine temple, the temple that was designated only for gods or god's special meetings. The lights in the temple were dim. The gods were coming from different directions. They were popping from the sky, going through walls, roof, because they were silhouette-like. You can only see their image but not with a physical full body. The night was dark and you can see the stars. The temple was fully secured by the winged, eagle-headed genies. The genies were quiet when the male and female gods arrived and they appeared to be waiting for them. All the gods then took their designated seats at the round altar—male gods on the right side and the female gods on the left side of the God Assur.

Few minutes have passed and suddenly, the genies rose. They started moving around and they were very excited. They can sense something was happening around the temple. At that moment, all the gods got up from their seats and prepared to welcome the God Assur. Suddenly, a strong wind entered the temple and in the middle of a dark cloud, a small opening appeared. It emitted a bright light and the God Assur came through the hole, still followed by the bright light. He then took his respected seat at the center of the altar.

All the gods had their heads bowed down. God Assur stood for a moment and opened his hand up in prayer. He then asked the gods to be seated by lowering his hand and his head. After which, he took his seat.

God Assur started the meeting and told the gods that he seeks to find a peaceful solution to the king of his country. The whole meeting lasted for more than two hours. They all decided to ask the Assyrian king to discuss the energy shortage problem that was happening on the whole planet. They would also discuss about the pure uranium, which the Assyrian controls 75% of. It was the only source of energy remaining on the planet and it was the only chance to supply Tiamat for more than 100 years. The Assyrian nation only has this in their reserves and the gods requested if the Assyrian king would allow to share the uranium with all the other countries, without discrimination, because the smallest countries get their energy from the nuclear reactor.

The God Assur requested that the kings of each nation that they should have their share, the distribution should be equal to the country's respective size. He asked the king to be merciful and to refrain from harming the other nations and help each other to live in peace because they all need the energy to survive.

The last request from the gods is that the king must initiate a general membership

meeting of all the countries to solve this crisis immediately. Otherwise, there will be a great destruction and devastation brought by a war between all nation.

When the meeting ended, the gods disappeared one by one. Only God Assur and three genies remained in the temple. He asked the three genies to approach the altar and ask them to take a message to the Assyrian king that on the first day of his return from the Akitu ritual, that the genies would read the meeting's agenda and he wants the genies to memorize every word. The genies understood the command, bowed to the God. The moment when the God Assur vanished, the temple then became dim.

ASSYRIAN GENIES

Assyria have two genie types, who were the protective spirits that protected the gods' temples and the royal family during religious ceremonies.

The first type were man figure genies. They were 6 ft. tall, with large wings like an angel. They can fly like birds and in ancient Assyria, they were called "Abkula."

They guard the entrance to the private quarters of the king. They always carry a goat and a giant ear of corn during ceremonies as a symbol of fertility. They wear kilts with long tassels hanging from it, indicating their semi-divine status; and fringed, gold embroidered robes, which were drawn around their bodies and thrown over their shoulders. This leaves the right legs exposed. They wear sandals and a bead necklace around their necks. They have armlets that sports animal head terminals. This type of genies can communicate via extrasensory perception or telepathy (to feel or receive impressions through body organs, sight, touch, talk, smell, or hearing). They are dedicated to protect the King and his family. They guard the palace, especially the throne room. No one can enter the throne room without the genies' permission. Usually when the king is in session with his cabinet or any foreign guests, six genies would be guarding the throne room—four at the main gate, with two opening the gate to the guests and another two to escort the guests to the king. They will not move until the king commands them to move away. The last two genies would stand on both sides of the king for protection.

The second type of genies are those with eagle-head and with large wings. They can fly very high. Their figures are the classic Assyrian type of protective magical spirits. They wear the same clothes as the other genies. They carry weapons because they protect all the Gods Temples. They attend all Gods meetings. They cannot talk but they can still communicate via extrasensory perception but with other genies only. This was actually good because God did not want any God's influence and decision to be known outside the temple as everything must be kept as secrets.

In the Royal Palace of Bet-Relutu, two weeks before the king would start his yearly ritual, the beautiful queen of Assyria—Ashurinu, was very busy preparing for husband, the honourable King Ashur-Adami I. Usually as a yearly custom, the queen would give a surprise get well party on the last day before the king leaves for his ritual. This was because she will not be seeing the king, her husband, for twelve days, during the Akitu ritual. So for this special occasion, the queen invited all the close family members of the king, her family, and their close friends—including the high-ranking military officials and their wives, cabinet members and their partners, as well as the religious leaders "Shish-Galu" of the country for the get well luncheon. Since the weather was good, the queen decided to hold the party in the Palace Garden. She ordered the palace gardeners to prepare the area and that the party was to be at the main fountain area. At the same time, she ordered the servants to prepare different types of delicious food, drinks, refreshments—including a wide selection of fruits and pastries—for the guests.

The Palace Garden is a few acres large and it is very beautiful. It is terraced with paving and ornamental flower beds, surrounded by ponds with fountains from reused cisterns that retrieved water from the palace. The spring garden continued the tradition of rotational flower displays in the spring and summer. The vibrant colours and exotic plants are on display from April to October when the garden is blooming its best. But for this spring, tulips, wallflowers, and pansies bloom. While during the summer months, geraniums, cannas, begonias and the likes provide vivid colours throughout the whole garden. The trees are coppiced or stooled, meaning, that they have been cut back to the ground. This was to preserve the original true stock and allows new stems to be trained over the new framework of the bower.

The Queen and her family love the Palace Garden and they usually use it every Sunday to walk around the flowery ponds. Once a month, the queen would invite her girlfriends for a tea party in a special location designed for the her and her friends.

But for the King, there were only four days remaining before he leaves for the Akitu Ritual. He has been very busy to appoint his son, Assur Tudiya, who's 35 years old, to take over his place as king for twelve days during the ritual. During the remaining days, the king spent most of his time in the throne room, working hard and having meetings with all his cabinet members, military, and other government officials. Friendly foreign dignitaries were present as well. This was done to prepare his government while he goes on leave.

The throne room was where the king conducted his government affairs and exercised his authority over a state. It is in the Royal Palace and is 100" wide and 300 ft long. It was one of the exciting rooms in the palace. Before you enter the throne room, there was the waiting room, where the guests would lounge before they are allowed to enter and see the king. The waiting room was very large and beautiful with a 100 ft x 100 ft area. It is decorated with window curtains in gold colour. The floor is covered with marble and the room is furnished with soft, plush sofas, seats and small tables with flowers on them.

Between the throne and waiting rooms is a large gate that is 15" wide and 20" high made of pure gold. This gate is always guarded by four eagle-headed genies—two outside to open the gate and another two inside to escort the guests close to the king.

The throne room was one of the most impressive rooms in the palace. The King's throne was three steps high that is 30 ft wide and 20 ft deep. Usually, there is only one throne. But on special occasions there will be two chairs next to each other. The wall at the back of the throne was decorated with the famous Assyrian relief called "Tree of Life". It was all in gold and on the top was the God Assur insignia, also made out of gold. The rest of the walls in the throne room were also covered in Assyrian reliefs. It can justly be acclaimed as a masterpiece inside the royal palace, with floors covered with decorated shining marble, six large chandeliers, two rows of chair on both sides of the room for the officials, dignitaries, and guests.

The Assyrian King was considered ¾ God and ¼ human. Usually, no one can take a step on the throne as it was forbidden because it was sacred. Only the king and queen can be on the throne and the genies who guarded them.

LUNCHEON

The year 432,000 was ending. Its last day of the year, the King of Assyria, Ashur Adami I, was very busy in the throne room with his cabinet members and religious leaders "Shish-Galu" debating the upcoming Akitu "Assyrian New Year". It was about ten in the morning. Suddenly, the throne room gatekeeper announced!

"Your Honour, the honourable Queen "Ashurinu", your son "Ashur Tudiya", and daughter "Atalia" and some guests are in the waiting room to greet you."

The King immediately stopped the meeting and all the cabinet members and religious leaders took their places. He then asked the gatekeeper to let his family and the guests in the room.

The queen, prince, and princess entered first. The rest of the guests waited in the other room. Immediately, two genies opened the throne room gate wide open and four beautiful people dressed in Assyrian costumes entered first, followed by the queen—who was dressed very elaborately in her traditional Assyrian royalty dress and her golden crown. A few steps behind her were her son and daughter. Atalia, the princess, was also decked in an elaborate gown. Following them were Assyrian dancers donning colourful dressed and were escorted by eight man-head genies.

The queen's entrance was very compelling to everyone in attendance. They all stood with their heads bowed down. The king; however, stood from his throne and went down the platform to meet his queen. He took the queen's hand and together, they went to the throne and assisted his wife in sitting on her chair. Meanwhile, both the prince and princess took their respective places behind the king and queen. The young dancers stood on both sides of the throne. The king then asked the gatekeeper to let the guests come in. The gatekeeper then started to call the names of each guest and escorted them to the throne to greet the royal family. There were a lot of guests. The gatekeeper continued to assist the guests one after another, and once they arrived at the throne, they bowed their heads in respect to the king and queen, then they turn left or right to join the rest of the guests.

The queen invited most of the royal family and the members of the royal palace—including the high-ranking officers in the government, as well as the king's good friends—like Chief Air Force Commander Azarah-Anu and his wife Anunitu, with their son astronaut pilot Mr. Abzu-Bet-Anu, who was a very good friend of the prince. In attendance was also the general of the Armed Forces, cousin of the king, General Tartaru and his wife Yoba. Adding to the guests were the Navy Commander Assur-Shar Shari and his wife Mami, with their daughter Bonita and son Dudu-Enlil, the Navy's lieutenant. Many other government officials, congressmen, councilmen, and religious leaders attended as well. All the invited guests were couples but some came with their sons and daughters.

The king was very happy and surprised to see all his good friends before he leaves to the Akitu ritual. He kept looking at the queen to find out what was going on! But the queen simply kept quiet and only smiled. It was evident that she wanted to surprise her husband.

By noon, all the invited guests were already inside the throne room. The two genies started to close the gate. Suddenly, the room became very quiet and a slow, Assyrian traditional music filled the room. The young dancers then took the middle floor and started dancing for half an hour. When the dance ended, the room lit up. Then the queen stood from her seat and went close to the king. Everyone in the room grew quiet. The queen was very beautiful. Aside from that, there was something in her, something that the people saw and recognized in her performance; like she exudes an aura of luminous quality—like a combination of wistfulness, radiance, and yearning.

The queen looked around the room and spoke. "Ladies and gentlemen, I would like to thank all of you for coming to this very important event. As you all know, today is the last day before my beloved, our king Ashur Adamu I, the great king of Mat-Assur, will be leaving for the Akitu Ritual for twelve days. This event has been a custom in the great Assyrian nation for thousands of years. We will have the Akitu Festival upon his return and everyone here in attendance is invited."

BONITA   PRINCESS MAHAA

QUEEN ASSURINU

Queen Assurinu walked a bit closer to the king and asked his hand to get up. While she was talking to the guests, the king was looking seriously at her, not knowing that his wife was giving him a surprise party.

At that exact moment, the main gate of the throne room opened and ten genies entered, walked up to the throne to escort the royal family to the garden.

The king, although quite confused, stood up from his throne and held his queen's hand. Together, they walked down the throne, followed closely by the prince Ashur-Tudiya and princess Atalia. The genies surrounded the royal family and the entourage was followed by the rest of the guests.

They arrived at the luncheon area and the palace servants were waiting for them, standing on both sides of the walkway from the palace to the luncheon area, with heads bowed down in respect to the royal family.

A special tent was prepared for the royal family, with two servants. Once they relaxed on their seats, the invited guests wanted to meet the royal couple. Everyone waited for their turns to introduce themselves to the king and queen. First to go were the family members, close friends, then the government officials, foreign dignitaries.

The King turned to his wife and said, "Thank you honey for this beautiful luncheon, and for inviting all my good friends." The queen looked at her husband and smiled.

The governor of Mat-Ashur, Ashur Shar-Shari, his wife Mami and their son Dudu-Enlil, approached the royal couple. They hugged each other as how close friends would do. Their son wanted to meet Princess Atalia as it was apparent that he liked her. He was ten years older than the princess. The princess was not interested in him and in fact, informed her mother about how she felt towards Dudu-Enlil.

After a few minutes, Air force Commander Azarah-Anu I, his wife Nahnita and their son, astronaut and Air Force pilot Mr. Abzu-Bt-Anu, approached them. Mr. Abzu was 35 years old and very handsome. He told his parents that he was very interested to meet the king's daughter. Mr. Azarah took the opportunity to introduce his son to the royal family, specially that the princess was present.

When the king saw them approach, he got up from his seat and happily greeted the family and exchanged greetings.

Azarah said, "Your honour, thank you for inviting us. I would like to introduce to you my son, Abzu-Bt-Anu. He is an astronaut and Air Force pilot, and is currently training our future pilots and astronauts for our new spaceship."

The king replied. "Abzu!! I heard so much about you. How is the training going, especially with the new spaceship?"

"Your honour, thank you for asking. It's all coming very well. In fact, we are training for 10 hours a day. and training new astronauts as well." Abzu replied. "We need to train twice as much astronauts as the spaceship can carry 150 astronauts or Annunaki."

The king was delighted to hear of the progress. "Very well. I will talk to your father in our next meeting." He then turned to the queen and told her about Mr.

Abzu, the son of Azarah, and how he was training to make a flight into outer space and possibly, to the blue planet.

Mr. Abzu happily extended his hand to the queen and said, "I am honoured to meet you, your highness."

To which the queen replied. "The honour is mine, Mr. Abzu. Your mother is a very good friend of mine. I am so glad that she has a son like you who is dedicated to serve our nation."

"It is my duty to serve my country, your honour!", Abzu replied.

On the other hand, Atalia was seriously looking at the man and listening to his conversation with her mother. She wanted to get in the conversation too. It was then the queen saw her daughter's interest in Mr. Abzu, so she introduced her to him.

"I am honoured to meet you, Mr. Abzu. My brother speaks about you very well. How do you know my brother?" Atalia inquired.

Mr. Abzu replied. "Thank you, princess. Your brother and I work together in the Air Force. We are assigned to train astronauts for our new spaceship. You should ask your brother to bring you to the training area so you could see the spaceship."

"I would love to come and see it for myself! Can I get inside the spaceship?" Atalia asked excitedly.

"Of course, I will be honoured to show you inside the spaceship." Mr. Abzu replied. He obviously did not want the conversation with the princess to end because he was already in love with her. He continued. "Atalia. I have seen you in numerous occasions but I never had the chance to meet you in person. I am so honoured to now finally meet and talk to you. You are very beautiful." He said all of this while looking into the princess's eyes.

Atalia blushed then looked at him and smiled.

The queen noticed the exchange and said, "Atalia?" But the princess appeared to not hear her mother and kept on looking at Mr. Abzu. Then she turned to her mother and they both smiled.

It was time to start the luncheon, which was prepared meticulously for the occasion. Once everybody was seated, the servants started to bring out the food. Some of the guests helped to more servings for themselves for there were plenty of food and drinks. Everyone was enjoying themselves. It was a really beautiful day and the weather was just perfect. The garden looked colourful and the flowers were in full bloom. One can even hear the sound of water flowing from the fountain in the background. Suddenly, Assyrian music started until it became louder and the dancers took the stage and started to dance traditional folk dances around the fountain. The music became frantic and many guests joined the dance. The royal family saw the dance and were enjoying it. Prince Assur asked his sister to dance with him. Together, they walked towards the dancing when he saw Mr. Abzu sitting with his parents.

Prince Assur called, "Mr. Abzu! Let us dance, come on!"

Mr. Abzu saw and smiled as he could not resist seeing the princess. "Wait for me, I am coming!", he called back to the prince.

Princess Atalia's heartbeat took a faster beat and she was happy. She never expected that she will be dancing with the gentleman she just met and like.

Mr. Abzu joined the royal siblings and happily joined the dance. They danced together to the beats of the Assyrian folk dance. The princess was surprised to see Mr. Abzu dance and she was very proud and excited at the same time. Unfortunately, the dancing did not last long as a hover craft suddenly circled the palace and the garden. In a few minutes, it slowly started its descent and landed at its designated landing area, just a hundred feet away from the festivities. The music stopped. The head genie created a walking pad from the tent to the hover craft for the king.

The Shish Gala, the religious leaders, suddenly got up and asked the guests that it was time for the beloved King Assur-Adamu I to leave to the Akitu Ritual. They asked everyone to stand up and pray for the king before he leaves.

The king stood up from his chair, looked at the queen for a second, and went close to her. He then looked at everyone, raised both his hands up to heaven and in an old Assyrian dialect, he started praying:

Ah Assur d'bwashmiya
Neeta Kadasha schmoch
Tay tay malkootha
Ne-whey t'savec-yanak eyekanna
d/bwashmaya apf-baraha
Now-lahn lachma d'soonahnan yow-manna
Ah Assur d/bwashmaya yow-manna
Wash wo-klan how-gane
Eye-kanna ddaph hahnan
Shwa-ken el-high-ya-bane
oo-la-tah-lahn el-nees-yo-nah
ella ph-sahn min bee sha
metahl dih-lah-kee mal-kootha
oo-high-la oo-teesh-boh-ta
la-alahm
ah-mayn

All the guests repeated after the king with the loud sound of "Ah mayn".

At that moment, two shish gilas went on both sides of the king and escorted him towards the craft. The guests all bowed down their heads when the king passed through. The king and the religious leaders arrived at the craft. The king turned to the religious leaders and shook their hands, then he went inside the craft and head off to the Temple of Assur or the Crystal Shrine, which was located on the Angel Tower. He will stay there on the first four days according to a refrain from the myth.

The luncheon party was then ended by the queen an hour later. The guests approached her and her son and daughter, one by one, to thank them for the invitation. At the same time, the queen invited all the guests to the Akitu festival when the king returns from the ritual. This will be held in the Palace Royal House on the 21st of Nisanu (April 21).

The guests gathered to greet and thank the remaining royal family. The genies stood beside them while the guests approached them. While this was going on, Princess Atalia was anxiously waiting to see Mr. Abzu before they leave the luncheon. Suddenly, she saw Azarah-Anu I, Abzu's father in the crowd, waiting to greet them. Mr. Abzu was with them but he appeared to be busy, talking to his comrade. He too, was anxious to see Atalia. He did not notice her since the genies protected the royal family well. The genies would hold off the guests 30 feet away from the queen's throne to make sure that every guest and family were attended to in an orderly fashion and take their time to see the queen and her family.

The queen has never seen her daughter so happy but she did not respond to the stimulus; she was busy greeting the guests. Atalia, however, was excited to see Mr. Abzu closely again. However, this gratification was delayed because the first to greet the royal family was the king's cousin, Governor Assur-Shar-Shari, his wife and son, Dudu-BT-Enlil, who was in love with the princess. He wanted to marry her but she refused his hand.

When the governor's family approached them, Mr. Dudu-BT-Enlil chatted with the princess and gave her a kiss on her cheek. It is apparent that he was still in love with her. But his advances were shunned by the princess, so him and his family moved on and paved way to the next guests.

Up next were the Chief of Military's family—General Tartaru, his wife and their lovely daughter, Bonita, who was engaged to Prince Assur-Tudiya. They were preparing to get married after the Akitu festival. Upon seeing his future wife, the prince stood from his seat and met Bonita before they approached the royal family's seats. He hugged and kissed her, then turned to his future in-laws and hugged them. The prince held Bonita's hand and introduced her and her parents to the queen. Atalia was happy to see her brother's future wife as Bonita was her friend. They chatted for a few minutes then left to give way to the other guests.

At last, Atalia's wait was finally over! For the Air Force commander's family was next. The commander and his wife greeted the royal family first. Mr. Abzu stayed a few feet behind his parents because he did not want them to see him smiling. He was seriously looking at the princess, who turned really quiet but excited with the silent exchange. The princess did not want her mother and brother to see the interaction but it was obvious that the love reaction between Mr. Abzu and the princess was overflowing. When he approached the throne, he asked for the queen's hand, held it and spoke, "Your honour, thank you for this beautiful luncheon. I am so honoured to meet my queen in person. And you have a lovely daughter."

"Thank you.", the queen responded. "I am glad you and your family enjoyed it. I would like to see you and your parents in the Akitu festival." She looked directly at Mr. Abzu's eyes while talking to him.

Mr. Abzu responded. "Thank you, your honor. You can expect us at the festival." Then he kissed her hand and moved to meet the princess. Atalia was standing right next to the queen with a huge smile on her face. Mr. Abzu then held her hand tight, looked her in the eyes and said:

"Atalia, you are quite a good Assyrian dancer. I really enjoyed it."

"You too, Mr. Abzu. I will be very happy to see you during the Akitu festival. Then we will dance more.", the princess replied.

"I would be very happy to attend. Thank you again for the invitation." Mr. Abzu said. He looked her in the eye with a smile on his face. He then kissed her hand and released it. He then moved to the prince and said, "Prince Assur, thank you for the lovely event." The prince and Mr. Abzu both shook hands. The two were good friends and worked together in the Anunnaki Training Center.

PRINCESS ATALIA

After that brief exchange of greetings, Mr. Abzu stepped away from the throne, but not without looking back at Atalia for one more time. While the silent exchange happened, the commander noticed it and asked Mr. Abzu. "Son, what is going on between you and the princess? Are you in love with her? Do you know that the king will never let you marry Atalia because you are not from a royal family? She is one of the Assyrian royal family!! It has been a custom for thousands of years. And you know our king is very strict when it comes to our customs and traditions!"

Mr. Abzu replied calmly. "Yes father. I am in love with the princess. She is very beautiful and I think she loves me, too."

Azarah sighed and tried to talk his son out of it. "Please son, stay away from her. If the kind finds out, she will be in trouble then you will be, too. I am sure the queen noticed your conversation with her daughter. Lucky for you, the king was not here." He spoke while holding his son's shoulder.

Sounding defeated, Mr. Abzu replied weakly. "Okay father. I will try to stay away from the princess."

His mother noticed the exchange and stepped in the conversation. "Azarah, my love, why do you discourage your son not to love the princess? She was looking and smiling at him the whole time. Yes, the queen noticed but the princess does not care. So why do you think your son should care?"

Turning to Mr. Abzu, she said. "I am asking you to be careful though. I know the king's attitude and it's true, he will never let his daughter marry out of the royal family. It's been an Assyrian custom for 1,000 years. My son, you know about this and the history of all our kings."

Mr. Abzu has never seen the princess in person before. That was the first time he met her. Previously, he could only see her in events that were shown on national TV stations and the royal family pictures.

Princess Atalia was the king's only daughter and it was apparent that the king loves her very much. She was very beautiful and only 28 years old. She is highly educated in Science and Technology. She has the typical Assyrian features—with blue eyes, black hair, and stands 5'10" in height. She was involved in the royal activities, especially with her mother, the queen. She arranged most of her mother's meetings and other social activities.

Atalia never married because she has not found the right man, plus the king appeared to be an obstacle in her marriage life. He always insisted that she has to marry a man from the king's family, and she was not able to find someone to love since most are way older than her or too young for her taste. Atalia was getting old and decided to follow her dream of marriage and look into the king's family, and now she found Mr. Abzu, the son of the Air Force commander.

On the other hand, all the guests have finished greeting the royal family. The genies loosened their protection and escorted the queen, prince, and princess back to the royal palace. When they arrived at the palace, the prince asked his mother to talk to the princess about her conduct with Mr. Abzu. Even though the prince and the pilot were friends and he liked Mr. Abzu, he was not comfortable with what was going on between his friend and his sister.

Atalia happily went to her room, singing to herself quietly and dancing slowly. She was happy that she met Mr. Abzu. While she was changing her clothes, her mother entered her room.

"Hi, mother!" Atalia said in a surprised tone. She knew she must have done something wrong to see her mother standing at her door. "Did you enjoy the luncheon today?"

The queen asked her back in a stern voice. "Did you enjoy the luncheon today?"

Atalia responded. "Yes mother, I did enjoy it! It was a very beautiful luncheon. We met new and old friends, even some whom we have not seen in a long time!"

"I am glad, honey.", the queen said. "But you were acting a bit strange when you saw Mr. Abzu, the astronaut. I would like to know—do you love him? I know he is quite the looker and from a good family, too."

"Yes mother, I love him. When my brother introduced us, he looked at me with so much love and respect. And it's true—he is young and very attractive." Atalia quickly responded.

The queen smiled but replied with a worried face. "I know he is good-looking, honey. But your father will never let you marry him. He is not from a royal family. You know how your father loves you and wants you to be queen."

Atalia fell silent for a moment and said. "Yes, mother. But I cannot find anyone else in our royal family, someone like Mr. Abzu. I am now 28 years old, how much longer do you think I need to wait?"

"How old is Mr. Abzu?", the queen asked. "He told me he is 35.", Atalia responded.

The queen then said, "Honey, you were lucky that your father was not here. Otherwise, he would have been very angry to see you acting like a child. Even your brother noticed your behaviour. You are a princess and you must act like one."

Atalia stood straight and said, "Okay mother. I love you and you are right."

The queen smiled and turned to leave but then she stopped at the door. She turned back to her daughter and winked, whilst reminding Atalia to apologize to her brother.

It appeared that the queen approved of her daughter's decision to fall in love with Mr. Abzu. But it was not really her decision to make. Atalia must still face her father, the king, if she really wants to marry Mr. Abzu.

Once the queen left her room, she quickly picked up her cell phone and texted Mr. Abzu.

I had a long conversation with my mother. Both she and my brother noticed our interaction during the luncheon. I think my mother likes you.

My dear, when I looked deep in your eyes, I can see how they every time you see me. My heart is filled with happiness and it feels reassured that all the affection I've devoted to you echoes in your kind heart. Love you!

Within a few minutes, Atalia received a response from Mr. Abzu.

This immense love is all yours, my love. I would like to open up my heart to you but I may lack the skill, or I may fall short with words. My heart harbours so many good feelings for you, that the dictionary seems to lack the words to use and express my love for you.

Also, I forgot to tell you. My parents noticed our love exchange at the luncheon, too. My father did not like my behavior, especially in front of the queen and prince. He was just worried of what the honourable might think and you know how my family has great respect to the king. But my mother likes you very much. I miss you, I miss you dearly. I wish I could be with you and fill you with kisses and tell sweet things in those pretty little ears of yours!!

Atalia was lying in bed, reading Mr. Abzu's love notes in her phone. Suddenly, she heard a knock on the door. She immediately put her phone away and went to open the door. She was surprised to see her brother, Prince Assur.

"Can I come in?", the prince asked. "Sure, brother.", Atalia said, gesturing her brother to enter her room.

The prince asked her, "How are you, sister? Did you enjoy the luncheon?"

Atalia tried to calm her tone and replied. "Yes brother. It was a very enjoyable luncheon."

"Mother told me everything. I know what's going on between you and Mr. Abzu. He is a very educated and knowledgeable person and under my command. He is the head of the Astronauts and trains them. His father is our Air Force commander. He is from a respected family and a hard-worker. I like him very much so I have no problem that you love him. But Atalia, you know how father will react to this. But don't worry, I will help you because I like Mr. Abzu." The prince told his sister.

Atalia was very happy to hear her brother's stance on her relationship with Mr. Abzu. She relaxed a bit and laid down on her bed. She then picked up her phone and sent a message to her beloved.

My brother likes you, too.

Mr. Abzu responded immediately.

Thank you honey for the good news and for letting me know. Your brother is my supervisor and I respect him and report to him every day. I like the prince very much and we are good friends. I am glad he approves of me. I was really worried, especially with how the queen will react to this.

She is your mother, the queen, and I respect her very much. I devote my life to serving the Assyrian nation and fly into space. I respect my king as well and I love you with all my heart

KING ASSUR-TUDIA BECOME A KING

Before he left for the Akitu Ritual, King Assur-Adamu I left his son, Prince Assur-Tudia, to be in charge while he was gone for twelve days. At the same time, he requested his son to report to him of anything that would happen to the nation, or anything new that would come through while he was away. The prince happily accepted his father's request to a temporary king and he promised that he will do his best.

After the luncheon, the king also requested his cabinet members, advisors, councilmen, and department heads to be in the royal palace throne room the next morning for a meeting with his son, the prince. When the time came, the throne room became full of the king's people and advisors. At 10am, the genies entered the throne room and took their place around the room.

Sin-Namir spoke. "The new king will be entering the throne. Please stand up."

Everyone stood to respect and honour the new king. Prince Assur-Tudiya entered the throne room, escorted by six genies, with three on both sides. He was wearing the king's uniform, jewellery, and crown. On his way to the throne, he waved to all the members and in return, everyone in attendance started clapping and shouting "Long live the King!" repeatedly until he reached the throne. The prince then sat on his father's seat for the first time. When everyone stopped clapping, he got up from his seat.

Prince Assur addressed everyone in the room and said, "Thank you very much, ladies and gentlemen. My father, the honourable and venerable King Assur-Adamu I, assigned me to govern the nation while he is currently away for the Akitu Ritual. With our God Assur's help and all of you, I will govern the Assyrian nation to the best of my ability."

"Our king requested me to give a full report from all ministries—including the military, Air Force, and the Navy. He needs a progress report about the three flying saucers that are under construction and the Anunnaki Training Center. This is because he would like to visit the space center after the holidays. I am asking all the departments to prepare a report and deliver it to the house speaker within ten days before the holiday ends."

"Another important thing is that I have asked the Air Force commander, General Azarah-Anu to be here to give you the latest update about the earth rover, which was launched six months ago. He will explain to you in details where it is now. Also, Mr. Assur-Ram is here, the head of the Assyrian National Space Observatory. He operates on the largest telescopes in our nation. He can tell us about the deepest mysteries of the impenetrable shadows, like the dark energy, dark matter, and black holes. The third gentleman to be join us is Mr. Abzu-Bet-Anu, one of our astronauts (Anunnaki) and is head of the Space Training Center. They are going to be here to answer any questions you wish to ask about space. Lastly, I would like to inform you that we will have a meeting every day from 10am to 2pm.", Prince Assur ended his speech.

The house speaker, Mr. Enlil Nirari informed the temporary king that the guests are here. The king told him to let them in.

He spoke again. "As you heard the speaker, the three space experts are here! They will enter shortly. In a few days, we will also have a full report from the festival committee. They are working hard to prepare and decorate our capital, Mat-Assur, and the rest of the country for the happiest holiday of our people. Once the honourable king leaves Easagila Temple, one million citizens will be waiting in Star Avenue to greet him. These people will wait for days just to see the King, and it is an Assyrian tradition for the last one thousand years that the people will have a way to express their love to the king and the country." He paused for a few seconds and then motions to the speakers to bring in three chairs for the guests.

The three guests entered the throne room and sat on their respective seats.

"Thank you, gentlemen. Everyone, please welcome our guests—the space experts!" The prince said and called them one by one for an introduction.

"Here's Air Force commander, General Azarah-Anu, then Mr. Assur-Ram,

head of the Space Observatory, and my good friend, Mr. Abzu-Bet-Anu, astronaut and head of the Space Training Center. Please help me welcome them!"

Everyone clapped in unison.

"As mentioned, they are here to answer a few questions about the mysteries of the universe. Our scientists have pierced together how the universe began and how it will end. But most of them would ask: *Is there life outside our solar system? Are we alone?* These questions are challenges for our astronomers, astrophysicists, and mathematicians, who formulated the hypotheses—the foundation of rigorous scientific theories and experiments. You can start asking now."

One of the chamber members, Mr. Erba Adad, asked a question. "What is the main objective of the rover?"

"The answer is this—the Earth Science Laboratory Rover (ESLR) will assess whether the earth has an environment that is capable of supporting life. Whether it is habitable and if life existed there. The mission by itself is not designed to answer as the ESLR does not carry experiments to detect active processes that will signify present day biological metabolism. It is part of a series of expeditions to Earth that will help us meet the three scientific goals:

Determine whether it is face for humans
Characterize the Earth's climate and geology
Prepare it for human exploration."

Another question was asked. "Were any of the Earth landings recorded on video and sent back here?"

"The ESLR has many cameras focused mainly on engineering and science tasks. Some help us land on Earth while other would serve as our eyes on the surface to drive around. We use others to do scientific observation and aid in the collection of samples. We have the following:

Descent Imaging Cameras (full-colour video)
Engineering Cameras
Science Cameras

These high-resolution cameras will be transmitting all the pictures and videos to the Tiamat Space Center the first day after the landing."

Next question went like this, "Who will get to go to Earth if all is well?" "The answer is obvious. We are training Anunnakis, which has a variety of Science, Technology, engineering, and mathematics background."

"How long will it get to planet Earth?"

"It depends on how you go; what kind of flying saucer is used. With our current technology, it would take 8-10 months to travel to Earth."

Q: "What kind of fuel are our scientists considering for this trip?"

A: "We are evaluating several kinds of fuel for this trip. The options include nuclear thermal, nuclear electric, and various chemical propellant."

Councilman Mr. Baryoom approached the podium to ask his questions.

Q: "What does it take to become an Anunnaki, to be able to travel in space?"

A: "You need to be trained by Mr. Abzu-Bet-Anu at the Mat-Assur Anunnaki Space Training facility, or otherwise known as the Assur Space Center. The ASC has trained more than 100 Assyrian astronauts and 10 from other friendly countries. The training process used today is the culmination of this considerable experience. The first phase starts with one year of basic training. Much of the training takes place inside a classroom, where candidates would learn about vehicle and space station systems. They would also study key disciplines— including Earth sciences, meteorology, space science and engineering that may be helpful in their work in space. Outside the classroom, astronauts must complete military water and land survival training, to prepare for an unplanned landing back in Tiamat. These candidates must be a good swimmer to be able to do the training as they will be treading water continuously for 10 minutes while wearing a flight suit.

Finally, astronauts would receive their mission and crew assignments when entering what is known as the advanced mission training phase. In the final 10th month of training, astronauts will mainly focus on activities, exercises and experiments specific to their mission."

Q: "Why do astronauts wear space suits?"

A: "Without the special suits, astronauts would not be able to leave their spacecraft, work on the moon, or work outside the space station. Space is very dangerous for humans as there's no air to breathe. It also has high levels of radiation, energy that can move through our bodies and make us very sick."

Q: "Why do astronauts wear helmets?"

A: "The astronauts' helmet protects it wearer from micrometeoroids, solar ultraviolet as well as infrared radiation. It is made of the protective shell, neck ring, vent pad and feed port. Protection from radiation is actually provided by extravehicular visor assembly, which is fitted over the helmet."

Next to ask questions is another councilman, Akki-Den-Ili. He approached the podium and asked his questions.

Q: "Can you describe a day on the job as an astronomer?"

A: "Astronomy was more concerned with the classification of phenomena in the sky. While astrophysics attempted to explain the phenomena, the difference between them is using physical laws. Today, that distinction has mostly disappeared. Professional astronomers are highly trained individuals who typically have a PHD in Physics or Astronomy, and are employed by research institutions or universities. They spend the majority of their time working on research, although they quite often have duties such as teaching, building instruments, or aiding in the operation of an observatory. The number of professional astronomers in the Assyrian nation is actually quite small.

The Assyrian Astronomical Society, which is the major organization, only has 5,500 members. These numbers include scientists from other fields, such as Physics, Geology, and engineering, whose research interests are closely related to astronomy. The International Astronomical organization comprises of 77,500—8000 members from all the friendly nations on the planet Tiamat."

Q: "What is planetary science and evolution of stars?"

A: "Planetary science is a virtual tour of the solar system and beyond the top scientists in the planet as your guides.

The milky way galaxy contains several hundred billions of stars of all ages, sizes, and masses. A typical star, such as the sun, radiates small amounts of x-rays continuously and larger bursts of x-ray during a solar flare. The sun and other stars shine as a result of nuclear reactions deep in their interiors. These reactions change light elements into heavier ones and release energy in the process. The outflow of energy from the central regions of the star provides the pressure necessary to keep the star from collapsing under its own weight.

A star collapses when the fuel is sued up and the energy flow from the core of the star. Nuclear reactions outside the core cause the dying star to expand outward in the "Red giant" phase before it begins its inevitable collapse. If the star is about the same mass as the sun, it will turn into a white dwarf star. If it is somewhat more massive, it may go under a supernova explosion and leave behind a neutron star. But if the collapsing core of the star is very great—at three times the mass of the sun—nothing can stop the collapse. The star implodes to form an infinite gravitational warp in space—a black hole.

I hope you understood my explanation on the evolution of stars.

To summarize, this tableau illustrates the ongoing drama of stellar evolution and how the rate of evolution and the ultimate fate of a star depends on its weight or mass."

Mr. Assur-Ram ended his speech.

The temporary king, or Prince Assur then said. "Thank you all! Commander Azarah-Anu, Mr. Abzu-Bet-Anu and Assur-Ram. Thank you for the lecture about space science!"

The three guests stood up and at the same moment, a councilman got up and soon, everyone in the room was up and gave them a standing ovation. Then two genies approached the trio and escorted them out of the throne room.

Prince Assur continued to address the remaining people in the room. "Ladies and gentlemen, we had a good and beneficial meeting today. We learned about the universe, Anunnaki, and our mission to Earth. Speaking about Earth, I was told that the Earth rover will be landing in a few days. I hope it will be successful that we can see the planet Earth for the first time via the rover's video camera transmission."

It was approaching 3:00 PM and it was time to end the meeting. The king, or Prince Assur, got up from his chair and the Assyrian National Anthem started to play. Six genies then approached the throne and escorted the king to his vehicle, then the rest of the people went to go their separate ways.

It was approaching Akitu Holiday, one of the happiest holidays of the Assyrian nation. But the shortage of energy on the planet was creating considerable problems to all countries, especially the smaller ones. The fuel was becoming very expensive and it was hard to supply for them.

But the King Assur-Adamu I pledged to the united nations assembly in the last meeting that he will try to help some of the smaller countries.

Five days remained before the ritual ends. King Assur-Tudiya, arrived at the assembly at 10am, escorted by six genies, to his throne. As usual, they stand up to welcome the king. He stood, bowed his head to the council, a sign of respect or thanking them.

Prince / King Assur then spoke. "Ladies and gentlemen, good morning. We have only four days before our nation will celebrate the Akitu festival.

Today, we will end our meeting. We will have two weeks off. Most importantly, as you know, every year for this event, hundreds of guests from friendly countries, Kings, head of the governments, dignitaries, would arrive at our capital to give love and respect to our beloved King and his family."

"Second, I received a call from the National Space Center that our Earth Rover has successfully started circling the Earth. In two days, they will try to land the rover on Earth. Preliminary pictures show that at one point, ice covered the northernmost part of Earth, but the south of the Earth looks fine. Scientists believe that the landing area of the Earth rover looks fine, and there is no reason to change it. The video cameras have taken spectacular pictures of the Earth's moon, but the instrument on the rover has recorded pictures that indicates that the planet has lots of water and air. The combination of air and water proves the atmosphere is safe for humans to land and live there. We all hope tomorrow, by the grace of our God Assur, that the rover will land softly on Earth."

King Assur-Tudiya left the council meeting in his vehicle. He called Mr. Puzur-Assur, the chief of security of Mat-Assur, to the palace. They will discuss the security for the 21st of April when his father, King Assur Adamu I, returns from the ritual. The Star Avenue from Esagila Temple to the Royal Palace will have one million people watching and enjoying the ceremony. They will give respect to the King once he leaves Esagile temple.

Queen Assurinu called her son on his phone, and King Assur-Tudiya answered. "Hi son. Bonita is here. Your sister called to have lunch with us. I was wondering when you will be coming home."

To which he replied, "I am already in front of the palace, mother. However, Mr. Puzur-Assur is coming. We have things to discuss."

The queen replied. "That is fine. He is welcome to join us since the lunch is ready."

When the king arrived at the palace, Mr. Puzur-Assur was already there, arriving a few minutes ahead of him. They went in together and headed straight to the lunch room where his mother, sister, and future wife were waiting. The king introduced the chief of security to his family and they all had lunch together.

After their meal, the king and Mr. Puzur-Assur went to a private room and discussed the security for the Akitu festival. He immediately left the palace after the meeting.

On the other hand, the queen started her preparations in the Royal Palace Hall for the festival. She was helped by her daughter, Atalia, and Bonita, the prince's future wife. Helping them were the palace maids. They were expecting 500 guests to attend the event—dignitaries from the friendly countries, high-ranking military officials and members of the congress. The queen planned to have special dishes with all types of cuisines, including desserts, coffee, cakes, and delicacies to entertain the guests.

She requested to have only Assyrian music played during the festival, with the Assyrian national dancers to perform a few traditional dances while everyone would be busy. Suddenly, her phone rang and Atalia answered it.

"Hello?", Atalia said. "Yes, I would like to speak with Queen Assurinu. This is the Queen of Mesren (Ancient Egypt)—Amasis.", the person on the other line said.

"Oh hello, Queen Amasis. This is Princess Atalia. How are you?", Atalia replied.

"I am fine. How are you? I know you must be very busy.", the Egyptian queen replied.

Atalia responded. "Yes, I am fine, thank you. My mother is keeping us busy. Would you like to speak with her?" To which the Anasis replied yes. Atalia called her mother that the Egyptian queen is asking for her and would like to speak with her.

Queen Assurinu picked up the phone and said, "Hi! How are you? What a lovely surprise!"

"We are fine. My husband, King Narmar and I would like to visit you foor the Akitu festival. The king told me to call you because he knows that King Assur-Adamu is still in the ritual. Also, my daughter, Princess Mehaa, is coming with us." Anasis replied.

"That is wonderful! Yes, you are very welcome and free to stay here in the palace. I will meet you at the airport, okay?" the Queen said excitedly. To which Anasis said, "Thank you, and we'll see you soon!"

Queen Assurinu ended the call and Atalia approached her. "Mom, are they coming here? Is Mehaa coming with them?" The queen replied, "Yes, they will be here on the 21st of Nisanu for the festival."

Meanwhile, King Assur-Tudia received a telephone call from the space center and head of the Earth Rover project, Mr. Isme-Dagan.

"Your honour, tomorrow at 10:00 AM, the Earth Rover will be descending to the blue planet as planned.", Mr. Isme-Dagan reported.

King Assur-Tudia asked, "That is good. Where will it land? I thought the northern part of Earth is covered with sheets of ice?"

"Yes, your honour. But we have carefully chosen a location that is very hot and is in the southern part of the Earth's equator. Our scientists believe that on this part of the planet, we will find life. For this, I would like to invite you to be here at the space center and see how the Assyrian scientists designed an instrument that can land the rover electronically by its own computer system.", Mr. Isme-Dagan said.

"Yes, I would be very happy to attend and witness this. I have been waiting for the last 8 months for this moment. Thank you for letting know and I'll see you tomorrow." The king dismissed the call.

EARTH ROVER PROJECT

At the space center: *Could there be life elsewhere in our Solar System?*

As far as we know, Earth is the only planet with life in our Solar System. But in the past few decades, we've had some tantalizing clues to the possibility of extra-terrestrial humans with life. "Here on Earth, humans came from a different planet."

Scientists still did not believe that Assyria came to Earth from another planet 6,500 years ago; that they arrived and turned savages into humans, created a God for them, gave the "Alphabet" language knowledge and used that to explore the extreme environments in the Solar System. If the Assyrians did not come from the planet Tiamat, the world would be 6,500 years backward. The Europeans stole our intelligence and took our secret and hid it in their music.

The Scientists of the Assyrian Space Center agency launched the Earth Exploration Satellite 8 months ago, called "Anu"; the Robotic Space Mission which is a rover to explore the planet Earth. This project was created because the astronomers detected changes on the Earth's surface—between 15,000 BC to 10,000 BC, the planet was white. It appeared that the planet was going through an Ice Age period; however, between 8,000—10,000 BC, the ice started disappearing. The Assyrian space scientists have been observing all the changes on the planet, so they decided to let the king and the council of ministers to know about the changes, and let the king decide what actions are to be taken.

King Assur-Adamu I had an astronomical mind. He always visited the space center and always talked about sending a satellite go planet Earth. Now that the scientists have seen drastic changes on the Earth's surface, they decided to show it to the king when he visited. So in one of his visits a few years ago, the king saw the change for himself and decided that they do an Earth exploration mission via a robotic rover.

The king's primary objective was to see if life existed on planet Earth. The scientists' objective, on the other hand, were the following:

1.   To search for geological clues to environmental conditions that existed when liquid water was present and is safe to humans.Determine the distribution and composition of minerals, soil, rocks surrounding the landing site.

2.   Search for iron-containing minerals, and to identify and quantify the amount of specific mineral types that contain water or were formed in water. Assess whether the environment was conducive to life.

King Assur-Tudiya planned to visit the Space Center. At eight in the morning the next day and while preparing for the visit, he had breakfast with his mother the queen and his sister.

Queen Atalia asked him, "Son, where are you going? You looked excited this morning!" And Atalia chimed in, "Yes mother, you're right about that!"

The king replied. "Sorry, I forgot to tell you. Today, our Earth Rover will be landing on planet Earth. Mr. Isme-Dagan called me yesterday about it."

The queen smiled at the news and said, "I wish your father was here. He initiated the program and he used to talk about it since it was launched."

Then Atalia said. "Brother, is it okay if I come with you? I want to see the landing, too." She was thinking of her boyfriend, Mr. Abzu-Bt-Anu, and thought that he will be there since he was one of the officers that worked and trained the Anunnakis. She thought that he will be there to attend the spectacular landing.

"Okay, if you wish to come, please prepare now. We'll be leaving at 10am as they are waiting for me." The king told his sister.

The queen asked Atalia, "Honey, do you have to go?"

Atalia replied. "yes mother, this is our first view of the planet Earth. I would love to witness it!"

"Okay Atalia, please hurry!" The king told his sister. "Alright, alright. Just give me ten minutes to prepare."

Atalia rushed to her room, singing and dancing while preparing. She knew that Mr. Abzu will be there but she wanted to make sure. So she texted him. *Are you going to observe the Earth landing in the Space Center?*

Mr. Abzu replied immediately. *Yes, I am already here! I miss you.*

Atalia then put her phone inside her briefcase, in case her mother would show up at her bedroom. Now that Mr. Abzu was in the space center, she wanted to look her best. In a few minutes, her mother came to her bedroom.

The queen told her, "Atalia, are you serious about wanting to go to the space center?"

"Yes mother. I would love to see the planet Earth.", Atalia replied nonchalantly.

"Or is there anyone you want to see at the space center?", the Queen asked her.

Atalia smiled and replied, "Maybe, I do not know. I'll let you guess then."

"Alright, please dress your best, and remember to behave like a princess." The queen said.

"Thank you, mother. I love you!", Atalia said and hugged her mother.

"Alright, alright. I love you too. Hurry up now, your brother is waiting for you."

Suddenly, a voice message came in Atalia's phone and the Queen heard it.

"Did you call someone, Atalia?", the Queen inquired.

Atalia looked at her mother and smiled. "Yes mother."

The queen smiled back at her and left the room.

Atalia dressed her best then went downstairs. King Assur-Tudiya was waiting for her and was surprised to see her outfit.

King Assur-Tudiya asked her, "Where do you think we are going? We're going to the space center. There will be a lot of officers and generals only and they will be very busy. There may only be a few ladies who work at the center."

"I know, brother. But I have to look fine and beautiful. There will be a lot of people. I must look and dress good." Atalia explained.

The king sighed and said, "Alright. Anyway, we are late. Come, let's go!"

Genies opened the palace door. The car was already in front of the palace and two genies opened the car door. Both the King and princess got in and drove away inside the king's personal car. The distance was 40 miles between the palace and space center. It was located in the mountain area. To get there, you must drive through Cinic Drive and the Space Center is halfway to the mountaintop.

Atalia had a few questions about the space center and she knew that her brother knows a lot, and it was the perfect time to learn about the space and the universe.

She asked. "Brother, what is the mission of the Assyrian Space Center?"

Assur was taken aback by his sister's sudden interest, but replied, "The Assyrian Space Center is the leading center for robotic exploration of the solar system, and has about 15 space crafts and 6 monitoring instruments, carrying out planetary and Tiamat science, plus space-astronomy missions.

Atalia asked again. "Brother, are we close to finding life outside or in our galaxy, like planet Earth or Venus?"

"The vast distance of space makes it very difficult to search for life elsewhere in the universe. But even if it exists, there's still a bigger question: if we find alien life on another planet, would we even recognize it?" Assur stated.

Atalia, confused, replied. "What do you mean by we cannot recognize it? Why can't we?"

King Assur replied. "In the last decade, we have discovered thousands of planets outside our solar system. We have learned that rocky, temperate worlds are numerous in our galaxy. The next step is, it will involve asking even bigger questions: could some of these planets host life, and if so, will we be able to recognize life if we see it?"

"My God, Assur, this is very hard to digest! I wonder how the scientists, astronomers, geologists, and leading researchers have done this. They must have a lot of patience." Atalia exclaimed.

"If we do not recognize life on a distant planet, then why are we landing a rover on Earth?" King Assur said. He continued, "Landing and operating the rover on the Earth's surface is just the beginning. We have many more missions to that planet. Our scientists have been looking on that planet for the last 10 years. They have seen water, a lot of ice, Rocky Mountains, and thunderstorms."

"The scientists believe there may be life existing on the planet. Yes, it is too far, but the rover will send us live pictures that will satisfy our scientists' curiosity, you got that?", the King asked.

Atalia nodded and said, "Yes brother. Thank you for explaining this to me." She began to look around the surroundings. "The road to the space center is quite beautiful. When are you we going to arrive?"

The king replied. "In another ten minutes. We can see the building on our next turn."

Atalia looked out and saw the space center. "Oh yes! I can see it now. It's on a really nice location. Can't wait to see what's inside!"

INSIDE THE SPACE CENTER

King Assur-Tudiya and Princess Atalia arrived safely at the Space Center. Their car was parked in front of the building. Over a hundred people, including the scientists, were waiting to greet the king and the princess. There were ten genies to protect them.

Two genies opened both of the car doors and the king and princess stepped out of the vehicle. At that moment, all members of the Space Center said in unison "Long live the King". They did this thrice and started clapping. However, when they saw the princess, they clapped even more since it was her first time to visit the center.

The head of the Assyrian National Observatory, Mr. Assur Ram, was waiting to greet the royal members. When he saw them, he said, "Your honour, welcome to the Space Center." Then he turned to the princess and shook her hand. He held on tight to it. It was apparent that he was happy to finally meet the princess. Then Isme-Dagan, head of the Rover Project, greeted the king and princess.

There were also a few scientists who waited to greet her. She was busy attending to the greetings when Mr. Abzu called her attention. She turned and saw him, looking surprised and happy. Then Mr. Abzu asked her what she was doing at the space center.

"Oh, you know, I like the space. And I wanted to see you.", Atalia said, and gave him a wink.

Mr. Abzu was elated. "You make me so happy, too! By the way, you look lovely. I'm so glad to see you!" To which Atalia responded, "Me, too!"

All the scientists and space center employees escorted the King and princess to their special room so they can watch the rover landing on the 10x6 inch screen. At the same time, Assur-Ram, head of the space center, asked everyone to congregate at the main control room.

"Your highness, all the instruments on the rover are working as planned. It has transmitted a message with lots of data an hour ago. One of the messages was that the rover is ready to land. This indicates that all instruments are waiting for our command.", Mr. Assur-Ram informed the king.

Isme-Dagan added. "I am sorry, your honour. Mr. Assur-Ram and I could not do anything without you here. We want you at this rover landing. We have to be in the main control room right now but I will be sending a few scientists to be with you and explain about the descending process."

The king responded. "That is fine. I know about the landing process, but can you send Mr. Abzu with the scientists? He can be a great help here with us."

Atalia suddenly wanted to say something. "Is there something you want to say, Atalia?", the king asked his sister.

"Yes, I think he will be just fine. Thank you, brother!", she told her brother with a smile. She started thinking that her brother must know about what was going on between her and Mr. Abzu. She was glad. Just like her mother, who showed her approval of her relationship.

Isme-Dagan and Assur-Ram excused themselves since it was time to start the descending process.

Isme-Dagan said, "Your honour, we will see you in an hour. I hope the Earth rover will land successfully. The control room has given the command to start the descent."

Suddenly, the large screen started showing the communication (commands) between the rover and the control room. This took 20 minutes.

Four scientists entered the room where the king and princess were observing. Scientist Belu-Bani, Nur-Ili, Enlil-Apil-Ekur, and Mr. Abzu greeted the king and princess. Mr. Abzu sat next to Atalia while the rest sat behind them. They started talking about the Earth rover.

Mr. Abzu spoke. "Your honour, I was surprised by how difficult it was to command a rover which was in flight to Earth. Just communicating with the rover was such a crazy task. Every day, the rover lander wakes up and it has a list of instructions. It's supposed to the instructions, but you don't know if it actually does them until the results come back to you. That takes hours and the time difference between Tiamat and Earth makes it more difficult to communicate. We always schedule our communication in advance because we are relying on an orbiter to pass over the rover, and the rover has to be turned on and ready to communicate with the said orbiter."

Atalia was amazed by this and asked, "Mr. Abzu, what is the orbiter and where is it right now?"

To which he replied. "It is a satellite that orbits around the planet Tiamat. We launched it two years ago that orbits around Earth. It was developed as a simulator with accurately modeled planetary motion, gravitational effects including non-spherical gravity, free space, atmospheric flight, and orbital decay."

He continued. "The orbiter consists of two multifunction displays and a head-up display. Each feature several modes of operation, with all commands given via the keyboard or mouse. Do you understand this, princess?"

The princess replied. "Yes, Mr. Abzu. It was a very good explanation. Thank you so much."

King Assur-Tudiya said. "The princess learned a lot about space and the Earth rover lander today, and now the orbiter & satellite as well. Thank you, Mr. Abzu."

Mr. Abzu responded, "Thank you, your honour. Thank you for bringing Atalia with you. She will never forget this day."

Suddenly, the big screen started to blink rapidly for a few seconds, then the Earth rover camera started blinking at the same time. Ismi-Dagh's voice was then heard and said, "Your honour, we have twenty minutes till the touch down on planet Earth. We have a slight problem with the pictures but we are trying to fix it."

In a few seconds, a clear picture came through via two cameras. One showed the Earth below it and the second camera showed a parachute opening. The main screen started showing two pictures at the same time. One, the view of Earth from above while slowly descending. A voice from the main control said that the rover is 700 ft from the Earth's surface, then 600, then when it reached 400, Mr. Abzu told the king and princess that they're going to the main control room. The king and princess went to the control room with Mr. Abzu.

When the rover was nearing touchdown, everyone in the room went crazy—all technicians and engineers started yelling and screaming from happiness. When they saw the king at the back of the control room, everybody ran to him and congratulated him and Atalia. The scene was unforgettable. The king was so happy and congratulated them one by one.

The successful landing of the Earth rover on the surface of Earth after its 8-month journey across space was a happy moment for everyone. It landed in Central Africa at 10 in the morning. Meanwhile, the happiest people in Tiamat were Mr. Abzu and Atalia while everyone was busy with the rover landing. Mr. Abzu took the opportunity to hug Atalia with her consent and kissed her many times. The princess was excited and happy as well.

The space command center suddenly became quiet. The TV screen went blank during the touchdown. The rover was waiting for a new command from the main control. The engineers concentrated on the rover and responded on what their next move will be. Isme-Dagan was so excited and busy that he forgot about the king and princess.

Isme-Dagan said to them, "Your honor, I am so sorry. I forgot about you. I want you to sit in the main control room. I have room for one only. Princess Atalia can sit with the engineers."

Mr. Abzu heard this and said quicky, "Don't worry, Isme. I will look after the princess. We will sit back here and look at the main screen."

Isme-Dagan thanked Mr. Abzu and turned to the princess, "Will you be okay, princess?"

Atalia responded. "Yes, Mr. Isme. I am fine. Mr. Abzu will surely explain to me all the details step-by-step. I am happy here."

Isme-Dagan, satisfied with the princess's answer, went to the main control room with the king. He then ordered the engineers to send a command to the rover to open all the cameras including Video camera, to see where the Earth rover has landed. After waiting for twenty minutes, all cameras were opened. The main screen lit up and a bright picture in colour came through, and what they saw was amazing and surprising. Everybody in the control room started yelling Wow! What they saw was ten to twenty black humans standing thirty feet away from the rover. It appeared that they were trying to attack the rover with rocks and sticks. The black humans were all nude without clothes. Some were young and some old, but most of them were women. They were covered with a piece of leaf in their front, but the men had nothing. It seemed the humans were scared of the rover lander as it landed next to their village. That was the main reason they were attacking.

The king asked Mr. Isme to please move the rover 500 meters away.

Isme-Dagan said, "Your honour, I am trying. But it takes time for the signal to reach Earth. The humans keep attacking it with sticks and small rocks. It will take a few minutes for the signal to reach the rover."

Once the signal reached the rover, it started moving. The humans ran away from it. The rover kept moving at 5 miles per hour, heading up north, away from the village. The humans did not follow it, but they were all looking at the strange object. It kept moving for twenty minutes without stopping. The country looked like a desert and it was hot. There were no trees and was no water.

The king was shocked to see the black humans, with tattoos on their bodies. This kind of humans did not exist on planet Tiamat.

Isme-Dagan spoke. "Ladies and gentlemen, the honourable king would like to make a brief speech."

The king said, "In truth, I was shocked when I saw a black, nude human and I want to express my personal view about the successful mission. But first, I would like to thank every one of you, especially Mr. Isme-Dagan, Assur-Ram, and my good friend, Mr. Abzu-Bet-Anu, for this successful mission on our neighbourly planet. This is not the first mission and we will have many more like this in the future. This was the first and we learned that Earth is a living planet, but we never expected the black humans. Anyway, thank you for your hard work. Please keep this mission a secret until my father, our honourable King Assur-Adamu, would return from his ritual. There are 3 more days until he comes back. Also, happy Akitu in advance to all of you!"

Isme-Dagan thanked the king and the princess.

The king and princess were preparing to go back to the palace. Mr. Abzu, Mr. Isme, and Assur-Ram and the engineers escorted them to their vehicle, which was guarded by two genies.

The king then said to Isme, "I want you to keep the rover landing video a secret until the Akitu festival. I would like to show the king and he will decide what course of action to take. Thank you again."

Mr. Abzu joined in the conversation and said, "Your honour, Atalia was scared when she was the black humans and I had to comfort her." To which Atalia added, "Yes brother, I was so scared when they came close to the camera. You can see the tattoos on their faces. What kind of planet is Earth?"

The king and princess then bade goodbye to everyone at the space center, while the engineers went back to work.

TENTH DAY

It is the tenth day of the ritual. King Assur-Adamu I arrived at "Bet Akitu." God Assur begins to celebrate with both the upper and netherworld gods (the statues of Gods were arranged around a huge table such as in a feast), then Assur returns to the city at night, celebrating his marriage to the goddess Isthar, where Tiamat and heaven are united. And as the gods unite, so is this union arranged on Tiamat; thus, the king personifies this union by playing the role of marrying the highest priestess of the Esagila where they would both sit on the throne before the population and they would recite special poems for the occasion. This love is going to bring forth life in the Spring.

The king and princess arrived at the palace. The queen was in the meeting with the Akitu festival committee in the Royal Palace Hall. There were ten other people, the queen's girlfriends. Atalia missed her mother, because of what she saw on planet Earth.

The queen asked Atalia, "Honey, how were things on the space center? Did the rover land on the Earth?"

"Yes mother." Very quietly, Atalia added, "I will tell you later, mother, okay?"

Atalia then joined the committee members. She shook hands with them. She knew most of the ladies as they were all friends of her mother. They were wives of high-ranking people in the government and very respected. Most of all, they loved the queen. While this was going on, King Assur-Tudiya entered the hall to see his future wife, Ms. Bonita. He first kissed his mother then hugged Bonita, then shook hands with the rest of the ladies.

The queen asked him, "Son, how was the Earth rover landing?"

The king replied excitedly. "Let me tell you, mother. We had a very successful landing on the planet Earth! Our scientists did a very good job. After waiting for 8 months, the rover finally landed safely. I can tell you a lot when the king return from the Akitu ritual, he will tell our nation about this mission, and you will see surprising things. We have two more days for the king to come out from the Esagila temple."

"I was wondering mother, how are the preparation for the Akitu festival coming along? We have a lot of dignitaries and kings and their families will be attending to this holy event to celebrate with our nation.", the king added.

The queen responded. "Son, everything is in order. The palace hall has been decorated. We have room that's enough for a thousand guests. The dancers, bands, food, and drinks are all planned perfectly. The palace security, Mr. Bayoom, was there to report that they are ready."

The king nodded and addressed everyone. "Mother, and all the ladies here, I want to thank you all for your hard work. I hope you will enjoy this year's festival."

Atalia and Bonita were sitting away from the committee members. They were busy talking quietly. The king saw them and thought that his sister was telling Bonita about the black humans she saw on planet Earth. He wants to keep this a secret first and only have his father to tell this.

He approached the ladies and said, "Atalia, Bonita, why are two so busy? What are you discussing about? I hope you are not talking about me." He wanted to stop Atalia from telling his fiancée about the humans on Earth.

Bonita responded. "No honey, we are talking what dresses to wear for the Akitu festival.

We are expecting a lot of kings and their families, high-ranking dignitaries and their families as well. So we are trying to look very beautiful too."

"Well, you are both very beautiful for me," the king said.

"Why, thank you brother." Atalia said and Bonita smiled quietly.

The king then said, "I am sorry but I have a big meeting the council member's tomorrow morning."

The queen said, "Son, why tomorrow? You know everybody is busy preparing for the holiday. They can wait."

The king sighed and said, "You're right, mother. I will think about it. Bonita, can I see you for a few minutes in my office?"

Bonita said, "Okay honey, I will see you in a few minutes."

The queen added quickly, "Son, tonight our guests are arriving at 6pm. The king and queen of Egypt, along with their daughter, are coming."

The king said, "Yes mother. We will be going together to meet them. Are the guest rooms ready?" To which the queen replied yes.

The king left the hall then went straight to his office. While the king was waiting, Bonita arrived a few minutes later. He got up immediately and hugged and kissed her.

The king said, "I am really sorry, honey. I have been really busy for the past twelve days. I did not have enough time to spend with you. But don't worry, tomorrow is the last day. About the dress that you and Atalia want to buy, just go and buy any dress you love. I love you."

Bonita understood and said, "Okay honey, I love you too. Atalia is waiting for me. I'll see you tomorrow, okay?" With that, she kissed him and exited the office.

At 5pm, the queen, king, princess and Bonita, waited for the security vehicles to escort them to the airport. They were leaving to pick up the Egyptian royal family. King Assur-Tudiya requested a full security at the airport and a red-carpet treatment to honour their guests. The Assyrian and Egyptians nations are very good friends, and they respect their sovereignty for each other.

In a few minutes, the Egyptian plane arrived. The welcoming genies approached the red carpet and opened the aircraft doors. The king and queen came down first, followed by Mehaa. The Assyrian queen approached first to greet the Egyptian royal couple. She hugged Queen Amasis and held each other for a few seconds because they were very good friends. They were all happy to see each other. After a couple of minutes of pleasantries, they drove back to the palace.

ELEVENTH DAY

The gods returned, accompanied by their Lord Marduk, to meet again in the Destiny's Hall "Upshu Ukkina," where they met for the first time on the eight day. This time, they will decide the fate of the people of Marduk. In ancient Assyrian philosophy, creation in general was considered as a covenant between heaven and Tiamat as long as the human serves the Gods till his death; therefore, a God's happiness is not complete unless the humans are happy as well. It is a human's destiny to give happiness, on the condition that he serves the gods so Marduk and the gods will renew their covenant with Babylon, by promising the city another cycle of seasons. After the fate of mankind is decided, Marduk returns to the heavens.

The next morning, it is the eleventh day of the king's ritual. King Assur-Tudiya called all the heads of the military to come to the palace for consultation. He contacted Air Force commander, Azarah-Anu I, and General Irkallu-Enlil, chief of Military of the Armed Forces, General Tartatu and Commander Kur-Kukku, and Navy General Assur-Kigal. Then he called Mr. Isme-Dagan, head of the rover project and Assur-Ram, head of the Assyrian National Observatory, and Mr. Abzu-Bet-Anu. He asked them to be at the king's office at 10am.

Unexpected, the queen entered the king's office. She looked excited. King Assur-Tudiya greeted his mother. "Good morning, mother." He got up from his chair and kissed her. "What are you doing here so early? You have guests to attend to."

The queen replied, "Why did you not tell me about the black humans that you found on Earth?"

The king was stunned. "Where did you hear it from, mother?"

"Atalia told me all about it. She was pretty shocked, too." The queen responded.

The king sighed and spoke again. "I told her not tell anyone about it. I want father to announce it to the world. Where is she?"

"She and Bonita went shopping. They should be back by 11am.", the queen answered.

"I just finished calling the military leaders to come here and tell them about it. However, I don't want them to hear it from someone else. Mother, if you wish to come, please do. We can show you the video that was sent by the rover."

"Is it scary though?", the queen asked.

The king responded, "No mother. They are black humans, but they're just like us. Only they are nude and have paint or tattoos all over their faces and chests, even women."

"Do you have any women in your meeting today?", the queen inquired.

The king replied, "No mother, they're all military leaders."

"Then why should I attend it? I will watch it when your father returns and announces it to the nation.", the queen decided.

"Okay mother. But when the guests are here, I will call for you. They would like to see and meet you. Also, please bring Atalia and Bonita with you. If the Egyptian royal family would like to come as well, please bring them too.", the king said.

"Okay fine. I love you, son. Please don't work too hard. See you soon!", the queen responded and exited the office.

The queen rushed to make sure that King Narmar and Queen Amasis and their daughter Mehaa are awake and ready for breakfast. She assigned three maids at their room, so if they'll need any help, they're at their disposal. On the other hand, Atalia was busy helping the queen, supervising the dining room, to ensure that everything was prepared well for their guests.

The queen asked Atalia. "How is the breakfast room? Did you call Bonita to come this morning?"

Atalia responded. "Very good mother. When the guests are ready, they can head straight to the breakfast room. Also, Bonita said she will be here any minute."

Suddenly, one of the maids spoke to the queen and announced that the guests are awake.

The queen quickly told Atalia to get her brother, so he can greet the guests and walk them to the breakfast room. Because of this, Atalia rushed to call her brother and informed him of the queen's orders. They all met at the guest suite. There were two genies and opened the doors for the queen, and they found the Egyptian king and queen sitting in the waiting room of their suite, waiting for their daughter to finish dressing.

The queen approached them and asked, "Did you sleep well?" To which they both replied, "Yes, we slept very nice. Thank you so much for your hospitality."

King Narmar added, "You have a very beautiful palace. I love it."

The queen was glad with the compliment. "Thank you, and I am glad you slept well."

King Assur-Tudiya then asked, "Where is Mehaa?"

Queen Amasis responded with a chuckle. "You know women; they always take their time to dress. She is only 23 years old and wants to look beautiful."

Atalia then said, "Can I go inside to see Mehaa?"

Queen Amasis responded, "Go ahead. She is in that room. She would love to see you."

So Atalia went inside and Mehaa hugged her when she saw her. They started talking loud and everyone outside can hear them, but no one listened to their chatter.

At that same moment, the suite doors opened and Bonita entered the room. The king went to greet her and introduced her to the king and queen of Egypt.

Bonita first kissed the queen of Assyria, then shook the hands of the king and queen of Egypt. She asked them if they slept well, to which they responded that they had a very nice sleep.

She then asked where Mehaa and Atalia were. The king said, "Can't you hear them? They are in that room. Mehaa is still dressing. Honey, why don't you join them there?"

Bonita agreed and said, "Excuse me, your honour." Then proceeded to join the girls. The voices grew louder as she joined the ruckus inside the dressing room.

The queen then spoke, "Those girls will not come out for a while. I know you must be hungry. Let us go have breakfast. It is ready."

King Narmar said, "That's a good idea, your highness."

Then Queen Amasis said, "Let me just tell the girls that we are heading down for breakfast." She then went in the dressing room and asked her daughter to come out and greet the king and queen of Assyria. Mehaa immediately came out of the room and apologized for her delay. "We will be there for breakfast, your highness.", she bowed to both the queen and king.

"Don't worry, Mehaa. Take your time.", the queen told her. Atalia came out of the room and said in a loud voice, "We will be there soon, mother!"

Two genies then opened the door and the four of them went out of the room and headed down to the breakfast room, walking very slowly.

The queen turned to the king and asked, "It's already 10am. Do you have time to eat with us?"

The king answered, "Yes, mother. The meeting will start at 12am. However, at around 11am, the guests should start to arrive."

King Narmar spoke, "You have enough time. It won't take long for breakfast. If you don't mind me asking, who will you be meeting with, your highness?"

To which the king replied, "Our military leaders and high-ranking government officials."

They were interrupted by the girls, who were only a few steps behind and talking animatedly to each other in loud voices. They were wearing colourful dressed and looked beautiful.

They arrived at the dining room of the palace. Two genies opened the doors. They entered the room and after everyone was in, the genies entered too.

The dining room was very beautiful and large. It can hold a maximum of 24 people. Most distinguished guests were invited to savour a mouth-watering menu of Assyrian cuisine. This elegant formal dining table with an expandable and decorative veneer top and carved double pedestals, the chairs have upholstered seats and back for extra comfort, and a large matching buffet hut that has etched glass doors and multiple shelves. All of the china were plated in gold.

King Narmar was surprised by the beauty of the room and said wow. Queen Amasis spoke, "Yes it's an elegant room. I absolutely love it!"

The queen replied and smiled, "Thank you, Amasis. I am glad you like it. Please everyone, take your seats. Breakfast will be served shortly."

The breakfast lasted for an hour. The king and queen of Egypt enjoyed the Assyrian breakfast. The girls were busy talking when suddenly, a genie approached the king and announced that the guests have started arriving.

The king said, "Okay, thank you for informing me. I will be there soon." The genie then left the room. "My apologies. I have to leave ahead of you. The guests have started arriving for the meeting. Mother, please come to the meeting briefly so you can greet the guests. They would love to see you. Please bring our honoured guests from Egypt as well. It will be my honour to introduce them to our military leaders and government officials."

King Narmar was delighted to be included and said, "We would love to come and meet them all."

The queen added, "Yes, my son. As you wish. We will all go to your meeting."

The king turned to the girls and said, "You too, girls. Please make sure to be there as well!"

King Assur-Tudiya immediately headed straight to his office to welcome the military heads, state officials, and space experts. The guests started arriving one by one as it was scheduled. The protective genies were very busy helping the guests from the vehicle to the king's office. The king was at his office to great them and they were all seated at their designated chairs. It was almost 12pm, and the king called the queen and asked her to come and meet the guests.

Queen Assurinu, Princess Atalia, Bonita, and the Egyptian Royal family, walked together to the king's office where the meeting was conducted. The king got up and welcomed his guests. He then told everyone in attendance that they have guests from Egypt who recently arrived to celebrate the Akitu festival.

He introduced them one by one. While he was talking, the genies opened the main door.

The queen's entourage then entered the king's office. When everyone saw the queen, they all chanted "Long live the Queen!" and all clapped for a few minutes. They would not stop cheering until the queen was seated. She then asked the guests to sit down.

She continued and thanked all the guests then said, "I would like to introduce you to the Egyptian royal family. Please welcome, King Narmar, Queen Amasis of Mesren, and their daughter, Mehaa."

All the king's guests clapped to honour the Egyptian royal family. Then the queen continued.

"You all know Princess Atalia, my daughter, and Ms. Bonita, my son's future wife." Again, everyone clapped for a few minutes.

After which, the queen requested for the cheering to stop and asked everyone to bow their heads. Then, she asked King Narmar and Queen Amasis to sit, as well as the girls. She then told the officials to take their respective seats.

She continued. "First, I would like to thank you with all my heart for your respect and for your consideration. Second, we have the king and queen of Egypt, together with their daughter, and they are our honored guests from the Kingdom of Mesren. They are here this week to celebrate with us our great Akitu holiday."

Upon hearing this, the officials got up and started clapping and cheering again for the honored guests. Then took their seats again.

"Then we also have my lovely daughter, Princess Atalia, and my future daughter-in-law, Bonita." The crowd cheered again until the king asked them to stop.

The king thanked his mother then addressed everyone in the room.

"Ladies and gentlemen, I would like to welcome our honorable King and Queen of Mesren and their lovely daughter, Mehaa. The queen requested that she cannot stay in this meeting. But if you would like to meet them in person, they will stay for 20-30 minutes. They they'll leave."

Once the king finished his announcement, the officials started to line up to where the royals were seated. Two genies were standing near the royal family to guide the officials while they approach them for their personal greetings. The line grew larger when the queen spoke.

"Thank you once again. I would love to stay with you, but unfortunately, I could not due to some pressing matters that I need to attend to. I have a lot of things to do tomorrow. The king will be ending his ritual. I hope to see you and your families in the Akitu festival party. I, along with Queen Amasis and the girls, will leave first. However, if they would like to stay, they can decide for themselves. Thank you all."

The government officials were waiting in front of the genies for the queen to end her speech. Once she sat, the genies started to accompany the officials one by one to the queen, her guests, and the girls. Even when she was busy, the queen noticed Mr. Abzu in the crowd of guests, waiting for his turn. She recognized him despite the sea of people in the room. Because of this, she turned to look at her daughter and saw Atalia smiling. When it was Mr. Abzu's turn, Atalia was very happy and excited. Because the royal family were busy in the past weeks, they did not have time to meet, but when he approached the queen, Atalia quietly talked with Princess Mehaa about him. When he got closer, Mehaa got excited as well and told Atalia that he was very handsome.

Mr. Abzu greeted the queen, "How are you and how do you feel, your honour?" He said this while holding the queen's hand. To which the queen responded that she was fine.

He continued, "I am happy to see you, your highness. You look lovely, as always." Then he bowed and kissed her hand.

He then moved towards the Egyptian king and queen. He saw King Assur-Tudiya sitting behind the queen and raised his hand to greet him as two good friends. Mehaa, on the other hand, was excited to meet him and anxiously waited to see him. When he approached her, he was looking at Atalia all the time, and smiling.

Mr. Abzu held Mehaa's hand. Meeha was frozen on the spot and Atalia came to her rescue. "Honey, this is Princess Mehaa of Mesren, the daughter of the king and queen of Egypt."

Mr. Abzu smiled and said, "I am honoured to meet you, your highness. Welcome to our country." He then kissed her hand and moved quickly to Atalia. "Hi honey, I missed you."

Atalia's heart felt warm to see her beloved. "Me too!" While this exchange happened, the queen was looking at them to see how her daughter would behave. At the same time, Atalia kept glancing at her mother to see if she approved of Mr. Abzu.

Mr. Abzu's time was up and told the love of his life that he will see her tomorrow.

The queen was very transparent of her satisfaction with Mr. Abzu since he was very handsome, a gentleman, and well-educated. Aside from that, he has a Bachelor of Science degree, has been awarded an honorary Doctorate of Science in Engineering from several colleges and universities. Mr. Abzu was assigned to the Assyrian National Space Task Group in the Mat-Assur Research Center. He has logged over 300 hours in space. He was a great Air Force pilot with 5,000 hours of flying time in a jet aircraft. He worked under Prince (now acting king) Assur-Tudiya, and was recommended to be the head of the astronaut training center by King Assur himself. He was the son of Air Force commander Azarah-Anu II and Naunitu Azarah. They were close to the royal family.

Mr. Abzu moved away from Atalia to make way for the other guests who lined up to greet the royal family. So he kissed her hand twice and told her "I love you. I will see you tomorrow at the festival party." Atalia responded with an I love you too. He then moved to Bonita, who was listening intently to their conversation.

Mr. Abzu said, "Hi Bonita. How are you?" He shook her hand and looked at her face. He could see that Bonita was smiling. He blinked his eye and saw that she was still smiling.

Bonita replied with a smile, "I am fine, Mr. Abzu. Atalia loves you very much."

Mr. Abzu was happy with the confirmation and said, "Yes, I love her too."

Bonita responded, "I know. Good luck." To which he said, "Thank you Bonita. And you look lovely."

After all the guests were able to greet the royal family and guests, they left the room. Then the king went up front to address everyone.

"Thank you for coming. I would like to give you good and bad news about our Earth rover, which was launched 8 months ago to planet Earth. The good news is, we landed safely and all instruments are working, including the video cameras."

With this news, all the guests clapped.

"The bad news, however, is that there are humans on earth. Although, it is great to know that there is life, water, and air. It is a living planet and it's somewhere we can visit in the near future without any special astronaut costumes like we used to go to Mars, our moon. But the only disappointment of this mission was when we found black humans. They were all nudes, without clothes, both men and women. What was most surprising was these humans had paintings on their bodies. Mr. Isme-Dagan, the head of the Earth Rover project, will show you a video. Mr. Isme, please come to the podium."

With that, Mr. Isme-Dagan got up and the guests proudly cheered him.

Isme spoke, "Thank you, your highness, and to everyone in attendance here today. The honourable king explained that the fact of this mission, we are happy we landed safely. We are now on the third day of looking at the pictures that we've been receiving from the rover lander. They are quite spectacular, I must say! The black humans attacked the rover when it touched the ground. The engineers and I were scared because we were worried that they will damage the instruments on board. But everything looks good. Now we will show you the video. At this time, I would like to call Mr. Assur-Ram to come up here and show us the video."

The video was then shown on the big screen, which was prepared for this occasion in the king's office. When the video was playing, it showed the part where the black, nude human looked at the rover and a few others who were throwing rocks. Some held long branches of trees, attacking the rover. When the officers saw this, everybody starting yelling and laughing.

Mr. Assur-Ram then spoke. "We were so excited we kept looking at this attack by the black humans. However, the king reminded us to move the rover immediately. So we did move it a quarter of a mile away from its original landing point. Luckily, the inhabitants did not follow the rover. We've been manoeuvring the rover for 3 days now and we did not see any trace of white people. This session's now ended and thank you all."

The king added. "Tomorrow is the twelfth day of the Akitu and the end of the ritual. It also marks the beginning of the Akitu festival. The Assyrian nation's holiday! We'll all be waiting for our beloved King Assur-Adamu I to leave the Esagila temple. Then we'll have the victory procession and the New year officially starts. The victory procession is our way to express our joy of Assur's renewal of power and destruction of the evil forces, which almost controlled life in the beginning."

THE END OF THE TWELFTH DAY OF AKITU

The last day of Akitu—the gods return to God Assur's temple—The Crystal Shrine temple" in the mountain and all the statues are returned to the temple. Daily life resumes in Mat-Assur, the capital of Assyria, and the rest of all Assyrian cities.

AKITU CELEBRATION

King Assur-Adamu-I, the great king of Mat-Assur, will soon be leaving the Esagila temple after twelve days of ritual. Then the Assyrian New Year festival will officially start.

It is the morning of 21 of Nisanu, a Sunday. It's a very lovely day and the Esagila temple was full of dignitaries, heads of military, city mayors, officials from friendly countries that were here to celebrate the sacred day with the king and queen of Assyria.

The Esagila temple was very large and can occupy up to a thousand people. The first row of seating was reserved for the royal family. In the middle of the first row was reserved for queen Assurinu, the king and queen of Mesren, Prince Assur-Tudiya, Bonita, and Princess Atalia and Mehaa. On the other side of the queen will be seated were the six high priests. They were all waiting for the honourable king to come out from the temple's prayer room.

Before the king leaves the temple, his entourage waited at the main gate of the temple. His entourage consisted of three golden carriages—the first were for the

King and Queen, the second for the Egyptian royal family, and the third for the prince, princess, and Bonita. There were also 50 more regular carriages for the guests, and the dignitaries if they wish to follow the king and the queen through Star Avenue then to the Royal Palace.

This festival was more than any other event in the Assyrian nation. It's humbling moment with all the population sharing progress to prove them procession was the people's way to express their joy at the king's renewal of power and destruction of the evil force which almost controlled life in the beginning.

The king's entourage will consist of six priests, including two high priests of the Esagila temple in the front of the King and Queen's carriage, walking on foot with 60 protective winged genies, 40 young Assyrian dancers all dressed in their traditional dressed, 8 musicians and 4 drummers. In front of the drummers were 20 of Atalia's girlfriends, all wearing beautiful Assyrian folk dresses and dancing in front of the entourage.

At exactly 10am, the guests in the temple and got up, shouting with a loud voice "Long live the King Assur-Adamu!". Two high priests came out first from the prayer room, followed by the King. The priest stood aside, and the king ran straight to his wife to hug and kiss her. He then turned to the King and Queen of Mesren and greeted them. He was happy to see them as well. Then he walked to his son, daughter, with Bonita and Mehaa. He hugged them one by one, and kissed them. The king also waved to all the guests in attendance. He held the queen's hand and moved slowly to the main gate where the golden carriages were waiting. The Egyptian royal couple followed suit, with the prince, princess, Bonita and Mehaa behind them.

When they got outside, the music started—Zorna and Dawala started with a very loud music and 40 dancers with their beautiful, colourful dresses started dancing. In the front of the entourage, followed by 6 priests and protected by 60 genies, all walking in front of the king's golden carriage. Half of a million citizens gathered on both sides of Star Avenue, cheering and waving to the king and queen. The king was standing majestically in his carriage, waving to the people with his hand.

The Star Avenue, between temple and the nation palace, was exactly one kilometre. It was one of the most beautiful avenues in Mat-Assur. 100-meter wide, decorated with all types of flowers and flowery tress, and palm trees on both sides of the avenue. It was decorated specially for this event. Halfway between the royal palace and the Esagila temple, there were two large Assyrian colossal lions (Lamasu) statue made of limestone. The size of each statue was 20m long and 10 m high, facing the Esagila temple. When the king's carriage arrived at the Lamasu statue, they stopped for a minute, then quickly moved toward the palace. The music and dancers continued to the palace as well.

Today was a very busy day for the king. He will spend a few hours in the throne room, meeting with all his cabinet members and government officials. His son, Assur-Tudiya, will give him a full report for the twelve days while he was in ritual. Then he will meet all the dignitaries, kings and queens from friendly countries as well, who came to celebrate the Akitu festival with them. At 7pm, there will be a big celebration and dinner party for all the guests at the royal palace dining room, which can hold 500 guests. Immediately after dinner, the queen arranged a dance party with the Assyrian singers and professional dancers to entertain the guests for this happy day.

The king's entourage slowly moved towards the royal palace. Half a million of its citizen's cheers and danced to the king and queen. At the palace, twelve genies stood guard at the entrance, and 50 more are stations to help stop the spectators that followed the entourage to enter the palace.

It was 10am, only a few hundred feet away from the palace. All the genies at the gate took their place. They can hear the music and cheering of the people. They opened the palace gate wide open so that all the dancers, carriages can enter.

At exactly 11am, the king's entourage arrived at the palace gate. All the participants went inside. It was a successful procession, albeit it being noisy from the Esagila temple to the Royal Palace via the Star Avenue.

The king and queen directly went to the throne room, followed by the prince and princess because all the cabinet members, dignitaries from the friendly countries, were already inside, waiting for their beloved king and queen to arrive. They haven't seen the king for 12 days because of the ritual.

Before the royal couple entered, 60 genies went in, followed by 6 high priests, who stood by threes on each side of the throne. The Assyrian National anthem was then played and everyone in the room stood up. The king and queen entered. The king looked very powerful and the queen, with her golden crown, looked very beautiful. They moved slowly towards their seats on the throne. Everyone in the room cheered and started clapping. The prince and princess followed their parents and the cheers did not stop for a whole ten minutes. While this was ongoing, the music started again and dancers danced the traditional folk dance in front of the royal family.

It was a festive entertainment. A few guests joined the dancers because the music was so festive and exciting. The king was happy, especially when the prince and princess joined the dance. Mr. Abzu also joined. This lasted for more than an hour and finally the music stopped. Everybody went back to their seats. It was time for the king to thank all the guests. He got up and addressed everyone in the room.

"Today is the day of creation and also the rebirth of nature according to our religion. The story of the creation has been described by our heavenly God and we've been obeying it for a thousand years. Every new year, I have to go through a ritual which led to my dethroning by the high priest in the presence of Assur, to confess that I have sinned against the land and have not neglected the divinity. My crown was returned by the high priest because I was humble to my people and to my country. For this, our kingship was extended for another year. Also, I would like to say Happy New Year to all of you. Most specially to my wife, the Queen Assurinu, my son Prince Assur-Tudiya, and my beloved daughter, Princess Atalia. Also to my special guests and friends, King and Queen of Mesren. They came a long way to celebrate the Akitu festival with us. I hope this year will be successful for everyone, and the happiest!"

The king ended his speech and immediately, the prince spoke:

"Ladies and gentlemen, honorable King and Queen of Mesren, I would like to welcome you to our Akitu festival. We have a small video to show you first, then we will move to the palace dining room for luncheon, and inner. I would also like to thank the queen. For 12 days, she has been working very hard preparing with all the palace ladies, while my father was still in ritual."

Father, I have great news to tell you. But before that, I would like to call these dedicated Air Force officials to come and stand next to the throne.

Mr. Azarah-Anu, Air Force commander

Mr. Isme-Dagan, head of the Rover project

Mr. Abzu-Bt-Anu, astronaut/head of the space training

Mr. Assur-Ram, Assyrian National Observatory Center

MR. IRKALLA (Airforce General)"

They all approached the throne one by one and stood in front.

The prince continued, "Your highness, these five scientists and many others in the space center, worked strenuously for 12 hours a day since the rover was launch 8 months ago. We would like to report that the rover landed safely on Earth. We will show you a video that was taken before the arrival and when it touched down on Earth.

Please bring the large screen down." He asked Mr. Enlil-Nirari and instructed him to dim the lights.

The video started. Everybody was quiet in the throne room, but when the scene of the black humans appeared, everyone started shouting from excitement. Some ladies wanted to leave because they were scared. They could not believe that there were black humans who existed since they do not have them in Tiamat.

Prince Assur-Tudiya asked Mr. Enlil to end the video and to turn on the lights in the room. Once the lights were on, everyone started clapping for the successful landing.

The king got up from his chair and moved to the edge of the throne. "Thank you for your hard work. Now we know that there is life on planet Earth. Now we can plan on visiting the planet. Mr. Abzu, how is our astronaut training coming through?"

Mr. Abzu replied. "Your highness, we have now about 150 astronauts under training every day. You must visit the space center to check them out."

The king was happy to hear of the progress. "I will, very soon. Thank you, Mr. Abzu." He then turned to Mr. Isme-Dagan and said, "Mr. Isme, what else have you found on Earth? And is it safe to visit in the future?"

To which Mr. Isme-Dagan responded. "Yes, your highness. We have found water, oceans, rivers, trees. It is a very safe planet to live in. However, we did not see humans like us as they were black. Maybe it's just in where we landed. I don't really know since Earth is very big. So we may find other types of human. It looks that the humans are savages on the planet, I mean Earth is a very new planet."

"Thank you, Mr. Isme, and thank you to all the space center scientists. Good job, all of you!", the king said.

The king went back to his chair. All five scientists bowed to him one by one and went to their respective seats. Atalia was sitting behind her parents and she was excited to see her boyfriend talking to the king. But when Mr. Abzu bowed to the king and queen, he smiled at Atalia, which the Queen noticed.

The prince then announced. "Ladies and gentlemen, in half an hour, we will be moving to the palace dining room. We will have a luncheon with the king and queen. Those guests who wishes to see them, they can wait where Mr. Enlil-Nirari is standing. Please register your names with him now so he can call you when your turn has come. Thank you!"

After the announcement, almost everyone registered their names so they can meet the king and queen personally.

PALACE DINING HALL

The spectacular dining hall was the largest on the planet Tiamat and can seat 500 guests. As its name suggests, the grand hall has sophisticated wood interiors, ornate crystal chandeliers. The stucco ceiling has inlaid mirror and gilding with real gold leaf. The room was designed to dazzle the guests. The walls were covered with pictures of the Kings of Assyria. The king used the state dining room for dinners for up to 200 guests, often in connection with the ball room, rather than the room which occupied 500 seats. On such occasions, the table and buffet used for magnificent displays of gold plates. The food served are usually Assyrian type as the king and queen loves it.

Most dignitaries wanted to see the king and queen and they took their turns, escorted by two genies from the standing point. When everyone was done with their greetings, the prince announced that they all need to go to the dining hall.

Six genies approached the throne and assisted the royal family slowly to the dining room. Gold plates were set on the table, the table cover was white and every 10", there were red flower bouquets, and the room's carpet was red as well.

The royal family sat on their special table, then all the guests sat on their designated tables. Before dinner started, the king requested the high priest to pray for their meal.

Through God Assur, our Lord, we pray.

Assur, we have gathered to share a meal in your honor. Thank you for putting us together as one family, and thank you for this great food. Bless it to our bodies, Lord. We thank you for all the gifts you have given, bless the hearts and hands that provided the eternity, own us and crown us heirs to thy kingdom. These favors and blessings we ask in the name of God Assur, our great Redeemer.

After the prayer, everybody relaxed and food was immediately served on the tables. Servings of Tabboulah, salad, marinated chicken and meat shawarma, jumbo shrimp skewers grilled to perfection, beef/lamb decorated with onions— they were followed by delicious appetizers—Baba Ganoush, DOLMA (Stuffed Grape Leaves), falafel, etc. The dinner lasted for one and a half hour, and every guest was happy with the food, and there was a wide array of beers and wine to select from.

Suddenly, the dining room became very quiet. Mr. Enlil Nirari stood and spoke. "Ladies and gentlemen, the honorable king Assur-Adamu I would like to speak to you. Please be very quiet."

The king stood up and opened his hand and prayed.

Dear Lord, as this new year is born
I give it to thy hand,
Content to walk by faith what paths I cannot understand
Whatever coming days may bring
Of better loss, or gain,
Every crown of happiness,
Should sorrow come, or pain.

Oh lord, if all unknown to me
Thine angel hovers near
To bear me to that further shore
Before another year.

It matters not—my hand in thine,
The light upon my face,
By boundless strength when I am weak
They love and saving grace.

"My fellow citizens of Assyria, thank you all. I would like to thank my family for their passions, specially to my dear wife, the queen. She worked very hard in the past 12 days. Thank you again."

Then the palace speaker announced "The Akitu celebration starts now!!"

Everyone moved to the palace dancing hall. The royal family were escorted by a group of dancers who were wearing beautiful Assyrian costumes.

When all the guests were seated in the dance hall, 12 dancers moved towards the king and queen, dancing a slow dance, with two musicians Zorna and Dawola. Thwen the dancers neared them, the king and queen got up and started moving towards the dancers. At this time, the music turned to folk and loud music. Suddenly, 30 dancers ran and joined the first dancers. The prince and princess joined in as well as other guests.

When Atalia saw Mr. Abzu busy talking with his friends, she called for him and waved for him to stand up and join. They danced all night. The Akitu celebration ended at 2 in the morning. Finally, the dance ended and Mr. Abzu asked Atalia to walk her to her father. She hesitated. She told him "Honey, we are enjoying the celebration. My father and mother are entertaining their closes friends. The music is also too loud, so my father will never hear you. Please, it's not a good time. Let's just dance and enjoy."

Mr. Abzu replied, "Okay honey, you're right. But see, your mother has been looking at us all the time." "Yes, because she likes you.", Atalia said.

While they were dancing, Prince Assur-Tudiya and Bonita joined them. Mr. Abzu asked

Prince Assur why Mehaa was not dancing. He replied that she does know how to dance.

The music was loud and exciting. All the guests were enjoying themselves.

The King has successfully returned from the ritual and they were celebrating the Akitu holiday. He was enjoying when a genie approached him and brought him with some news.

"A week ago, in the "Shrine Temple" there was an emergence Gods meeting which was requested by the God Ashur and he asked three eagles to remain in the temple. After the Gods meeting ended the three eagles headed genies approached gods Alter. God Ashur asked them to take his message to the king Ashur-Adamu -1 when he returned from Akitu-Ritual."

While the celebration was going full blast and everybody enjoying themselfes; suddenly, two protective genies approached the Kings and the genies sense through physical perception that something is going to happen very soon outside of the palace. The three head genies were seen flying from the Shrine-Temple to the king palace, to take their god message to the honorable king. The three genies landed at palace gate, all the guards at the gate immediately stood in command. The guards knew these genies were sent to see the King only, no other officials! The Palace guards knew that the three eagle-headed genies have more authorities and position in the government, so all the guards stood in command to great the three genies.

The three genies landed in front of the palace, all the guards stood head down as the genies walked between them toward the large gate as two guards open the gate, the genies walk through the guards without question. They head down a hallway towards the Ball room, passing through the government officials as they bow to the genies; though the palace is so large with many hallways So immediately the three genies headed to the Ball room where the king is celebrating Akitu festival with his guests.

The honorable King and Queen of Assyrian standing with the honorable King and Queen of Meseren including the Prince and Princess Mahaa and Bonita, watching a group of professional dancers perform while everyone else was very concentrated. Suddenly two genies approached the King Ashur-Adam 1 and the protective genies of the King immediately communicated with the three eagle-headed genies and they turned to the king and told him that they have a message from the shrine-temple. The King immediately apologizes to his guests and asked the protective genies to tell the eagle-headed genies to follow the King to a private room behind where they were standing only being 20ft away, which is quieter then the dancing hall.

The King asked the protective genies asked the eagle-headed genie what the message is, as the two genies stood face to face for a few minutes and by extrasensory perception they communicated Gods message. When they finish, the king's protective genies turn to the King and said "your honor, the genies were sent by the God of Pantheon, God Ashur sense a trouble to the Kingdom because of the severe energy shortage of Energy on the planet, he asks you to be a leader and call a special national meeting to solve this problem as soon as possible and God Ashur believes that you and other nations; which control most of the energy, can come with a peaceful solution to this crisis. God Ashur has full trust in your leadership and wants you to follow through with his command."

Once genies ended God message, King Assur-Adamu excepted the God message, he bowed his head for both genies. The two eagle head genies immediately left the room they join third genie, which was waiting outside. then all three flow back to Shrine Temple.

Taken by surprise, the King stayed in the room for a few minutes, anxious and uneasy, not knowing what may happen. He raised his hands and lifted his head up to God Assur and decided to thank Him for his reminder of the severity of the crisis. He then left the room to join his family and guests, the two genies in tow.

The festivities continued.

There was dancing and merrymaking all around. They celebrated with Assyrian music and dance until 1 PM. The King's son, Prince Assur Tudia headed the celebration along with his fiancée, Bonita, Mr. Abzu, and Princess Atalia. All the boys and girls joined in as the music grows louder and the dancing even merrier.

The King of Mesren, in the midst of all the excitement could not help but admire the dancers especially Princess Atalia and her partner.

"Your majesty, you have a very lovely daughter who is a graceful dancer as well. Her partner is a good dancer as well." He praised.

"Thank you! Indeed, she loves to dance. That is her boyfriend she is dancing with," The Queen responded.

The King was also observing the Princess in the dance floor. He noticed that she was dancing with the same gentleman since the beginning. They were holding hands and seems very affectionate. He turned to the Queen and asked who he was.

"That is Mr. Abzu Bet-Anu, the head of the Astronaut Training Center and the son of Air Force Commander Mr. Azarah Anu. He is a loyal friend of Assur and Atalia likes him very much.

"He is an excellent dancer. I am glad he has mastered the Assyrian dance," the King said.

"What a beautiful couple!" King Harar exclaimed.

"How about Prince Assur Tudia, when is he getting married?" Queen Amasis inquired.

"They have not set a date yet but I will let you know for sure once they do." The Queen promised.

Meanwhile the Queen decided to focus her attention to Mehaa.

"Meeha, there are many young gentlemen in this party, why don't you mingle. Maybe you can find a boyfriend who can teach you Assyrian dance." The Queen teased.

"I think they are afraid to approach me I am not Assyrian. They know I am from Mesren. There are a lot of handsome men in the hall, I noticed." Mehaa replied.

"Ah yes and you are wearing the Mesren National dress. It is beautiful! Like you, our girls here in Assyria love wearing our National dress during parties and celebrations like this." The Queen said.

"Atalia tried to introduce me to one gentleman earlier but I did not want to get close to anyone because we are going home in a few days. I love being a guest in your Kingdom but we will be going home in just a few days." Mehaa shared.

"You should have met with him. You'll never know!" The Queen answered.

While the Queen and Princess were busy trying to find a match for Mehaa, King Assur Adamu approached the King of Mesren, the honorable King Narmar:

"Can you stay another week? I am calling for a special UN meeting to discuss the energy crisis. I have already sent my deputies to call all the presidents of the world for the gathering."

"Of course, your honor! I am honored you asked. I came here not just to celebrate the Akitu Festival with you and your Kingdom but to also discuss with you the energy situation. We need to work together to find a solution that will be amenable to everyone otherwise, we are looking at worldwide chaos. We don't want countries going to war against each other." King Narmar pointed out.

"Thank you, I appreciate you coming here. It is indeed nice to see you again. The family missed you. And you are right, we need to find a solution soon before chaos breaks. Our planet is getting old and our population is doubling every 10 years. The planet can no longer sustain the demands of the booming population." The King replied.

"Thank you, your majesty for your hospitality." King Narmar said.

Meanwhile, Abzu Bet-Anu decided to show off and get the attention of the King so he can show him that he loves Atalia. He took Atalia's hand and headed towards Mehaa. Atalia was hesitant to go along because she did not want her father to see her with Abzu. Abzu however wants the King to see them both together so he dragged her along towards Mehaa, never letting go of her hand:

"Mehaa, I apologize for not coming to you soon. We have been so busy. We want to teach you the Assyrian dance so you can enjoy the festivities just as much as we do."

"Yes, please Mehaa." Atalia plead.

"Go ahead Mehaa, let Abzu and Atalia teach you. It's better than standing here all night by yourself." The Queen joined in.

"No, thank you! I don't want to make a fool of myself. It is embarrassing, there is just too many people. I don't want to disrupt the dance for everyone." Mehaa protested.

Prince Assur Tudia and Bonita showed up:

"Abzu, why did you and Atalia leave the dance?" The Prince asked.

"We came to get Mehaa. We want her to join the dance and offered to teach her the Assyrian dance." Abzu replied.

"Oh great! Come on Mehaa, let's go! We will teach you. I promise you will have fun." The excited Prince exclaimed.

"No, thank you Assur. I am enjoying the party from here. I love watching you four on the dance floor," declined Mehaa.

Prince Assur Tudia turned to Abzu and asked:

"Did you meet the King yet?"

"No, he is with King Narmar. I did not want to interrupt," answered Abzu.

"Come on, I will introduce you!"

Prince Assur grabbed Abzu's hand and brought him to the King:

"Father, I would like to introduce Mr. Abzu Bet-Anu, son of Air Force Commander Azarah Anu. He works as the Astronaut Training Center and an air force pilot as well."

"I know. Your mother told me," the King told the Prince. He turned to Abzu:

JOHNSON KARAM

"I heard good things about you Mr. Abzu. I hope you are enjoying the festival."

"Your majesty, it is a great honor to meet you. I would like to congratulate you and your family for the success of the Akitu Festival." Abzu bowed.

The King turned to King Narmar and introduced Abzu to him:

"This is one of our astronaut and air force pilot, Mr. Abzu Bet-Anu."

They shook hands then King Narmar said:

"We are sending 10 new Air Force graduates over to you for training. I talked to Prince Assur yesterday. He will discuss this with his majesty and we will talk about it next week. I am glad to meet you Mr. Abzu."

"It is a pleasure to meet you, your highness. We will be honored to trained your graduates. We currently have 150 astronauts in training." Abzu said.

Atalia was with her mother observing very closely, trying to listen to the King and Abzu's conversation. She was so nervous for Abzu and worried that the King might not like Abzu. She really likes Abzu and wants the King to like him for her. The Queen noticed how nervous her daughter was.

"Relax darling, everything will be fine. Mr. Abzu seems like a very charming and smart gentleman. I am sure he can handle talking to your father. I can see that he loves you so I am sure he will do his best to impress your father and will not do anything that will disrespect or turn him off. Don't worry." The Queen assured her.

Princess Atalia never took her eyes off Abzu and the King. As soon as Abzu was done talking to the King and King Narmar, Princess Atalia run to her father's side to investigate. Meanwhile, Abzu approach Queen Azurinu to pay his respects.

"Your Grace, I am happy and honored to see you today. Congratulations for the successful festivities! Everything is splendidly beautiful. I hope every year will be as successful as this year or even more so," praised Abzu.pect. He kissed the Queen's hand to show his res.

"Thank you, Mr. Abzu! I am happy you are here to celebrate with us. I hope you are enjoying the festival," teased the Queen.

151

"I am, your Grace, very much so. Thank you for your generosity and for the invitation." Abzu bowed down as he moved back to signal his leave, greeting Queen Amasis of Mesren on his way out of the Queen's circle.

Curious, Queen Amasis turned to the Queen;

"What a handsome gentleman. He seems very smitten with Princess Atalia. I must say, your Grace, they look good together. They will make a lovely pair," Queen Amasis commented.

"He is indeed! He is a smart, responsible young man. He loves my Atalia and I approve of him. I think he is a good match for the Princess," replied the Queen.

"Does the King know?" asked Queen Amasis.

"No, he does not know yet. That's why Princess Atalia is so anxious tonight. She is afraid Mr. Abzu might slip and tell the King his love for her. She knows the King wants her to marry from a royal bloodline. She does love Mr. Abzu just as much as he loves her, so she worries even more," explained the Queen.

"Is there a potential match for her from a royal bloodline? Someone within her age range?"

"There is no Prince but the King's cousin, Governor Assur-Shar-Shari has a son, Dudu-Enlil but he is 45 years old and she does not want to marry him. He is too old for her and besides, her heart is already set for Mr. Abzu. Personally, I don't see anything wrong with her being with Mr. Abzu. He is a fine gentleman who holds a high-ranking position in the space center. He works closely with my son Prince Assur-Tudia and he talks highly of him. I do not know how the King will feel though. We will see..." said the Queen.

By 2AM all the guests, Royalties, dignitaries, Government officials, family and special guests, started lining up to congratulate the King and Queen for a successful festival and to wish them a happy new year before they all go on their way. This marks the end of the Akitu Festival.

All the servants made a 2-line formation to give way for the King and Queen and their entourage. Three genies lead the way - one in front, two behind. They escorted the King and the Queen to the quarters followed by the Prince and the Princess. They also sent the King and Queen of Mesren, who are the King's special quests, to their quarters along with their daughter Mehaa.

Inside their private quarters, the King turned to the Queen;

"My love, I noticed something tonight and I am not sure how I feel about it. I want you to tell me the truth because it bothered me all night."

"What is it, my King?"

"I noticed Princess Atalia and Mr. Abzu Betu-Anu were dancing and kept to each other all night. They were holding hands, being cozy like they are a couple. They seem very comfortable being like that in from of the Prince too." The King stated a matter of factly.

"Yes, I noticed that too but Honey, our Atalia is 28 years old. She is old enough and more than capable to choose a life partner. I think she is ready and I trust her judgment. She has always been a good daughter. I am sure she will not do anything or choose anyone that will bring shame or embarrassment to her and to our family. Mr. Abzu comes from a noble family, holds a high-ranking position in the Air Force. He works closely with the Prince, that is why they are comfortable around him. The Prince talks highly of Mr. Abzu. He loves Atalia and she loves him too. They are happy together. Your daughter is happy." The Queen said defensively.

"How long has this been going on?" asked the King.

"I don't know. You should sit down with her and discuss this. Prince Assur do know about their relationship from the start so you should talk to him too, but the fact that Prince Assur is not opposed to the match says a lot about Mr. Abzu and their relationship."

The King was pensive for a moment. "I hope she remembers our ancient rule about marrying within the royal bloodline."

"My King, there is no match for here within the royal family. The closest to a match is Dudu-Enlil and he is 45 years old. He is too old for her and she doesn't love her. You don't really want your only daughter to go into a loveless marriage, do you? Besides, I think what we have about royalty marrying royalty is an ancient tradition and not a law. Will you talk to her and discuss this?" Pleaded the Queen.

"Yes, I will." Assured the King.

The days after the Festival was hectic for the King. First on the agenda is to discuss country affairs. He called for all his councilmen and legislators to the throne room for a special meeting. He also asked his deputy, Mr. Ninos Ninurta to call a UN meeting to discuss the energy crisis that planet is facing.

"What we have here is a CRISIS and an OPPORTUNITY. This crisis offers for us an opportunity for a shift in consciousness which goes beyond changes in energy policies. We need a solution that is grounded in Heo Humanism. It is a global spirit that maintains the balance of all beings in nature." the King started.

"I am speaking of a problem that everyone is experiencing, either at the gas tank every day or every family at the end of month when they receive their energy bill."

"We will discuss this in the UN meeting as we explore quick fixes and permanent solutions to the problems the world is facing today. Problems like Social Justice, Climate Change, Food shortage, Energy shortage and many others. We need to find ways to use an Integrative Model for all countries. During the meeting I would like to focus on true progress that takes care of our people's spiritual and physical well-being. This will be achieved by finding balance in providing for our needs and taking care of our natural resources. I have prepared a list of solutions and basic guidelines that will be discussed during the meeting. I have asked Mr. Ninurta to arrange the UN Meeting as soon as possible. It will probably take a month or two to get every leader from every country to agree on a schedule but what is important is that we have initiated the process."

The King received a standing ovation from the room. Everyone knows the imminent danger brought about by the energy crisis.

"Thank you. What we have is not a simple crisis at hand. We are facing imminent danger. Our energy resources are running out and finding a solution will take a lot of hard work and dedication. Keep researching and keep praying. Thank you!" The King stood up and took his leave while every stood up as he walked past.

The Sergeant at Arms, Mr. Sin Namir took the floor;

"In two weeks, we will meet again. As for now, the King needs us to be vigilant. The King has a lot of work to do and he needs our help. Let us do our job and do it well. The King will be visiting the Space Center and the Flying Saucer Factory to check to progress in hand. And until the next week, the King will be hosting the King of Nesren and his family. So let us make sure we are able to assist the King the best way we can."

After the meeting, the King went directly to his Palace office and summoned his children, Prince Assur Tudia and Princess Atalia. The King wanted to address any issues he has with his children as soon as possible before he will be swamped with so much work on the energy crisis. His children arrived within minutes, eager to know why their father summoned them with such urgency. The two genies opened the office doors for the royal children and they went in to give their father a kiss and a warm embrace.

"Father, is anything wrong? Why the urgent call?" Prince Assur asked, worried.

"Sit down," the King ordered. "I called you both because I miss you and I wanted to talk to you about something very personal and very important. But before that, I want you both to know that I care for you and that I love you both with all my heart."

"We love you too, father." Both replied in unison.

"Atalia, I noticed during the Akitu festival that you and Mr. Abzu-Bet-Anu we very cozy the whole night, dancing exclusively with each other, holding hands and looked very much like a couple. And you my son, was there right next to them and did not say or do anything to stop that which makes me think you know what is going on with the two." The King said accusingly.

Atalia was taken aback. She was not expecting a confrontation from his father. She was lost for words and could not speak. She just bowed her head in submission and did not say a word.

Prince Assure came to Princess Atalia's rescue;

"Father, Mr. Abzu is a good man with exceptional character. He is a highly educated officer and holds a high-ranking position at the Astronaut Training Center. He has 150 young officers under training and he is the best officer under my command. I have watched him work under me for over 5 years and I can attest to his outstanding character. I cannot get in between the two of them because I do think Mr. Abzu is a great match for my sister. I have also seen how he cared for Atalia. I know he has pure intentions and loves my sister very much. I have seen how happy my sister is since they have been a couple. I only have high praises for Mr. Abzu. I approve of him for my Atalia."

"I am sure he is the best officer in the Space Center, I have no doubt about that. I also know he is from a noble family. I know all that, but he does not hail from a royal family, he does not have a royal bloodline. I want my daughter to be a Queen one day and that will only happen if you (looking at Princess Atalia) will marry a Prince or someone from a royal family." the King said firmly.

Atalia wanted to burst out screaming to defend her choice and her relationship with Abzu but she kept her cool. She raised her head and started speaking politely to her father.

"Father, I understand your position, I really do. But I want to live my life with someone that I love not with someone society dictates. I love Abzu and he loves me. I cannot marry someone I do not love. I know that tradition dictates I marry Dudu-Enlil but I cannot marry someone just because that's what society and tradition dictates. I have to marry the person my heart choses. Abzu may not be of royal descent but he is noble in every way."

"Atalia is right, Father. We cannot force her to go into a loveless marriage. I do not want to see my sister to live a miserable life. I only want what is best for her and for her to be happy. And if Mr. Abzu is the person who can bring her happiness, I am all for it. I have never seen Mr. Abzu disrespect my sister or anyone. He is a good man." Prince Assur interjected.

"Alright, alright!" The King surrendered. "Let us continue this another time. We are not yet done talking about this and we will talk about this again in the future. For now, Assur, I need you to go to the Space Center and check on the progress of the Annunaki Training. I, on the other hand, will be visiting the Flying Saucer assembly factory."

"Okay, Father. We have finished one Flying Saucer so far. You will be pleased to see it especially the interior. It is beautiful," boast the Prince.

"Okay, let's do it tomorrow. Make sure everyone will be there." Ordered the King.

"Can I come too, Father?" asked the Princess. She wanted to see Mr. Abzu one more time and feels embarrassed to ask.

"Yes, you can sweetheart. Please bring Bonita with you. I don't want you roaming around in the Space Center alone." replied the King.

"Father, what about Mother?" asked Atalia.

"Your mother will be busy accompanying the King of Mesren and his family meeting some dignitaries and friend's tomorrow. She will have her hands full with them for the whole week." the King answered. He turned to Prince Assur, "And please make sure everyone is there tomorrow." he ordered.

"Yes, your highness." replied the Prince.

By 10am the next morning, everyone was up and ready to go -the King, Prince Assur, Princess Atalia and Bonita. The King's limousine was ready to. They were escorted by two genies to the limousine and went on their way. By 11am, they arrived at the Anunnaki Training Center. They could have arrived earlier but security was very tight. When they got there, Mr. Abzu Bet-Anu was there along with his 150 Astronauts-in-training all lined up in front of the building to greet the Royal visitors. As soon as a genie opened the limousine door for the King, Mr. Abzu run down to greet him. He greeted the Prince next, Bonita and Princess Atalia last.

Mr. Abzu knew that Princess Atalia is coming to the official royal visit to the training center. She called him right after they had the talk with the King to give Mr. Abzu a heads up. Mr. Abzu was excited all night and all morning to see Atalia again. He was also nervous to see the King, afraid about the King's stand on their relationship.

Mr. Abzu wanted to spend time with Atalia and show her around but he cannot do anything because he has to accommodate the King, let him meet the trainees and show him around the facility.

As they walked around the facilities, the King turned to Mr. Abzu;

"How is the training? How many more Anunnakis do you need for training?"

"Your Majesty, we are always happy to accept more trainees. The training is hard and most trainees will quit in the first 2 months. Training is hard and living in space is even harder. They have to be strong and committed to the training program and the space program itself. This batch will end training in a few months. All 150 are basically ready to fly and serve. We have maintained a 75% retention so if you can send in more trainees our way, we are always happy to accept." Mr. Abzu nervously answered.

"Mr. Abzu, I am proud of what you have done here. I have heard good things about you from the Prince. He is quite happy with your service and your team's performance. That makes me happy too."

All the while, Princess Atalia has been keeping close, listening carefully to Mr. Abzu explain things to her Father. She is quite pleased with how things are going so far. The Princess cannot help but keep a sweet smile on her face.

Mr. Abzu then turned to Princess Atalia and Bonita;

"Your honors, can I interest you both to go into the Space Training Program? I will be happy to accept you as my students." Urged Mr. Abzu.

"I will have to ask my fiance." answered Bonita.

"How about you, Princess?"

"Do you have a training program for women?" asked Princess Atalia.

"Yes, we do. In fact, if you are interested, you can start tomorrow." Urged Mr. Abzu.

"Where is your training facilities for women?" asked the King.

"In the next building, your Majesty. We have 15 women astronauts in training. They are all doing really good." Mr. Abzu proudly answered. "By the way, your Majesty, we have prepared a banquet for you and your royal entourage."

"Mr. Abzu, Bonita and I would like to see your training facilities for women." Atalia interrupted.

"I can take you there after lunch, your Grace." Mr. Abzu happily answered.

The King interrupted their moment, "We have seen enough for today. You and Bonita can visit the women facility some other time with your brother. Right now, we have to visit the Flying Saucer Factory. They are waiting for us there right now."

"Princess Atalia, I can take you to see the women's training center anytime but you must see the Flying Saucer Factory first. It is amazing." said Mr. Abzu.

Mr. Abzu turned to the King;

"Your Majesty, lunch is ready, please follow me."

They all followed Mr. Abzu to the dining area which was beautifully decorated especially for the King's visit. All 150 trainees were there waiting for the royal family. As the King entered, everyone stood up and waited until the King was settled in his seat before they sat down.

Mr. Abzu stood up and nervously started to talk;

"Today, it is with great pride that we welcome the Great King, who made all these (gesturing to the facility) possible. We would like to thank you, your Majesty for giving us a free space for us to train but for future generations as well. This space program you started will not just be of used to us today but will help bring our future to greater heights, to other planets, even other galaxies. One day, we will find other life forms, other habitats… For God did not just create us and our planet, he created other universes too. Thank you, your Highness. Let us also welcome Prince Assur Tudia, his future wife, Bonita and Princess Atalia."

They were given a standing ovation once again.

"Thank you, Mr. Abzu. Thank you for your hard work and dedication for the Training Center and for the Assyrian Nation as a whole. The Great God Assur gave us wisdom and knowledge serve our nation and help our people advance to greater heights. And we have just started. Our exploratory team just landed on a planet called "Earth." We found life forms who call themselves "humans." They are different from us. We are still trying to find out if they are friendly intelligent species. We will know soon with your help and service. One day, you will travel to planet Earth. With our Flying Saucer Factory fully operational, we soon will have enough ships for each of you to travel to Earth and back home. Today, the country will call you "Anunnaki," the chosen ones blessed by the God Assur. And when you get to Earth, use your training, your instinct and your knowledge. Your Journey will be hard, that I know. You will encounter resistance and hardships but be courageous. You were chosen to make these heavenly trips for a reason. You have endured your training; this means you are fully equipped to take on this responsibility. You have in your hands, the future of our generation, the future of the Assyrian people. Be strong, be vigilant."

"As far as we know, they are a black race. You cannot change their color but you can start a new race with them, mold them and show them the blessing of God

159

Assur. Create an Assyrian Empire as soon as you land. Build the Empire with your courage and knowledge. Do not fail us. Be strong and may God Assur bless you now and always!"

Another standing ovation for the King and then the food was served.

After lunch, the King took time to meet and greet the Anunnaki. He made sure he met and shook hands with all 150 of them. The trainees were ecstatic that their King gave them special attention and was very nice to them. They were secretly hoping however that the Princess will do the same. They were all smitten with her beauty. If only they know that their very superior has already won her heart.

When it was time to go, the two genies appeared to escort the royal entourage back to the limousine and take them to the Flying Saucer Factory.

200 Scientists and workers were waiting for them at the Factory. As soon as the King stepped down from the limousine, two head Scientists of the Factory met him so they can escort the King and his entourage inside the Factory. They lead them straight to a special room in the assembly building so the King and his children can be comfortable while being briefed for the day's site visit. Scientists Burshmu and Balsu were the ones giving the briefing. They spend about a good 20 minutes in the briefing room before they headed out to meet the people in the factory and saw the production line and the finished flying saucer Prince Assur was raving about.

Meanwhile, outside the briefing room, everyone in the factory was excited to meet the King and see the Prince and Princess.

After the briefing, Mr. Burshmu led the King to the Flying Machine (Flying Saucer). As they exited the briefing room, they were met with a loud applause from the factory workers who were all happy that their great King took time to visit them and their facility. Princess Atalia took time to smile and wave at the workers which made them even more excited and happy.

About 200 feet and a few minutes' walk, they got to the Flying Machine. It looked majestic standing on its 3 huge wheels about 3 meters high. As soon as they got close, Scientist Balsu pressed the remote control in his hand which opened the stairs to the machine. Once the stairs came down, Mr. Burshmu asked the King to follow him to the stairs and asked Prince Assur, Princess Atalia and Bonita to follow suit.

There were 10 steps going up the machine. As soon as the King stepped into the first floor, he was taken by surprise at the beautiful craftsmanship, engineering and modern technology all poured into the machine. It must have taken outstanding teamwork for everyone to produce such superb machine.

Finding the first floor, it was a tad small, the King turned to Mr. Burshmu;

"Where are the pilot seats?"

"The seats and accommodations are on the second floor, your Majesty. We will use the elevator going up to the second floor. It can only take 4 people up so let's make 2 trips to accommodate everyone. This way, you Highness." Mr. Burshmu politely directed the King.

"Yes, Atalia, come up with us. Mr. Burshmu said the elevator can accommodate 4 people."

The King, Princess Atalia and Mr. Burshmu took the first flight up. Prince Assur, Bonita and Mr. Balsu followed right after.

As soon as they got out of the elevator, the King was overwhelmed by the sheer beauty of the space. The second floor was large and beautifully crafted.

The King could not help but exclaimed; "Wow, it's huge!"

"It is beautiful!" exclaimed Princess Atalia. "How many seats are there?"

"150 seats for all 150 Anunnakis. All seats have TVs at the back so the Astronauts can keep themselves occupied and keep them from being bored. The TV is also functional since it doubles as their technical screen where they can see all the data they need." answered Mr. Burshmu.

"Mr. Burshmu, what is the maximum travel speed of the flying machine?" asked Prince Assur.

"10,000 miles per hour within our space and 30,000 to 40,000 miles per hour in outer space." Mr. Burshmu said proudly.

"Do we have pilots ready to fly this?" the King inquired.

"Yes, Father," Prince Assur answered. "I asked Mr. Abzu to train 10 pilots who will man and fly this machine. They should be ready anytime."

He turned to the two scientists to explain;

"Mr. Abzu is under my supervision."

"Ah yes, your highness, we are aware. Mr. Abzu is a smart young officer who is dedicated to the program. He is exceptional at what he does." said Mr. Burshmu.

"Your highness, the second Flying Saucer is nearing completion. We will be needing your signature for the release so that Mr. Abzu can start training in it." continued Mr. Balsu.

"Are you saying Mr. Abzu has flown this space ship before?" curious Atalia asked.

Yes, your Grace, many times. We had to test the machine's overall performance so Mr. Abzu had to fly it several times for many hours to make sure that all instruments and engines are working properly." Answered Mr. Burshmu.

"Has this been tested within our planet's atmosphere or in outer space?" Atalia couldn't help but ask.

"We have only taken it up to 50 miles and it was Mr. Abzu who piloted each time."

"Do you want to try flying it yourself, Atalia?" asked the King.

"No, Father, it is too big for me." She turned to Mr. Burshmu, "Where is the Control Center?"

"Right this way, your Grace." Mr. Brushmu showed them the way. "It is in the third floor, so if you step right up here...Mr Balsu will explain all the electronics and gadgets in here. He is our resident expert when it comes to electronics and has designed all these himself."

The Command Center wasn't what the King expected. In fact, he was not sure what to expect at all. Everything was too modern, it seems like something Prince Assur would fully understand. He was pleased and impressed nonetheless.

"Good God, what is this?" the King exclaimed. He was not sure he even knows what everything is called.

The Command Center was fairly small but is pact with gadgets and gizmos the modern times can provide. There were TV and computer screens all around, navigators, communication equipment and many others.

"This is the Command Center, your Majesty. Once the ship starts its engine, the pilot can see all around the ship and can communicate to anyone within. This gives the pilot total control and full access to everything and everyone on the ship." explained Mr. Balsu.

"Thank you both for showing us around," the King gestured to the two scientists. We are looking at the future right here. One day, this ship will allow us to discover and explore neighboring planets in our galaxy, all thanks to your engenuity, hardwork and dedication."

"Thank you, your Highness, we are honored to serve." answered the flattered Mr. Burshmu.

"Your Majesty, you ordered 6 space ships to be built. This one is ready to fly, one is nearing completion while 4 others are still in the assembly line. Soon enough, we will be doing multiple flight tests to make sure the machines are in good running condition. We will notify you of the schedules so you are in the loop. Prince Assur is in charge of all the flight tests."

Mr. Balsu cleared his throat and said: "Your Highness, please let me know if you have any questions about the program, the machine or the process. I will be glad to answer them all for you." He turned to Princess Atalia:

"Princess Atalia, your Grace, are you still interested in flying the spaceship?"

"Oh yes, Mr Balsu. I like to be the captain and have Bonita as my second in command and my communications engineer, right Bonita?"

"I will have to ask my future husband first. I will let you know soon." Bonita answered nervously and jokingly.

They all chuckled, amused at Bonitas nervous reaction including the Prince. He jokingly adds;

"Let me think about about it my love, give me a few days."

The King turned to the Scientists Burshmu and Balsu;

"Thank you for accommodating us today. I think we have seen enough. Shall we go down?"

"Let's go down through the elevator, your Highness." said Mr. Balsu.

After getting off the elevator and out the spaceship, the King walked around the ship to inspect it from the outside. He finds the ship majestic and still can't believe that his people built it themselves.

A few minutes later, they were heading back to the Palace. While enroute, Princess Atalia sent a message to Mr. Abzu;

"I can't believe you did not tell me about you piloting the spaceship for its test flight. I am so proud of you Abzu!"

Mr. Abzu was quick to respond, as if he was waiting for her message all along;

"I'm sorry I did not tell you about, my love. I am just used to being a pilot, it is what I do. Every day I train and fly different spaceships, big and small. I do agree the Flying Saucer is a big one and there is nothing like it, at least not until the other 5 will be finished. If you want, I can tell you all about it. I didn't realize how much you love the flying machine" responded Mr. Abzu.

"Yes, I love it. It is amazing! But I love the person who flies it even more." Messaged Princess Atalia.

"I love you too, my Princess."

The King rode on a separate limousine from his children. He was in a hurry and arrived at the Palace first. He was greeted by the Queen as soon as he got off the vehicle.

"How was the tour? Where are the children?" asked the Queen.

"They are coming. They were in a separate vehicle right behind me," answered the King.

"What took you so long? I thought the tour will be quick. You were gone for about 7 hours."

"We had to visit the Space Training Center first and meet the Anunnakis. We spent some time with them and Mr. Abzu. They also prepared a luncheon for us so we had to oblige. We got to the Flying Saucer Factory only after lunch. We did not notice the time while we were there. The Flying Machine was amazing. You can get lost exploring that thing. I was mesmerized the whole time. It was sleek and modern, it was beautiful. Extraordinary! I will bring you there and show it to you one day. Princess Atalia and Bonita had a great time too, especially inside the Flying Saucer." shared the King.

"You do remember we have guests, right? The King of Mesren and his family came here to spend time with us, especially with you," reminded the Queen.

"I know, I'm sorry I forgot. We just lost track of time earlier. Today was busy. Where are they now?"

"They are in the living room, relaxing. They are waiting for you. Mehaa is waiting for Princess Atalia and Bonita. She is getting bored without them. I should have asked her to go with you earlier today." said the Queen.

Princess Atalia and Bonita came through the door, interrupting the royal couple.

"I'm glad you are here. Did you enjoy the trip?' The Queen asked both Princess Atalia and Bonita.

"Oh Mother, it was amazing!" and then whispered to the Queen; "Did you know that Abzu was the pilot who did the test flight of the Spaceship? He also is in charge of training the Anunnakis. His job is very important to the program."

"I know that he is in charge of training the Astronauts but I didn't know he flew the Flying Saucer to test it. Mr. Abzu is a fine, smart man, I am not surprised. What do you think about Mr. Abzu, Bonita?" Turning to Bonita for her opinion.

"He is a good man, your Grace. One of the smartest officers under Prince Assur. The Prince thinks that without Mr. Abzu, the Space program will not be as successful. It was impressive to watch him in action, training the Anunnakis. And when Mr. Burshmu and Mr. Balsu told us that it was only Mr. Abzu who was allowed to test the spaceship, we were so impressed. But I guess it should not come as a surprise, the Prince thinks Mr. Abzu is the best person for it." Answered Bonita.

"That is great! He is a deserving young man." She turned to Princess Atalia;

"Were you able to talk to Mr. Abzu during the trip?"

"Yes, but not so much. Abzu was busy with Father, showing him around and introducing him to the Anunnakis. We did mesaged each other after the trip." She whispered to the Queen:

"He told me he loved me and I said I love him too!" she whispered excitedly.

"I am happy for you, my dear. By the way, Mehaa is waiting for you and Bonita. She has been waiting for you both since this morning. She was getting bored. I should have asked her to go with you earlier." The Queen continued.

"Oh, poor Mehaa! Where is she now, Mother?" the Princess asked.

"She is in the living room with her parents. Your Father is in there now. Go ahead, hurry."

They wasted no time to ge to Mehaa. They all feel bad that she was left alone all day while they were busy enjoying their trip. The Queen went along with them to the living room. Mehaa was happy to see them.

"Oh Mehaa, we missed you! I am sorry you were alone all day. I wish we had you come with us to our trip." They both hugged Mehaa and then went to greet the King and Queen of Mesren. They then grabbed Mehaa by the hand and they went off to Princess Atalia's bedroom.

Meanwhile, the King and the King of Mesren were busy talking about the economic problems, energy crisis and many other issues affecting them and their people and the Planet as a whole. They are aware that the problem at hand is not a simple one. That it will take cooperation with other leaders to come up with a solution if they are to save the planet. They were brainstorming and discussing all night until about 1am.

"I have already called for a UN Meeting. I was just told it was scheduled for next week. I am glad everyone cooperated for the schedule and treated this with such urgency." said the King.

"That is good news! I am sorry I will not be here but my deputy will be here on my behalf. I am also happy we are able to discuss this today. You know I feel the same way and stand by what you think is the right thing to do. You have my full support." The King Narmar assured the King.

They spent all night and early morning in the living room discussing important matters until it was time to go back to their quarters to rest.

"Your Highness, I want to tell you before I forget, that we are leaving tomorrow. I know we are supposed to stay for one whole week but something urgent came up. I am needed back home." King Narmar was genuinely sad that their trip is cut short especially since Mehaa is having a good time with Princess Atalia and Bonita.

"I want to thank you and your family for hosting us. Your hospitality and kindness is unmatched. I hope you and your family will have time to visit us soon. We would love to host you and return the favor.

The King felt sad that they are leaving so soon. "I wish you could stay longer but our state affairs always come first. We have a responsibility to our people so I understand. I apologize for the days I was not able to spend time with you when I was busy. Please know that I always enjoy your family. My wife and my children love having you here."

The two leaders shook hands and gave each other a pat on the back, headed back to their quarters and went straight to bed.

The next morning, the King and the Queen was awaken by the noise outside their private quarters. Two messenger genies were outside asking for the King's audience with a sense of urgency.

"What is going on? What is so urgent that you have to wake me up?"

"Your Highness, your Grace, I apologize for the intrusion but there is an emergency. One of our Nuclear Plants was attacked. It was the depot mountains. 10 Armed men in an unmarked vehicles raided the depot and stole all the fuel and all our nuclear rods." The Genie reported in panic.

"Was anyone injured?" worried the King.

"Two of our guards were killed your Majesty."

Prince Assur Tudia came rushing in the room already aware of the news. The King turned to the Prince and barked his orders;

"Send 10 bird-head genies to track and follow the hostiles. Make sure they catch them and bring them to me."

"Call Air Force Commander Azarah-Anu and Military Chief, General Tartru. Call them immediately so we can take action."

Everyone jumped into action. The Prince supervised the manhunt and took orders from the King. By 8am the next morning, with the combined efforts of the Air Force and Military under the supervision of the Prince, the thieves were captured and put in prison. The King was immediately notified of the progress.

The Assyrian Nuclear Facility is 100 miles from the Capital, Mat-Assur. It is situated in the dark valley of Dumuz, in the highest mountain peak. The Nuclear Depot was built as a deep tunnel with 3 15-meter-high, 20-meter wide heavy metal gates manned by Special Military Guards. It was built specially to store nuclear fuel, nuclear rods and other nuclear materials for energy use.

The facility was built up the highest mountain to keep its location a secret and away from the public. The road to the facility rough and dangerous. You have to travel up the treacherous path 20-feet wide road. The pathway is equipped with security cameras and heavily guarded by armed personnel. It is one of the most secure facilities in the country. For the people to attempt to raid it, they must be very desperate and brave. No one in their right mind would ever think of robbing the place. But then again, desperate times calls for desperate measures.

It is the day that the Royal family of Mesren were leaving. The King, the Queen, Prince Assur and Princess Atalia was up early to send the family off. They all started with a hefty breakfast. King Assur-Adamu asked his family not to discuss the Nuclear Facility attack in front of their guests. He wanted to make sure their guests have a lovely time until the very minute they leave. He doesn't want to worry them about the attack.

And so they had a lovely breakfast. The topic was light and everyone was friendly.

"We are going to miss you Mehaa. I will miss you! I wish you can stay one more week so we can have more time together." said Princess Atalia.

"I know. I wish I can stay longer but I have to go back to school. It is my last semester in college. I hope to come back one day. Maybe you and your family can visit us back home." Mehaa gor closer to Princess Atalia and whispered, "Don't forget me when you marry Abzu." she teased Atalia.

Princess Atalia blushed. "For sure! I will call you." Princess Mehaa turned to Prince Assur;

"Where is Bonita, Assur? I am going to miss her."

"She will meet you at the airport to send you off," answered Prince Assur.

"So when are you guys getting married? I like Bonita. She is pretty and kind. SHe is fun to be around too. You two look good together. You better get on it before Atalia get married first." said Mehaa jokingly.

"Oh, I hope not! We are planning the wedding right now. It is a lot of work, you know." said the prince.

The Queen overheard them. You are right Mehaa, Bonita is a great lady and is perfect for my Assur. We are planning their wedding and hopefully we can finish the preparations and they will be married next month. I cannot wait to meet my grandchildren!"

The King stood up and raised his glass.

"To the King Narmar, the great King of Mesren and a good friend. Thank you for celebrating the festival with us. We love having you and your family here. I am sorry you have to leave soon but we shall see each other again in no time. Here's to you, the Queen and Princess Mehaa! Have a safe journey.

Everyone raised their glasses to toast for the royal guests.

"Thank you, your Highness. Thank you for your hospitality. Thank you to your family as well." he tipped his glass to the Queen, Prince Assur and Princess Atalia. Everyone drink to the toast.

"Where is lady Bonita?" King Narmar asked.

"She will be at the airport later, your Highness, to send you off." Prince Assur replied.

King Narmar continued his speech…

"Thank you everyone with all my heart. This has been a wonderful week for me and my family. Please visit us soon. I know you are all busy but please find time to visit us."

Soon after, the guests have to leave for the military airport. They were escorted by the genies to their limousine. King Assur Adamu, the Queen and their children followed behind.

When they arrived at the military airport, the King said his goodbyes to his guests and then went straight to meet his top officials to discuss last night's incident. The Queen, Prince Assur and Princess Atalia stayed with the guests and waited for their departure. Soon after, Bonita arrived to join them. They sent off the royal family before heading straight back to the Palace.

The King went straight to the meeting room where his high-ranking officials were waiting for him. They were ready to give him their reports. The King wasted no time adn started the meeting right away.

"What happened last night? How did the thieves get in a very secured facility? Who are they and where are they now?

General Baryoom stood up to answer;

"8 people from a private militia, your Majesty. It looks like they have been planning this attack for months and were planning to sell the fuel to other countries for a big profit. These are well trained personnel, probably ex-military. That might be why they knew of the facility's existence and location. They did not expect the road to be treacherous and security to be tight. They were surprised when the genies caught up with them. The genies flew straight to them and plucked them from the sky straight to prison. We had them interrogated right away and their two vehicles in our military barracks for more investigation. If you wish to meet the criminals, your Majesty, I can arrange that for you. Otherwise, we have retrieved the the stolen merchandise and have them back in the facility. All has been restored, security has been upgraded and I can assure you nothing like this will ever happen again. Kudos to the Eagle genies, Security personnel and the military and the Airforce for the quick response."

The King stood up;

"Thank you everyone, good job! I am beaming with pride at how fast the response was dring the incident. Indeed, your training is paying off well. Thank you for your service and dedication. I will let you have a few more days with the prisoners to get more information. Submit your briefs and findings before Friday so I can pass judgement on all 8 of them. Let us schedule their trial on Friday 10am at the throne room."

"That will be all. Thank you!"

Meeting was dismissed. The King shook hands with his officers and exchanged short pleasantries before he headed back to the Palace for his other duties.

Before 10am Friday morning, everyone was waiting for the King. All the legislators, cabinet members and important military officers are all in the throne room waiting for the King to pass judgement to the 8 thieves. The thieves were brought to the Palace as well but they were locked in a room separate from the throne room. Special guards and genies run a tight security around the thieves to make sure no one get away.

At exactly 10am, four genies escorted the King to the throne room where everyone is waiting. As soon as he came in, everyone stood up and bowed down. The King looked around to see who is present, nodded some courtesies and sat down. Everyone sat down after the King.

The King turned to General Baryoom;

"Are the prisoners here?"

"Yes your Majesty, they are here. They are in a separate room waiting to be called." Answered General Baryoom.

"Did you find out who they are and who they are working for?" the King further inquired.

"Your Highness, 4 of them come from the Kingdom of Eshnuuna and the other 4 are from the Kingdom of Esin. We did not, however, find out who they are working for. They insist that they are only working for themselves. That they are just trying to make money from the energy crisis. I am doubtful they are telling the truth." General Baryoom replied.

"Did you call the Kingdom of Eshnuuna and Esin and inform them about the crime their citizens committed here?" asked the King.

"Yes, your Highness. We have informed both Kingdoms. Both are willing to cooperate in the investigation and help us find out the bottom of all this. They are willing to send officers to coordinate with us. They are just waiting for your orders."

The King was happy to hear that both Kingdoms are cooperating.

"The kingdom of Eshnuuna and Esin are good neighbors and friends of Assyria. I am happy that they are not covering up the crime. I am pleased with that. We have always maintained a good relationship with both Kingdoms. In fact, we have sent help along their way several times. Just last month, they were asking for fuel donations since their energy shortage is much worse than ours. We are in negotiations with them to find ways to help. This could affect that in case their governments are involved although it seems that they are not." He turned to General Baryoom;

"Send in the thieves one by one. Make sure they are on their hands and knees. Have the genies escort them and invite the eagle genies who caught the thieves in here too."

"Right away, your Highness."

The 8 eagle genies marched into the throne room and bowed to pay respect to the King. Everyone in the room gave them a standing ovation and congratulated them on a job well done. Right behind them is General Bayroom and his deputies.

"Your highness, we have the prisoners outside."

"Bring them in one by one." Commanded the King.

General Bayroom signaled to his deputies to bring in the first prisoner. They brought in one prisoner and had in in front of the King's throne on his hands and knees. The King stood up and approached the prisoner. The prisoner is on his hands and knees, his head bowed down. The King put his foot on the prisoners shoulders and pressed on him hard.

"Who sent you to steal and attack our facility?" The King pressed on his shoulders harder. The prisoner is exhausted and very weak. They were up for a few days and nights being interrogated by the military. He did not answer.

"Answer the question and I will go easy on you. Keep quiet and you will be thrown in the dungeon for 10 years." The prisoner bowed his head lower and did not answer. The King pressed harder. The prisoner finally collapsed on the floor and passed out. The King turned to General Bayroom;

"Bring in the next prisoner."

General Bayroom signaled his deputies. They brought in the next prisoner and put him in front of the King's throne on his hands and knees. They did the same thing to each prisoner and each one of them did the same thing. They did not talk or answer the King's question of who sent them.

It took the assembly three hours to discuss with the King the punishment the thieves deserve.They eventually agreed on 10 years imprisonment and sent the prisoners back to the dungeons where they belong.

As the King was about to dismiss the assembly, his deputy Ninos Ninurta approached the King;

"Your Majesty, the UN Meeting you requested is scheduled to start at 10am Monday morning."

"Thank you Mr. Ninurta." The King got up and left the room. This signaled everyone that the assembly was dismissed and they all went on their way.

The next morning, the King, Queen and the Princess Atalia was enjoying the beautiful weather by the garden. They were having a lovely, quiet time until Prince Assur-Tudia came to find the King and interrupt their reverie. The Prince received an urgent call from Mr. Assur Ram from the Assyrian National Observatory Center, looking for his Father. He was roaming around the garden trying to find the King, until his mother, the Queen spotted him first.

"Good morning son. What is wrong?"

"Good morning, Mother. I am looking for Father." he replied.

The King came out of nowhere. "What is it Assur?"

"Father, I received a call from Mr. Assur Ram from the Assyrian National Observatory Center. He said an urgent matter regarding a star they have spotted a million miles behind the sun. He wanted to discuss the possibilities and repercussions before it is too late. He wants permission to come over and talk to you in person."

"Why the urgency? Is this a threat to us, to our planet?" The King panicked.

"I hope not. But we better invite him over as soon as possible so he can tell us about the star and if we are in danger." answered the Prince.

"Tell him to come for lunch at 1:30 today so we can talk about it. I would like to know more about this. Make sure you are here for that too." ordered the King.

"Yes, Father, I will be here. He is bringing his assistant with him along with Mr. Abzu Bet-Anu," answered the Prince.

"Mr. Abzu is a pilot, why is Mr. Ram bringing him along? Oh, never mind. Let them come. This should be interesting." said the King.

The Queen and Princess Atalia was quietly listening in the corner. Princess Atalia light up when she heard Mr. Abzu is coming.

"Be ready Atalia, your friend is coming." The Queen teased the Princess.

Princess Atalia blushed and kept quiet.

Meanwhile, Prince Assur went ahead and sent Mr. Assur Ram a message confirming the schedule the King wanted.

"Father, I just confirmed with Mr. Ram our lunch meeting today at 1:30 here in the Palace."

Princess Atalia was excited to hear that Mr. Abzu was coming for lunch. She sent him a message immediately to confirm.

"Are you coming here for lunch?"

Mr. Abzu responded to her with a confused message.

"I don't know. Am I supposed to?"

"You will find out soon. Wait for it." She replied.

Fifteen minutes later, Princess Atalia received a message from Mr. Abzu.

"I am coming, my dear. I can't wait to see you again!"

Princess Atalia can hardly contain her excitement. She is ecstatic to see her boyfriend again. Mr. Abzu is very busy; they hardly see each other.

Fifteen past 1pm, the guests arrived at the palace. Mr. Assur Ram, his assistant and Mr. Abzu Bet-Anu was greeted by the genies and was led towards the palace main entrance where Prince Assur -Tudia and Princess Atalia was waiting to welcome them.

"Welcome Mr. Ram, we are honored to welcome you to our home." He shook his hand and gestured towards Princess Atalia;

"This is my sister, Princess Atalia."

Mr. Assur Ram bowed his head as a sign of respect for Princess Atalia.

"It is an honor to meet you, your Grace. Your Highness, your Grace, this is my assistant, Mr Irkallu-Enlil."

The Prince shook Mr. Enlil's hand while Princess Atalia gave him a quick courtsy.

The Prince turned to MR. Abzu and said;

"You know my sister, right?" He teased.

Mr. Abzu opened his arms towards Princess Atalia while the Princess quickly came to his embrace. Mr. Abzu gave her a quick kiss on the lips.

"Be careful, do not let Father see you two like that." warned the Prince. The Prince highly approves the couple's relationship and supports them both. But the King has not officially given his approval so they still have to be careful and respect his boundaries.

Princess Atalia blushed at his brother's warning. She did not realize she run to Mr. Abzu's arms that quick and the kiss just happened naturally. She is head over hills in love with Mr. Abzu and she has trouble hiding it.

Mr. Abzu gave the Prince a warm hug. They are good friends and have missed each other a lot since they have not seen each other for almost two weeks. Both have been busy with their respective tasks and duties that they did not have time to catch up and spend time as friends.

Together, they walked up to the King's office. The King and the Queen was waiting for them. The Royal couple stood up to greet them. Mr. Assur Ram approached the King and paid his respects, his assistant right behind him. He formally introduced himself and his assistant to the King and Queen. He was about to introduce Mr. Abzu Bet-Anu to the King but the King stopped him;

"I already know Mr. Abzu quite well Mr. Ram. In fact, we have spent time together on several occasions."

Mr. Abzu greeted the King and went on to kiss the hand of the Queen.

"It is lovely to see you, your Majesty. Your look beautiful today."

The queen smiled and gave Princess Atalia and knowing look.

They all settled around the King's office table and started small talk. The Queen excused herself to check the servants progress in the dining room.

"My son told me you have something urgent about a star coming towards our Galaxy. Can you tell me more about that?"

The Queen came in and interrupted them. Lunch is served and they were all asked to move to the dining room.

"Let's continue this after lunch. Meanwhile let's go enjoy our meal." The King lead them to the dining room where a sumptuous feast awaits. No one discussed serious matters during their meal. The Queen made sure everyone enjoyed their meal and that everyone had second helpings. The food was so good they almost forgot they were there for a serious matter.

Lunch lasted for over an hour. When they were done, they went back to the King's office, got settled and started the meeting again.

Assur Ram wasted no time.

"Your Highness, I asked to come here to speak with you because I think our recent discover will significantly affect all of us, not just your Kingdom, our country but our planet as a whole. I wanted you to be the first to know." He started.

"As you know, we at the Assyrian National Space Center houses all kinds of telescopes and equipment that allows us to have a closer look at our outer space. Our observatories have been instrumental in avoiding possible tragedies of astronomical proportions and find solutions to existing ones. We help monitor and find solution on current situations like pollution, light energy, distortion of electromagnetic radiation, ultraviolet frequencies, X Ray and Gamma Rays."

Recently, Mr. Abzu Bet-Anu came to my office to report that during one of his routine flights with our spaceships, he noticed this small star from afar that he used to see during several flights, now seems larger and closer. He called my attention to see if this is something relevant and needs further investigation. Ever since then, I have been observing the star's movements. Each day the star seems to grow bigger and closer to our Galaxy. It seems to be travelling towards our Galaxy at an alarming speed."

The King turned to Abzu Bet-Anu;

"Mr. Abzu, what do you think?"

Mr. Abzu was surprised that the King was asking for his opinion.

"Your Majesty, I have always noticed this star during my flights. I paid it more attention when I noticed that it seemed to be growing bigger every time, like it is getting closer. I am not an expert so I called Mr. Assur Ram's attention so he can study and keep an eye on it."

"Thank you Mr. Abzu. It was a good call to get Mr. Ram's attention regarding the star. I appreciate that." He turned to Assur Ram,

"Mr. Ram, this seems to be a serious matter. I need you to focus on this and gather enough data so we can come up with a course of action. Give me your full report in a few days or weeks or however much time you need. If a star is headed towards our atmosphere, we need to be ready and make sure we are able to change its path."

Listening intently, Princess Atalia grew weary, she asked,

"Father, if the star enters our orbit and heads straight towards our planet, what will happen to us?"

"Right, what will happen, Father?" joined the Prince.

"This is why we need to monitor the situation so we can keep track of its orbit and where exactly it is heading so we can avoid a full collision with our planet. This is why I need Mr. Ram to dedicate his time and his team on this and give me regular reports. The star might just be another meteor that will pass by our skies. The Galaxy is riddled with meteors and meteorites and other celestial bodies floating around the Galaxy. Some pass by other planets, some will collide. We had our share of that. Our Space Program has always been on top of these situations and avoid possible catastrophes."

"But Father, Mr. Abzu said the star is getting bigger and closer to us!" cried Princess Atalia. She can't help but worry. The thought of a giant star colliding into the planet is scary.

"Let's not worry for now. I trust Mr. Assur Ram and his team will do their best to find answers and help us find solutions if there need be. What we need is more information and not panic. It will do no good for our people and our race if we panic without doing more research and study. Let us wait until we have more data." The King then turned to Mr. Assur Ram and shook his hands.

"Thank you for coming Mr. Ram. Thank you for your service." He shook Mr. Abzu's hand next and thanked him for his vigilance.

"Thank you Mr. Abzu. because of your vigilance, you might have just saved us all."

He shook Mr. Ram's assistant's hand the dismissed everyone.

Prince Assur-Tudia ad Princess Atalia escorted the guests out of the office to their vehicles. The Prince continued the discussion with Mr. Ram and his assistant, while Princess Atalia and Mr. Abzu were busy whispering sweet nothings and holding hands.

"Before we go, can we see the Queen so we can thank her for the sumptuous banquet?" asked Mr. Abzu.

Prince Assur forgot that their Mother did not join them back in their Father's office. He asked Atalia,

"Where is Mother, Atalia?"

"She is probably in the living room" she answered.

"Let's go see her then." Prince Assur lead the way and everyone followed. The Queen greeted with as soon as they entered.

"How was your meeting? I hope you enjoyed the feast I prepared especially for you all."

Assur Ram kissed the Queen's hand and said,

"We did not want to leave without thanking you for the lovely luncheon, your Grace. The meeting with the King went well."

Mr. Enlil, Mr. Ram's assistant and Mr. Abzu expressed their gratitude to the Queen as well.

"It was my pleasure." The Queen smiled. She then whispered to Mr. Abzu,

"Are you happy you came today?"

Mr. Abzu blushed and turned to Princess Atalia and answered,

"I am very happy, your Grace."

"Hush Mother! We have guests." Princess Atalia was embarrassed at her Mother's teasing. She did not want the other guests to know about her and Mr. Abzu especially since they have not received the King's blessing yet.

Prince Assur and Princess Atalia walked the guests to their vehicles to send them off. They shook hands with Mr. Ram and Mr. Enlil while the Prince and Princess gave Mr. Abzu a warm hug to bid him goodbye. They always love seeing Mr. Abzu, especially Princess Atalia.

After the meeting, the King stayed in his office to think and work on the various issues his country is facing. He lost track of time until the Queen interrupted and reminded him that he has been in his office for a long time.

"My dear, your guest are long gone yet you are still here. You have been here for 3 hours since they left."

"I have to work to do, my Queen. We have the UN Meeting on Monday. I have to prepare for that. The energy crisis in our top priority so this meeting is very vital. I was also thinking about what we discussed during the meeting earlier. It seems like there is a giant star headed our direction. It was Mr. Abzu who discovered it and called Mr. Ram's attention so he can monitor the star's movement and gather more data. If it is indeed headed straight our way, then we have another major problem on our plate."

The Queen was saddened by the news.

"Are we in danger?

The King took a deep breath and said,

"We don't know yet. We don't really have hard data yet. This is a recent discovery so I have asked Mr. Ram to monitor and gather enough data so we can know for sure. But if it is headed our way travelling at high speed, we are in danger. Not just us but he whole planet, maybe even our neighboring planets could be in danger. Mr. Ram's work moving forward will be very vital. I hope we won't let us down."

"Oh my God, what is happening? First the energy crisis and now this? What are we going to do, my dear?" worried the Queen.

"Now, dear, the star is still a million miles away. We still have plenty of time to prepare. Besides, we don't have hard evidence to prove that it will collide or at least pass our atmosphere. Let's not panic yet. Let's pray and trust that the Great God Assur will not forsake us." Assured the King.

"What will happen if the star continues is path and enters our atmosphere? Are we going to die?"

"It is still a million miles away, do not worry. It is passes by the sun, it's gravitational pull will propel it towards our orbit and might collide into our planet but if it stays away from the sun, it might just go on a different path away from us." explained the King.

"God help us all!"

"Don't think about it too much. How about we enjoy the rest of the afternoon and have tea? Let's call the children so we can have tea together," said the King.

The Queen called for the Prince and Princess and invited them for tea in the dining room. Prince Assur and Princess Atalia arrived to join them after a few minutes.

Usually, the King and Queen have afternoon tea exclusively to them but the news today made his heart heavy and made him long to spend time with his loved ones.

"What is the occasion, Mother? We never have afternoon tea with you." asked Princess Atalia.

"After that long and serious meeting, your Father wants to relax and unwind with his family. When one is plagued with worries, one seeks the comfort of family. Your Father just want to enjoy a quiet afternoon with us." explained the Queen.

"Ah yes, we were in that meeting too, Atalia and I. The thought of a star travelling at the speed of light heading towards colliding with our planet is disconcerting, a nightmare! But I have been thinking, the star is still a million miles away. It hasn't even passed the sun yet. We have a big Universe with a vast number of galaxies, that gives us a slim chance of getting hit by the star, don't you think?" said the Prince.

"Are you worried, Father?" asked Atalia.

"I was just thinking. If in case the asteroid is headed our way, we better prepare." The King replied.

"Prepare what, Father?" asked Prince Assur.

"Prepare to save our people, our race. In case the asteroid will hit us, I want to make sure that our race lives on. That Assyria lives on. This is the reason we have our Space Program, to discover other planets and other life forms for when the day comes that our planet can no longer sustain us, we have somewhere to go. Mr. Abzu has been training our people. He now has 150 full pledged Anunnakis ready to serve. In fact, an exploratory team has already landed on the planet Earth and their findings are great. Earth can be our future, your future."

"How many Anunnakis do you want to send to planet Earth, Father?" asked Prince Assur. "We only have 5 Flying saucers in production. Each ship can only accommodate up to 100 Astronauts."

"Son, we only need to send 300 Anunnakis, 200 civilian men and 100 women." the King said.

"You really are serious about this Father, aren't you? So does this mean 4 of the Flying Saucers will be for the Anunnakis, men and women, while the fifth ship is for us?" Princess Atalia is now curious.

"No Atalia, your Mother and I will be staying here. We will be staying with our people."

"How long have you been thinking about this and hatching this plan, Father?" Prince Assur probed.

"Not long. Only after our meeting with Mr. Ram. What if the asteroid will collide with our planet, what will happen to us? Where will we go? We have nowhere to escape to. And then I realized we have planet Earth! This is a serious threat, my son, so we have to take this very seriously. You too, Atalia. I pray to God nothing will happen but we have to think about the possibilities." The King obviously have thought about every possibility.

"What about the UN Meeting, Father?" The Princes asked. Not knowing how to express his discomfort over his Father's desire to stay behind along with their Mother, if the asteroid hits.

"I am preparing for that too. I am writing my speech right now. I want to bring some experts with me to the meeting. Some scientists, a Petroleum Engineer, my deputy Ninos Ninurta and you, son." The King wanted to make sure the other leaders fully understand the situation and the consequences."

"Maybe we should bring Mr. Assur Ram too, Father," the Prince reminded his father.

They were interrupted mid conversation by Queen Assurinu and Bonita. They came to take everyone to dining room. Prince Assur-Tudia was happy to see his fiancée. They have not spent a lot of time together lately because the Prince is so busy.

"Thank you for bringing my fiancée with you, Mother." He hugged Bonita right away and said,

"Thank you for coming, my love. Oh how I missed you! I am sorry I have been so focus with work lately, my Father has been keeping me busy."

They all went to the dining room for lunch. Despite the news, they all enjoyed their dinner and were happy in each other's company.

King   Deputy

The next morning, the King had an early meeting with his deputy Nino Ninurta. They started their preparations for the UN Meeting so they started early in his office.

"Good morning, your Highness," greeted deputy Ninos Ninurta.

"Good morning, Ninos," replied the King.

"You are early, my King."

"Ah yes, I am always early Ninos. I always start my work at 7am in the morning. Every day, I wake up 6:30 so I can be here by 7am and start my work. By 9am I will join my wife for breakfast. It is good to follow a strict routine. Eventually, your body will unconsciously follow them like clockwork." explained the King.

"Anyway, Ninos, I want you to attend the UN Meeting with me. I also need you to get in touch with the Petroleum expert Mr. Enlil. We might be needing his expertise when I present my report. The Prince will be join us too."

"That is a good choice your Highness. Mr. Enlil is a top Petroleum expert and will come in handy during our presentation.", Ninos said.

The King took out his papers and showed them to Ninos. "I am preparing my speech. I am calling it "The End of Fossil Fuel: Crisis and Opportunity."

"You mean to discuss how our energy shortage can be an opportunity to change our energy policies and help save the planet and our race?", Ninos inquired.

"And I will explain in detail how our today's problems can be solved by changing social behavior.", the King explained.

At exactly 10am on Thursday, all cabinet members and advisors were at the King's office, waiting for their leader to get ready to go to the venue. The Prince, Mr. Ninos Ninurta and Mr. Enlil were also at the palace early. All three were waiting at Prince Assur-Tudia's office. A few minutes before they headed to the King's office to join him, the office door was opened and Mr. Assur Ram came in. They were happy to see him especially the Prince since he was the one who requested to the King if they can bring Mr. Ram.

They were discussing the agenda of the UN Meeting and briefing Mr. Ram of the protocol for these meetings, when the King's office rang to let them know that the King is ready. They all headed to the King's office and greeted the King. Prince Assur greeted his father and the rest followed suit.

After the short greetings and pleasantries, they then headed to their limousines and were taken to the UN Meeting venue. When they arrived, they all gathered in the room while waiting for everyone in the congregation to be present.

Then the meeting started. They talked about the Annunakis. They have been training for the last ten years under the Air Force pilot, Captain Abzu-Bet Anu, the head of the Annunaki Squadron. All the men under the squad were trained solely for this purpose.

Assur said, "I apologize. Mr. Abzu won't be able to attend the meeting. Our honourable king requested that the meeting be for the councilmen only, so we need to schedule this for another week. Then we might have a better understanding of Nibiru's location." He continued, "We'll call in the experts—scientists, astronomers, the head of the National Observatory Assur Ram, head of Project Rover Isme Dagan, and Mr. Abzu. In that way, everyone will have a chance to ask questions."

"Oh, I forgot to mention Mr. Adini Enlil. He's the head of the company that are manufacturing flying saucers. As of now, they have built 6 saucers and these were already tested by Mr. Abzu and his squad. They're ready to fly them anytime." he continued.

At this time, the King got up from his chair. This signaled that he wanted to address the assembly before him. Turning to the prince, he spoke, "Assur, my son. I want you to be in charge of the Nibiru Project. It is your task to hold all meetings, gather the necessary people that are involved in this project. We have 12 months before this object reaches us. We need all your cooperation. Please inform the families of those involved as well. Is this understood?"

To which Assur replied, "Yes, your majesty."

The King continued, "Now that's settled, let's talk about more pressing matters. I have met with several Tiamat leaders and we discussed the energy shortage. However, we are now facing a much bigger dilemma, which is detrimental to the loss of human existence." With a sad face, he said, "I hope this Nibiru will take a different direction. I can't imagine that our planet will cease to exist because of it."

He then shook his head, suddenly tired from thinking too much about this problem. The rest of the people in the assembly grew quiet, not knowing what would happen to them and their families if they won't be able to stop the collision.

Assur then stood up and spoke loudly. "The King is very disheartened about this situation, and he now needs to rest. Let us end the meeting today, and I will call upon you for our next assembly. Thank you."

Suddenly, four genies appeared in front of the King. It appears that they felt the King's suffering and wanted to comfort him. A few councilmen were alarmed and tried to go near the throne; however, the genies would not let them.

Assur said, "Don't worry. The King is just fine." While he continued speaking, the Queen, Bonita, and Atalia, entered the room, accompanied by the sanitors and two genies. They quickly approached the King, while Atalia tried to hug her father, but they couldn't because of the genies protecting the King.

Atalia felt like crying and was comforted by her mother. To which the King looked up and felt relieved upon seeing his beloved wife and daughter. The Queen then spoke, "Honey, are you alright? Can you walk with us to the palace?" The King replied, "Just give me a few minutes. Let the sanitors leave first then we will slowly follow."

Atalia then approached her father and hugged him tight. "Oh Father!" she exclaimed, while giving him a quick kiss on the cheek. "I love you so much, you know that right?" The King nodded and smiled. He then asked his wife, "Honey, what will we have for dinner?" The queen replied, "Anything you want, my love."

Atalia then said, "Well, mother made Bushala and we weren't able to finish all of it since we ate loaf instead."

Assur chimed in. "I'm sorry. I finished it all off after you both left. I was really hunger." he said apologetically then turned to the King and said, "Sorry father."

The queen then said, "Oh, that wasn't all. I actually left some in the freezer because your father likes it one day old." They all laughed and Assur said, "Now that we still have some left at home, let's all go and eat what's left of the Bushala."

The King then told everyone, "Your mother is very smart." To which, everyone laughed a bit more. He then stood up, his hand tightly held by the queen. They walked slowly, with two genies up front and two more at the back, guarding the royal entourage. After 15 minutes, they arrived safely at the palace.

When they arrived, the King was already in a good mood, especially when he was able to eat his favourite Bushala with his family. The queen also made hot tea, and they all sat talking until 10 in the evening. They had fun, but the King did not mention to his family about the current problem—the planet that's heading towards the solar system and possibly wiping out their planet's entire existence.

Sometime past 10, Assur stood up and spoke. "I will now be taking Bonita home. Father, please take some rest. It is good for you." He then headed out with Bonita on his tow.

A few seconds later, Atalia's phone rang. She quickly moved away from where they were sitting and answered the call from Mr. Abzu. "Hi honey, how are you? It's 10:30pm. Why are you calling at his hour?" "I know. How is the king? Is he well?", Mr. Abzu replied. "Yes, he is fine but he looks upset with something." she answered worriedly. Mr. Abzu said, "I see. Well, say hi to your mother and father for me. I love you." Atalia responded, "Me too. I'll make sure to tell him you called. Bye."

She then walked back to where her parents were sitting and said, "Father, Mr. Abzu extends his wishes. He heard from one of the officials that you weren't feeling good."

The King raised his eyebrows and asked, "That was Mr. Abzu, the pilot? He is a good man." Atalia smiled and replied, "Yes father, he is a very smart gentleman."

It was time for the King and queen to sleep, so they headed upstairs to their bedroom. The King was tired as he had a very long day. Deep in his mind, he knew that the object will do great damage to the solar system, and completely destroy the planet Tiamat.

Two weeks have passed and the prince received a call from Assur Ram. "Yes, Mr. Ram, how are you? Do you have good or bad news for me?", he said as answered the call. Assur Ram excitedly replied, "Your highness, please come quickly to the space center! You should see what's happening. The object has now passed through Neptune and nearing Uranus. It is now within our Solar System!!"

The prince was dumbfounded. In a few seconds, he finally spoke again. "Do you have any proof of this. that this has already passed Pluto?" Assur Ram replied, "I am very certain of this. Mr. Abzu and Mr. Kakku-Dacn have been telling me about this for the past days, that the object is in our solar system. We have been using a very advanced technology so we can now see it in full color on the screen. We can even measure its distance to the planets."

"Very well. Can I bring along the King?", the prince asked. "I am not sure. During the last meeting, I heard he got very ill. I don't want this to worry him." replied Mr. Ram.

The prince then said, "The King wants very much to know what's happening, so I'll make sure he gets looped in on this matter. Please tell Mr. Abzu to meet us there."

He proceeded to look for the King. "Father, I just received a call from Assur Ram. He wants us to go to the space center immediately and see the object on the screen." "Good! I have been waiting for this." the King responded.

"We need to be there in two hours," the prince responded. It was then Atalia heard them and asked to come along; to which the King responded that he was okay with it. So the three of them prepared for their short journey then drove in the King's car.

They arrived at the space center on time. Waiting for them were Mr. Ram, Mr. Abzu, and all the employees. They were ushered inside a spacious room full of computers and big screens. Assur Ram gestured for the King to sit on a chair in front of the large screen at the center of the room. He then sat beside him with the prince Assur on his right and the princess, then Mr. Abzu at their backs.

Assur Ram then called all those who are involved in this project - the scientists, astronomers, and astronauts (the Annunakis), who have been training under Mr. Abzu. They were all introduced to the King. When it was time for the Annunakis, they were called one by one on the platform. When they were all complete, they bowed together in honor of their King. Mr. Abzu then spoke, "Thank you for gracing us with your presence, your highness. Training to become an Annunaki is one of the toughest jobs there is. They would train 12 hours a day, knowing that you stand by them in this endeavor, and gave them the opportunity to become volunteers of this nation." To which the King replied: "You distinguished yourselves as judicious stewards and never flinched in the face of difficult decisions, such as travelling to another planet." "Thank you, your highness, and your family.", Mr. Abzu replied while he bowed to the King. The Annunakis followed suit, and they clapped at their director after the introduction. At the same time, Atalia stood up and clapped her hands for the nice speech.

Assur Ram then went up on the platform. "Thank you, Mr. Abzu. I know your job is hard, but you're doing an excellent job with it. We, and the Annunakis, all appreciate the hard work you have done." Turning to everyone in the room, he said, "Now it's time to show you what you have all been called for. If you look at the screen, you can see the object we have been tracking for months. It is not just any object; it is actually the large planet. We call it Nibiru. As of now, it has now entered our solar system."

The King look worried at the revelation, then asked. "Is this planet going to collide with Tiamat?"

Assur Ram replied. "Your highness, our scientists created a few a program to create the planet's course through our solar system. It is generated by the system based on calculations made. However, it is not a guarantee to be precise since we still need to key in a few factors like its weight, size, and speed, which could affect which direction its taking. We also need to check its distance to the sun to properly calculate its path. A few scientists here are assigned to work on that and we are yet to receive a successful calculation to determine its true course. We need to get an accurate reading as it is really dangerous for a large planet like this to be floating and travelling in space."

He continued. "Now your highness, as you can see on the screen, the planet Nibiru looks a bit faded on screen. We deduce this as a result of travelling at a very high speed across our solar system. We have been getting this image through the largest telescope for our observatory. As of the moment, it is currently between Neptune and Uranus."

Meanwhile, Mr. Abzu was busy explaining the same information to Atalia and Mr. Ram noticed this. He got a bit irritated and told them off. "Our King would like to know more about our current discovery. There are some points that I still need to discuss. I would appreciate it if you could tone it down so we can continue with this. Mr. Abzu, please come sit next to me."

Mr. Abzu looked a bit flushed but said, "I apologize, Mr. Ram. I assure you that this will never happen again." Then looking at Atalia, he said. "Princess, please sit with your brother so we can continue with this important discussion."

Assur Ram, satisfied, continued with his presentation. "This image you see before you is transmitted by our satellites and is transferred in the highest resolution possible." The room suddenly became quiet when they saw the King transfixed on what's on the screen. The King was in awe with the planet Nibiru, which means "the crossing planet" in the Assyrian language.

However, the spell was broken when a white, circular image appeared on the screen. It was Nibiru, with its long tail. Everyone in the room was shocked and surprised, and they all talked loudly and excitedly to each other. Atalia, on the other hand, got really scared seeing the planet for the first time.

She unconsciously grabbed Captain Azbu's arms for support, to which the latter assured her that it was okay.

The King was disturbed to see the planet in full view, and he stood up and asked the room to quiet down. Turning to Assur Ram, he asked. "How far is this planet from us?"

"Your highness, as you can see at the bottom of the screen, this planet is still 2,600 billion miles. However, it would still change as we would need to factor each planet's movements around the sun. Now if you look at the large screen, you can see the location of each planet on the other side of the sun. So we can assume it is more than the estimated distance of 2,600 billion miles. The time and location is very essential to computing this, and to how our solar system works, since all planets are moving in a circular manner around the sun." Assur Ram said.

In a more somber tone, he added. "Your highness, this planet, Nibiru, does not follow any rules of space. It's really scary. It's a lost planet which follows its own course. We can also expect this to bring in a lot of disturbances within our solar system and the eclipses. It could also bombard us with comets, which would miss or hit us with full force. Therefore, we need to see where each planet is, their position in the solar system, so we can determine and somehow predict what could possibly happen. Now Nibiru is possibly travelling on a straight path, that we are hoping for, so it is very likely it will only pass us once and give us a really good chance to survive."

Mr. Abzu then spoke. "Mr. Ram, can you please show his excellency what we have worked on a few days ago? It is the possible collision of Nibiru and Tiamat. As we all know, Tiamat cannot change its course as its path is already set with the gravitational pull of the sun, keeping it in place around the sun while it revolves around it. However, as Mr. Ram mentioned earlier, Nibiru is travelling in its own course. Its speed may change and can greatly affect its direction." Then turning to Mr. Ram, he said. "Please continue to explain to his highness about the program we've worked on."

Assur Ram nodded at Mr. Abzu. "Your highness, Captain Azbu is right. Indeed, we studied the possible collision." He then tinkered on the buttons in front of the screen and proceeded to explain. "You see, the planet Nibiru is 10 times larger than our planet. So when this hits us, it will completely destroy our planet and tear it into a million pieces; killing everything in it. Your excellency, we need to send the Annunakis to planet Earth. They are our only choice in saving humanity, most especially the Assyrian race."

The King turned pensive. He thought about how he appreciates Assur Ram and his patriotism; however, this does not hinder the fact of the possible extinction of their race and the rest of humanity as well. Because of this, he stood up and addressed everyone in the room. "My beloved people. Mr. Assur Ram, Mr. Abzu, I thank you for your hard work and your love for our nation. I most certainly appreciate the time you've put in to help explain about the possibilities of the collision. I am not well, thinking of the loss of humanity; how I fear not seeing my wife, my children, and all those I care about." He got quiet then spoke again, this time to Assur Ram. "Mr. Ram, to what percentage can we expect a collision from this Nibiru?"

"Your highness, I have been watching this planet's every move ever since it was discovered by Mr. Abzu. I have been hoping that it will directly hit the sun. However, based on the recent calculations, there is a strong possibility of it colliding with us—a 75% chance and its happening is inevitable." Assur Ram replied with a somber face.

It was then Prince Assur spoke. "How did you come up with this calculation, that... that it is estimated to be a 75% collision rate? How far do you think it is from us at this moment?"

"Well, as mentioned, we have been closely monitoring its movement. Based on the recent calculations, we still have 18 months before the possible catastrophic event." Assur Ram replied.

Everyone was shocked at this news. He continued, "However, we will continue to monitor the planet Nibiru. We will send weekly reports to the palace and if anything alarming comes up, we will call you right away."

The King rose from his seat and spoke again. "Thank you, Mr. Ram. So you see, Tiamat is in deep trouble. Whether it be 12 or 18 months from now, the inevitable is happening if we don't find a way to stop this thing from coming to us. Now we ask ourselves 'when do we panic?' Well, the panic has already begun - it started with our planet running low on fossil fuel, now it is amplified by the coming of this treacherous planet that is coming towards us. I do not know what we've done to deserve, but why, oh god, is this happening to us?" He cried out in desperation, with arms outstretched before him. He bowed his head out of frustration, then looked up again, composed himself, and spoke. "We have 50 countries in Tiamat and none of them deserves this. Please god, help us! Save us from this apocalyptic event!"

Assur Ram gave a quick pat on the King's shoulder and said, "We will help you, your highness. We will all make sure this does not happen to us."

The King then gave the signal to end the meeting. While he stood up, he saw Atalia crying. He tried to comfort her but she started sobbing loudly. She was afraid of what might happen, about the finality of humanity's extinction. Her brother, prince Assur, tried to comfort her as well but to no avail. It was then Mr. Abzu approached her and tried to calm her. Sensing her beloved, she threw her arms around and continued to sob uncontrollably.

The King then waved a hand to all the other people in the room, bidding them farewell. He then turned to his children and told them that they need to go. Two genies appeared to escort the King and his children to their vehicle. Suddenly, prince Assur stopped in his tracks and called out Mr. Abzu. "Would you like to ride with us to the palace?" Mr. Abzu did not want to go because he just saw his girlfriend's grief over the death and destruction of their planet if the collision will indeed happen. However, since he could not refuse the prince, he relented and rode with the prince to the palace.

The King and the princess arrived first in the palace, closely followed by prince Assur and Mr. Abzu. The King went straight to his office, while Atalia searched for her mother and when she saw her, she ran straight to her arms and cried again. The Queen hugged her tightly, assuring her that everything will be fine.

Meanwhile, prince Assur and Mr. Abzu stayed at the living room. Assur called up his future wife, Bonita, to come to the palace. After which, he then told Mr. Abzu never to mention anything to his beloved about the collision. The Captain asked, "Why not tell her now? It's better to let her know earlier than later." To which Assur responded, "My mother or Atalia will tell her anyway, so let's leave it at that." So they both nodded in agreement.

Suddenly, a genie opened the living room door and Bonita strode in. Prince Assur stood up to meet her, then hugged her and kissed her tight. It was then she knew something was wrong. She pushed him gently and saw tears in his eyes. She asked, "Honey, what's happening? Why are you crying?" "Your highness, please come sit. You too, Bonita. I will tell you everything." Mr. Abzu told the couple, gesturing to the seats across him. Both the prince and Bonita sat on the couch while holding hands while they waited for Mr. Abzu to start. After a minute, Mr. Abzu finally spoke. "There is a planet we have named Nibiru. It is 10 times larger than Tiamat. It is currently in our system and there is a 75% chance of colliding with our planet, destroying everything completely."

Bonita was stunned by the news. She asked, "When will this happen?"

"In 18 months." Mr. Abzu replied.

"So are we all going to die?" She inquired.

To which Mr. Abzu replied in a somber tone. "Yes, we all are."

Bonita could not believe her ears. It was then the shock turned to panic and she cried loudly. She turned to her beloved prince Assur, and they both hugged each other tightly, crying their sadness and desperation of the current situation they are all facing. Mr. Abzu tried to comfort them, but he felt their pain and instead, cried along with them.

He tried to wait for Atalia to come out of the Queen's chambers; however, it appears that the mother and daughter were still busy comforting each other. So he decided to go home and break the unfortunate news to his parents. He thought that in exactly a year from now, civilization will come to an end. Nibiru will collide with planet Tiamat and it would be the end of everything he loves in the world. He shook his head at the thought, and with a lot of pain in his heart, hope that his prediction is wrong.

KING STORM'S DREAM

The King got very busy since the day he came back from the meeting at the space observatory. He was visited by delegates from across the country - the Airforce General, Chief of Military, astronauts, Navy commanders, politicians, scientists, and government officials. Because of this, Prince Assur tried to help his father in entertaining the guests and to make sure that the meeting would go smoothly and all agendas are addressed successfully. Meanwhile, the queen stayed with Atalia, who was still not feeling well. The princess suffered greatly because of the news. In fact, Prince Assur even asked Bonita to help comfort her sister, and requested his beloved to visit Atalia in her bedroom.

At the meeting, the King informed the guests about the current situation with planet Nibiru. Chaos erupted when everyone heard the news and he tried his best to calm everyone down. Although his efforts were futile, he told them to quiet down. "I know how everyone is panicking right now. At this time, I ask you all to be calm and brave. Our God Assur will not leave us to be destroyed, that I can tell you. He will help our nation in times of need, and we must keep our faith strong for him!" Looking around, he continued. "It is in times like this that we need to keep a tight faith. Most of all, we must work together to find a way to resolve this current issue we are facing. I believe that with hard work and cooperation, we can get past this and save our beloved Tiamat."

The guests were still not satisfied but they all agreed with him. Finally, he quickly ended the meeting with a note that he will call to them if the need arises.

At past nine in the evening, the King searched for his wife and daughter. Not knowing where they are, he asked prince Assur of their whereabouts. "Where is my wife and daughter? I miss them and I worry about them." To which the prince replied, "Father, they are in Atalia's bedroom. Come, let's both go to them and see what they're up to."

"No, I am tired. Please get them and let's all gather here in the living room." The King requested. So prince Assur went to his sister's bedroom. When he opened the door, he saw his mother, sister, and beloved all sitting on the bed. Upon seeing him, Bonita immediately rose and ran up to him and hugged him. After which, he pulled away and approached his mother. He hugged and kissed his mother. He then sat next to his sister and asked, "How are you, Atalia?" To which she responded with just a nod to show that she is fine.

"Father wants us all outside. He misses you, mother and sister." Prince Assur said. The queen then rose from the bed, straightened herself and spoke to her daughter. "Atalia, we must compose ourselves and go outside to see your father. He misses you and worries about you." The prince then held Atalia's waist to hoist her up from the bed, with Bonita holding her left hand. "Let's go, honey," he said. The queen walked ahead of them and they followed. When the genies opened the door to the living room, they all entered slowly.

In the middle of the living room, seated at the royal couch, the King sat and waited for them. When he saw his family, he anxiously stood from his seat and walked straight to his wife. He then hugged and kissed her. He hugged Bonita next. When it was Atalia's turn, she sobbed uncontrollably in his father's arms. Everyone tried to comfort her and eventually, her sobs died down and she was able to compose herself. The King then requested everyone to take their respectful seats.

He then spoke to address his wife. "My queen Assurinu, please sleep with Atalia tonight." "I know, sweetheart. I was actually thinking about it," the queen replied. "Are you sure you are okay with your mother accompanying you tonight?" The King asked Atalia. In response, she simply nodded and spoke softly, "I really do not want to be alone tonight." With downcast eyes, she then stared at the floor beneath her.

Bonita saw that the royal family is having their moment, so she spoke to excuse herself. "I am now going home. Thank you for having me here, and Atalia, I hope you feel better. If you need anything, I'm just a phone call away." She then rose from her seat and hugged Atalia, then curtsied to both the King and Queen. She then turned to prince Assur, who took her hand and he drove her home.

Obviously tired from the meeting and the situation with Atalia, the King went to his bedroom. He thought about his daughter, how she's still so young and beautiful, and how worried he is about the looming doom. He thought how Nibiru could completely destroy them and kill everyone on their planet. He thought to himself, "A few months from now, I can see a looming world crisis that could fuel and bring society to its knees. Once the public knows about the collision, chaos will surely erupt and I don't know what to think about what will happen." He shuddered at the thought. Suddenly growing very tired, he slowly put his head on the pillow. In a few seconds, he drifted off to sleep.

KING DREAM

The King twisted and turned on his bed. He was in a dreamlike state. In his dreams, he saw himself on top of the highest mountain. He had his hands up and prayed and worshipped the God Assur. In the middle of his prayer, the sky turned dark and the wind blew really hard. He felt himself shiver, seeing that he was still wearing his nightgown and sandals. He hugged himself to lessen the cold, but the sky grew darker and the wind blew harder. Although he was unable to see anything, the King stayed in his place, raised his hands again and continued praying. Suddenly, lightning struck the dark sky. It struck so hard that part of the sky opened - it opened so wide that a beam of light shone through it. He could not believe it! It was so radiant that he almost covered his eyes at the shiny display. But then, the Assyrian winged bull came flying out of the opening. Flapping its large wings, it swooshed straight from the light and onto him. The king panicked! He did not know what to do so he stood transfixed at where he was standing. When the bull came near him, a meteoroid with a long tail suddenly came out of nowhere and like a bullet, hit the bull. It instantly killed it and blasted it into a thousand pieces, some of which fell to the King and almost crushed him to death. He was flailing and yelling loudly. Then he slowly got himself up, shaking and shivering. He positioned himself on the edge of the bed.

When they heard the King scream, the queen and prince Assur immediately ran to his bedroom. "Father, father! What happened? Are you alright?", the prince asked his distraught father. He saw that his father was not fully awake yet so he shook him again, repeatedly asking if he was alright, until he finally opened his eyes, as if he was in a trance.

The prince spoke. "Father! You look weak and shaken. Did you have a bad dream?"

"Yes son. It was a very bad dream. Terrible. Frightening." The King responded in a trembling voice.

The queen then asked, "What was it, honey?"

"I am fine now. I think I need a cup of tea. Please ask one of the maids to bring one for me." The King requested. "Alright, honey." The queen replied and immediately rang the maids for the King's request.

The King spoke again. "Atalia, is she feeling better?" "Yes. She hugged me while trying to sleep until she finally did. She's sleeping soundly as we speak." The queen assured her husband.

The tea finally arrived and the King immediately drank it. He felt good as he tasted the tea and felt the warmth of the cup on his hands. Satisfied, he turned to his wife and said, "I can sleep now, honey, now that I had tea. Go back to Atalia and make sure she's fine. Take lots of rest, too. I will be at the office now since I'm feeling better and I'll see you in the morning."

The prince asked, "Do you need anything, father? If there's none, then I would like to retire to my room." The King waved him off and told him he got everything he needs. "I will call upon you tomorrow. Please contact all the religious leaders, the chaldeans. I want to speak to them about my dream and have them explain it to me."

"Can you tell me about it right now, father?" the prince asked. "You will hear about it tomorrow, my son. I will tell the chaldeans about it and they'll interpret it if it was a good or bad dream." "Alright, father. I'll see you tomorrow then. Goodnight." The prince then left the bedroom.

THRONE ROOM MEETING

At ten in the morning, the religious leaders and chaldeans have already gathered in the throne room. The deputy, Mr. Ninos Ninurta, along with Prince Assur, waited for the King to enter the room. Meanwhile, the King and Queen were still inside Atalia's bedroom. The King wanted to see his daughter first before he meets with his religious constituents. After staying for a couple of minutes, he then headed out to the throne room.

Six genies escorted the King and Queen to the throne room. Looking around, the King saw 12 religious leaders and the top 10 chaldeans. They were all standing when they entered the room, paying their respects to the royal couple. They remained standing until both the King and Queen sat on their respective thrones.

The room fell silent. Then finally, the King spoke. "It is a great honor to see you all gathered here today. The queen and I are delighted to offer you a warm welcome. Today, we ask that we put aside our differences and instead, celebrate the reason why were are here today." He smiled at everyone in the room, then continued.

"I called you all here today for a special reason. Last night, I went to bed really tired. I thought I would sleep peacefully but instead, had a terrible dream." He told them in detail about his dream and when he finished, he said, "Please do not hesitate to let me know if you have any questions. I just need someone to explain to me and interpret my dream. Take your time to think about it and let me know once you have an explanation."

The religious leaders then gathered on the left side of the room, contemplating on what the dream meant. On the other hand, the chaldeans congregated on the right side, discussing about the possible of the dream. Around 10-15 minutes later, the chaldeans dispersed from their small meeting and told the King they already have an interpretation; about the same time that one of the religious leaders approached him as well with a possible explanation of the dream.

So the King called them both and ask them to discuss their interpretation and come up with one explanation. After the two leaders have finished, the chaldean representative spoke. "Your highness, the dream actually looks good. As we know, we are the largest nation and the most advanced country in Tiamat. The Assyrian winged bull represents the Assyrian people in the last thousand years - its protector, guardian of the palaces, the savior of mankind, the King & his family." He continued, "Then a meteoroid suddenly came into the picture, zooming at a very high speed from the sky. Since the meteoroid is small compared to our planet, we believe that a larger object, a planet, will enter our solar system; one that will destroy and annihilate our existence."

Everyone in the room shuddered at this interpretation, most especially the King, since he very well knew about Nibiru. He urged the chaldean to continue, who was looking at him with a confused facial expression. "However, your highness, you were saved in your dream. You were not hurt in any way. Therefore, we believe that the Assyrian people will not be eradicated but rather, saved from this catastrophe."

The King then asked, "And how do you suppose we get saved then? How will the Assyrian race survive?"

"Your highness, you are the father of our nation. If you were not hurt in your dream, then we strongly believe that the Assyrians will survive. How, that I cannot explain further. Thank you, your highness."

The King agreed. "Very well, thank you for that interpretation, Mr. Shmash. And thank you all." He was about to dismiss the meeting, when he suddenly remembered about the flying machines and thought deeply about what the chaldean meant about them surviving.

Excited, the King rose from his seat and paced the front of his throne. The Queen noticed this and asked his husband about what he was thinking. Then the King spoke. "Honey, I just remembered something! I will tell you more about it after I have done some thinking!"

Prince Assur then stood on the throne platform and spoke to everyone in the room. "Our honorable guests, the King and Queen would like to invite you for lunch. Everyone, please follow the royal couple as they will lead you to the luncheon room."

All the people stood up. The royal couple were escorted by 6 genies from the throne room to the dining area. The guests then followed suit. Once seated, the King called Prince Assur and asked him to get Atalia to join them for lunch. The prince obliged and went straight to his sister's room. Upon arriving, he saw that Bonita was with Atalia, and that his sister is busy talking to Mr. Abzu on the phone. Seeing his brother, Atalia ended the phone conversation and turned to see Assur.

Prince Assur first spoke with his future wife. "Honey, when did you come in?" "Oh, around a half an hour ago, while you were still in the meeting. I came straight to Atalia's room to check on her and keep her company." Bonita replied.

"That is good. Atalia, father wants you to join him for lunch." Turning to Bonita, he motioned for his beloved to take his hand and join him. So the three of them headed to the luncheon room.

When they arrived, both the King and Queen stood from their seats. The royal couple hugged and kissed both women and motioned for them to take their respective seats. Atalia was seated beside her mother, so the Queen asked her how she was feeling. "I am feeling better, mother. Thank you for taking care of me and for sleeping with me last night. I felt really secure." Then in a whisper, the queen asked her how Mr. Abzu is. "Well, I spoke to him earlier before Assur came to get us for lunch. He told me not to worry and promised that he will take care of me." Atalia replied. "I'm sure he would. He loves you very much." The queen responded with a smile at her lovely daughter.

The luncheon ended and each member of the religious sect and the chaldeans came up to the royal family, and thanked them for lunch. The King, in return, thanked them for their time, and promised to call upon them should a situation arise. Then the guests left the room.

When they were finally alone, the King spoke to prince Assur. "My son, I have had a serious thought about their interpretation of my dream. Therefore, starting tomorrow, I would like you, your sister, and Bonita, to train and become part of the Annunakis. We will have your training supervised by Mr. Abzu. You, my son, I want you to train hard and master how to use and navigate the flying machines. Now I know and believe that if anything would happen to our planet, we can always escape using the flying machines. We can go to Earth since there is life on that planet. Understood?"

He looked at them one by one, until they all nodded their heads in agreement.

The prince then said, "Father, I have already been testing and flying out the saucers with Mr. Abzu. I just need to get approval and pass the flying test."

TEST FLIGHT

"That is fine, my son. Be on top of it. Make sure you can start flying it yourself.," the King replied.

Atalia chimed in. "Father, since Mr. Abzu will be training Bonita and I, can we call him for dinner tonight?" Her father chuckled. "Well, your brother here is his supervisor, so he can order it himself. However, I don't really mind him joining us for dinner, so that is fine."

Turning to the prince, he said, "I want you to call Mr. Adini Enlil, the head of the company that manufactures the flying saucers. Please have him in next week's assembly." "I will arrange for it right away, father.," the young prince responded.

The queen, with Atalia and Bonita, left the King and prince, to further discuss about the meeting. As they were leaving, they felt happy - they even danced while walking. The young girls were confident about the turnaround of events and how they still have a chance of continuing their life on another planet, that is is Tiamat will take damage from the possible collision with Nibiru.

Suddenly, the princess was bothered with something and asked her mother. "Mother, will you and father be coming with us?" To which the queen replied, "Well, we only have 6 flying saucers, each can carry 50 Annunakis. So that's a total of 600, with you and Bonita included. There would be no more room for your father and I, but don't worry. We'll never know what will happen, so let's keep positive. And you still have to invite Mr. Abzu for dinner!"

Atalia resigned and said, "Okay, mother. Remember that I love you."

THE ASSEMBLY

A couple of weeks later, an emergency assembly meeting was scheduled. Those in attendance included the military, Airforce and Navy commanders and generals, Mr. Assur Ram from the National Observatory Center, the chief of security, the head of Project Rover, and Mr. Abzu and the Annunakis.

The King entered the throne room with 6 genies accompanying him, followed by the prince and his deputy. The Queen opted to miss this meeting since this is strictly for the men to discuss about the current situation at hand.

Once everyone was in the room, the deputy ordered everyone to be quiet.

Then the King spoke.

"Mr. President of the General Assembly,

Mr. Secretary-General,

Head of the State and Government,

Distinguished delegates,

I call upon you today to tell you some really bad news. I understand that some of you are already aware of what's happening but I want everyone to be on the same boat.

I have been monitoring this news for quite some time new and I believe now is the best time to let you all know. The bad news is - there is a wayward planet that recently entered our solar system. It is currently speeding to our planet. Our experts call it "Nibiru" because it's crossing from one side of the solar system to our side. Our space experts have been telling us that there is a 75% chance that it will collide with Tiamat and completely destroy our planet."

Chaos erupted and everyone was talking excitedly, albeit the panic in their voices. The King signaled for everyone to hush down and continued.

"This planet, Nibiru, is now between Uranus and Saturn, as we speak. We are closely monitoring its path, and our experts have been sending me reports of its movement and whereabouts. We are highly concerned of the high chance rate of collision; however, let us not lose hope. Our experts are looking closely into this. And our God Assur will surely not leave us to suffer and be involved in such a climactic event."

He paused for a while, then spoke again. "There would be nowhere to run or hide when this happens. We cannot help you, only our God Assur can. I hope he takes mercy on us all and redirect this planet and let it stray from its path and not hit us! The universe is a strange and dark place, and no one, not even us, can predict its movements, nor protect us for whatever heavenly bodies it sends our way. We lived on this planet for thousands of years and suddenly, here comes this large planet, threatening our very existence with its coming."

"My friends, it is with great sorrow that I bring you this awful news. However, I am honored and privileged to have spent my entire life knowing you... serving you. We have worked side by side in this very chamber. At this time, I wish the God Assur would help us all and our nation."

"We often say that the hour of death cannot be forecasted. When we say this, we imagine a time when our inevitable death would be years away. We never thought it would come sooner."

There was no applause. Everyone was stunned. They all stared at the King as he sat back on his throne, obviously depressed and heartbroken to be the bearer of such terrible news. Then some of the guest wept, grieving for what's to come to them and their families. They all sat like this for a few minutes when the prince spoke. "Ladies and gentlemen, let us conclude this meeting. It is time for you to go to your families and explain to them about this problem we are all facing. Thank you."

"When is this going to happen, your highness?" one member asked.

The prince replied, "In about 12-18 months. We will provide you an update every week. It is the King's order to make sure that everyone is updated."

Six months have passed since the last assembly. Time was passing really slow and every citizen of the great Assyrian nation were all waiting for word from the King. They were anxious to know about Nibiru's movement and if it was anywhere near their planet. The palace has been giving them updates but they want to know more about it from the experts. So the King ordered the head of the national observatory, Mr. Assur Ram, to hold an assembly with the people in every city, every month. This is to provide them with the latest updates on Nibiru's location and how far along it is from colliding with Tiamat.

Aside from this, a lot have been happening across the nation. Schools and workplaces were closed. Some people have committed suicide. Everyone felt the hope drained from them. They had no answer to their children when asked about what was happening. One by one, the people were simply waiting to die. Some were desperate and constantly prayed to their God Assur to stop this cataclysmic event from happening. In the end, they all wanted to be saved.

Mr. Assur Ram, along with the scientists involved in Project Nibiru, have scheduled a special meeting to those who wished to hear on what will happen to Tiamat when the stray planet would be near them. They held the meeting in a large stadium, one that can occupy 10,000 citizens. Among those who attended were the people from the TV and radio stations, who helped broadcast the meeting live. The King did not attend the assembly, but he sent prince Assur and princess Atalia on his behalf, along with Mr. Abzu. They sat together in silence, and the people were anxiously waiting to hear what the experts have to say. So they all waited for the meeting to start.

Assur Ram stood on the platform and started the meeting with: "What will happen when the planet Nibiru will get close to our planet Tiamat?"

This introduction caught everyone's attention, and every person in the stadium hung on to his every word. He continued by stating the sequence of events, from the day they discovered Nibiru up until its entering the solar system.

"Once this planet approaches ours, there would be nothing we can do to stop the impending doom. There will be nowhere to run or hide. You'll be surprised at how everything you love would be taken away from you - your house, your money, your family, and children - we would all come to an end. Yes, we have been living on this planet for thousands of years with no problem. But now, we are to be vanished completely from the universe, not only humans, but every living thing on Tiamat."

He paused to see everyone's reaction, which was full of anguish. He continued. "Since a large planet is heading towards us, it will result to chaotic effects. Things will start to occur on a slower time scale, an astronomical time scale. For example, our planet is rotating at 1,000 miles per hour. However, we cannot feel this due to its sheer size. But a collision with another planet would rock us to our very core. It is like getting hit by an asteroid, only on a larger scale, and a chain of events will surely take place. It would start really slow then would eventually spread out, taking much worse damage. To give a more concrete example, we would factor in the speed and direction of both Nibiru and Tiamat. When the collision happens, it will be like fireworks. To make it easier to understand, you can imagine two planets free falling towards each other with a speed of 3km/sec as a point of reference."

"To make it short, once Nibiru will get near us, a lot of catastrophic events will take place. From lightning storms to tornadoes, hurricanes that are off their categories. The gravitational force between the two planets will cause earthquakes. When Nibiru gets closer and closer to its collision phase, those living in the part of the planet where it's nearer the location of impact would immediately get vaporized by the raw energy caused by it. Our planet, as we know it, will be destroyed into a billion pieces and vanish from the universe. Thank you."

You could hear a pin drop from the eerie silence that followed the end of Mr. Ram's discussion. After a couple of minutes, the cries of the people have become audible. People started to get up and leave the stadium, holding onto each other with hunched shoulders. The desperation is palpable and Assur Ram felt their pain as well.

The country fell into despair. Even the King's palace, with all its grandeur, became quiet. All activities and meetings were stopped. Businesses have closed due to the people's disinterest. A lot of minds have gone unstable, with people often asking whether they should kill themselves, their children, or their pets. It was a sad time for the Assyrian people. As much as Assur Ram tried to pacify the situation, he cannot bear any longer withholding the information about the impending tragedy that will befall their beloved planet. He often has to evaluate whether to respond to such claims and requests, while weighing the values and reassuring the scientists and the public of the risk with granting further exposure to completely non-scientific ideas.

He also believed that the solar system is potentially a violent one. New computer simulations revealed that there is a strong chance of a disruption with the planetary orbits and this could possibly lead to the collision of Nibiru and Tiamat in the next few months.

Venus and its moon, Mercury, in their diminutive location and sizes, pose the greatest threat. According to the model, when Nibiru first passes Venus, it will cause Mercury to stray from its orbit, making it independent and free-falling in space. Unless the gravitational pull of Nibiru is strong, it pushes Mercury to the sun instead, therefore, creating a massive collision which could cause chaos within the solar system.

These thoughts constantly occupied Assur Ram's mind, and at this moment, he does not know how to create a solution for it.

Prince Assur and Princess Atalia returned to the palace, shortly after the meeting at the stadium. Atalia was still heartbroken upon hearing Mr. Ram's speech, so when she saw her mother, she ran straight to her and sobbed uncontrollably. She remembered everyone in the stadium and their reaction to the bad news - people crying hysterically, losing all hope, as they exited the venue one by one; clearly not knowing of what the future might bring to them - if it's catastrophic or salvation.

The King, upon hearing his daughter's cries, ran out of his office. Outside, he saw the mother and daughter clinging to each other, with the latter still crying loud. He said, "Honey, I understand how you feel. We are all crushed by this news and the impending doom that our God Assur has brought upon us. Our hands are tied and there is nothing we can do but wait for our fateful tragedy to come."

Hearing this, Atalia let go of her mother and hugged her father. "Honey, everything will be alright. You and your brother will be saved. You will be escaping to another planet, I promise you that," the King said.

Atalia cried, "Father! I will not go without you and mother!"

"There, there. I know we all want to be together. But this time, your father and I would want you and Assur to be safe. Whatever will happen to us, we will be in heaven watching over you both as you start anew in the new planet.", the Queen assured her.

Prince Assur then spoke to the King. "Father, I have started flying lessons with Mr. Abzu. We flew over to Egypt and back. Also, both Atalia and Bonita will start training to be Annunakis soon. They should be ready to fly in a few months."

"That's good, my son. But remember, flying to Earth is not the same as flying from here to Egypt. It will take about 6-10 months to travel in space. We do not know what to expect once you arrive on that planet. For all we know, there are black people residing there. Other than that, we are completely blind. I hope God Assur will help you all in that journey.", the King replied.

"Oh, King Narmar and Queen Amasis called me earlier. They were worried about the collision and would want their daughter Meeha to fly with you, son.," he quickly added.

Prince Assur responded. "That's not going to be a problem, Father. In fact, the Egyptians already have 30-40 of their people training to be Annunakis. Father, you promised to help the Egyptians in case trouble will arise."

"I know, son. Which is why I want to know how many flying saucers do we have?", the King asked.

"We currently have 6, Father. However, 2 will be added in the next month. So that makes it 8 in total.", the prince answered.

"Good, good. We will give them one saucer so they can fly and navigate space by themselves when we start our journey towards Earth.", the King said. "In fact, I will call King Narmar now to inform them about this. I'm sure they will be happy to know that they will have their own flying machine to use."

The prince added, "Mr. Abzu and I will be flying out to Egypt again tomorrow. Please inform them that we'll be picking up Princess Meeha so we can bring her back here for training. She will be joining the flying classes with Atalia and Bonita."

TEST FLIGHT 2

At this time, Atalia was elated to hear this news. "That is absolutely great. We'll start training and have flying lessons in the morning. Can I call Mr. Abzu and Bonita about this?"

"Yes, you can call them about this great news.", the prince replied.

So Atalia called Bonita first, who was happy to know that they have something to do in their waking hours. After which, the princess called Mr. Abzu, who was just happy to hear his beloved's voice.

Meanwhile, as promised, the King called King Narmar of Egypt regarding the news. He told him that he will be giving them their own flying machine, which they can use on their journey to Earth. King Narmar was shocked, and told the Assyrian king, "Your highness, my queen and I would like to express our sincere appreciation to you and your family. We are honored to be acquainted with a royal family like yours. We are forever grateful as well for giving our daughter, Meeha, a chance for a new life in another world. On behalf of my queen and myself, we thank you so much for everything you have done to help us."

When her father and the Egyptian king finished talking over the phone, she immediately called up Meeha. On the first ring, the Egyptian princess answered and Atalia quickly told her that they will be picking her up first thing in the morning for their training.

The next morning, the Egyptian king and queen prepared their military airport to receive their Assyrian guests, who were flying. They also arranged a red carpet for the Annunakis to walk on.

The flight to Egypt was successful and they landed at the airport smoothly under Prince Assur's captainship. The king and queen were waiting for them, accompanied by over a hundred military officers. Once they disembarked from the flying saucer, Prince Assur and Mr. Abzu gave the royal couple and a few military officials a tour inside the machine. The Egyptians were clearly in awe of the Assyrian technology.

A few minutes after their arrival, they all headed to the military for a luncheon prepared by the king. It was a festive meal and they exchanged stories about their nations. When the time came for them to leave, the king and queen stood up first, followed by their daughter. When they approached the flying saucer, they both gave Princess Meeha a hug, knowing they will never get to see their daughter again.

So the Annunakis, now with the Egyptian princess on board, bid their last farewell and flew off into the skies - heading back to the great nation of Assyria.

Meeha started training with Atalia and Bonita. The three girls were excited to be able to fly out in space. They worked hard during their training and after 4 months, they were ready. When that time came, they graduated with flying colors and finally embraced as part of the Annunakis.

The end of Tiamat was drawing near. The people wished it would not come sooner, but at that moment, Nibiru has become visible to the naked eye. Everyone who looked up to the skies could see it hovering above them, a signal of inevitable death and destruction. This brought about more desperation in the hearts of the people, most especially the King's family.

At the end of the month, a report came the National Observatory. It read: As predicted, in 3-5 months, the planet Tiamat will see drastic changes in the environment. Oceans will behave like thunderstorms, pulling in warm surface air from all directions. The seas will rise unexpectedly and without warning, causing giant waves to crash down the shores, engulfing the land it reaches. Violent weather is to be expected as well. Dark clouds and heavy rains would last for minutes and sometimes, it will stretch for hours; bringing with it lightning and thunderstorms. Temperatures will become erratic. The heat energy from the equator will rise up to the opposite poles.

Your Highness, the more we are aware of what Nibiru can bring upon us, the better we can prepare for our people. This is to minimize whatever possible damage we might take, including the loss of lives. —Mr. Assur Ram.

After reading the report, the King immediately called upon the prince and his deputy. He then requested his son to contact Mr. Abzu as he would like to hold a meeting with all of them present and discuss about Mr. Ram's latest report.

When he was done with his commands, he sat back and thought to himself, "Why, why God Assur? Why are you punishing us? Take my life and please save my people. They don't deserve to be vanished into this world. Please God Assur, take mercy on us."

It was already tea time and the queen brought the King his favorite tea. However, when she entered the room, she found her husband mumbling to himself, looking agitated about something. Worried, she placed the tea and scones on the table, then rushed to her husband's side. She hugged and kissed him until he came to his senses. She looked at him in the eyes and saw them filled with tears. She was surprised as this was the first time she's seen him in this state. So she asked him, "Honey, why are you crying?" She hugged him tighter and continued. "Are you still dreaming about Nibiru? Honey, it's the will of the God Assur. He rules the universe and he is the Supreme Being. There is nothing we can do if he commands it to be."

"Yes honey, I am crying. My heart bleeds for the millions of families, especially the children. They do not deserve to die like this! And you are asking me why I am crying?" He cried out loud.

"I know, honey. But we are all going to die." The queen responded softly. "It hurts me to think about the fate of our nation, the great Assyrian people; and how quickly our lives will end because of one wayward planet!" He replied in desperation.

The tea has gone cold on the table, yet they both sat side by side. Minutes have passed and they still held onto each other for support. They stayed in this state for a few more minutes when their children, along with Bonita and Meeha entered the room. Atalia rushed to her mother and father and kissed them both. The rest simply greeted the king and queen.

The queen then spoke to them, "Girls, how is your training coming along? Are you ready?" To which Atalia responded, "Yes mother. Mr. Abzu has been careful in training us. In fact, we have already graduated to be Annunakis!"

"That is fantastic! I am so proud of you, sweetheart, and to you girls as well." The queen beamed at her daughter, Bonita and Meeha.

Then the King asked Prince Assur, "Where are Mr. Ninos and Mr. Abzu?" "They are here, Father. Should I call them in?", the prince replied. "Yes, please let them in the room. Ladies, I would like to ask you to leave the room."

The women nodded in agreement and went straight to leave the room. Meanwhile, Prince Assur ushered Mr. Ninos and Mr. Abzu to the office. The King did not wait any longer and asked the men before him to take their respective seats.

"I called you here today for a very important reason. However, let us first talk about the training. How is it going?", he spoke to Mr. Abzu.

"As you can see, the girls are really happy. They have been very obedient and attentive to the training. They have already graduated and are now Annunakis. In a month's time, they will be ready to fly in space. We have also made space suits for everyone.", Mr. Abzu replied.

The King was happy with the result of the training. He quickly asked if it was true that his son, Prince Assur, have been flying one of the saucers by himself. To which, Mr. Abzu responded. "Yes, your highness. He flew by himself to Egypt when we went to get Meeha. I was his co-pilot and there were three communication engineers with us in the machine. He successfully took off and landed the flying saucer with no issues. Even Atalia wanted to fly the machine and I let her sit as a co-pilot for 15 minutes. She really enjoyed it."

"That sounds really good. I am so proud of my son and daughter. I thank you for your help." The King said. "Now, I would like to know how many saucers we currently have?"

Mr. Ninos responded. "From what I know, we already have 6 saucers ready to fly. There are 2 that are in the final testing stage. I believe Prince Assur and Mr. Abzu knows more about this matter."

Prince Assur agreed to that statement and spoke. "Father, Mr. Abzu and I, along with the engineers, have tested the two flying saucers. They have passed and are now ready for flight. We just need to finish adding the things that are necessary for the long journey."

"The two new saucers are updated with the latest equipment. I can assure you that they are in good condition for flying into space.", Mr. Abzu added.

"Very well, that is some really good news. I asked about this because I promised to give two of our flying saucers to Egypt. Will the remaining 6 be enough for the Annunakis?", the King inquired.

"Yes, father. There are currently 300 Annunakis, with 10 crews for each flying saucer. Add the 3 ladies, that will be a total of 363 people for the 6 flying saucers, carrying 60 people per machine.", the prince answered.

Mr. Abzu then said, "Your highness, are you and the queen flying with us? We have more than enough room to take you with us."

The King sadly replied. "Go where? And leave my people here to die? No. The queen and I have decided that we will be staying here with our people until the end of our days. Atalia, Assur, Bonita, and Meeha will be going with you. I am positive that once you have all reached the planet Earth, my son will build a strong Assyrian nation just like what we have now."

"Thank you, father. We are sure to arrive safely there. I promise to create a new world for the Assyrian and build a nation as strong as this one.", the prince said.

The men all nodded in agreement when Prince Assur's cell phone rang. "Hello, Mr. Ram? Do you have anything important to report?"

"Yes. I would like to come to the palace. Something strange is happening to the planet Nibiru and I would like to explain it in detail.", Mr. Ram answered.

The prince relayed this information to his father, who agreed. He then told Mr. Ram to come to the palace immediately.

They all reflected on what that strange thing is happening with Nibiru. While they were thinking, the King told his son to have the queen prepare for tea and snacks for themselves and the guests. At the same time, Mr. Abzu wondered about naming the flying saucers, so he asked the King about this.

"You know; we were so busy that I never thought about this. Perhaps we can think about the names while we are waiting for Mr. Ram to arrive.", the King said.

It was then the ladies entered the room, carrying with them several cups of tea and pastries. They served the men their tea and offered scones and sandwiches. While doing this, the King told his wife. "Honey, we are trying to think of names for each of the flying saucers. Maybe you could help us out with this."

Atalia perked up upon hearing that they were to name the saucers. She whispered to her mother about suggestions, which were quickly declined,

judging by the way the queen shook her head. So she said, "Father, we can name them in our Gods' names. "Anu No. 60", "Exilil No. 50", "EA No. 40", "Sin No. 30", "Shamash No. 20", "Adad No. 10", "Antu No. 55", and last "Ishtar No. 15."

Everyone in the room was surprised at how quickly the princess was able to come up with the names. Mr. Abzu clapped loudly and praised her. The King told his daughter, "Honey! How did you come up with the names? You are really smart. I am so proud of you. I think the names are marvelous!"

"Oh father! I proposed the names to mother first and she liked them. I thought that since we are flying out to another planet, I believe we should bring with us our gods. Just like Shamash, the sun god. Anyway, I'm so glad you like it, father. I did not include Assur though because he doesn't have a number associated with him.", Atalia replied.

The ladies left the meeting room just in time for Mr. Ram's arrival. He quickly greeted the King and everyone in the room. After which, he immediately went straight to business.

"Your highness, something happened in our solar system. As you know, we have been closely monitoring Nibiru's movement. Yesterday, at its most critical point, it has already passed the sun. It was originally far from the sun; however, the sun's gravity pulled it and caused to change Nibiru's direction. It has already passed Venus and as what we initially believed, it would cause Mercury to hit the sun. However, this was not the case. Mercury went on its own path, following a newly created orbit and is now starting to revolve around the sun. The downside is, this paved a better way for Nibiru and it is now heading straight towards us in a very high speed!"

The King grew quiet, as well as everyone in the room. Then Prince Assur spoke, "So you mean to say, we now have 8 planets revolving around the sun, seeing that Mercury has now become a planet?"

"Yes, your highness. I have never thought that such a phenomenon would happen.", Mr. Ram replied.

"Very well. We must now take action and do the preparations. First, we must assign a captain to each of the flying saucers, and the Annunakis that will be accompanying him. Then we need the names of the crew members so everything will be properly organized and everyone is well accounted for.", the prince commanded.

Mr. Abzu replied, "That is a great plan, your highness. We must assign a captain for each flying saucer. However, I must say that the prince should be the head of this mission."

The prince was surprised by this proposal and quickly said, "No, Mr. Abzu. You have been spearheading this mission since it first started, plus you have been the one training the Annunakis, including me. You know better on what to do with the flights and I believe you will take us all safely to Earth."

"Thank you all. Thank you, my King. I will do my best to get everyone safely to Earth, especially your beloved son and daughter. I know it's a long journey from here to there, and I have been constantly checking the distance. Based on the calculations, it will take us much longer to reach our destination planet. However, we are ready to take off any day, at your command.", Mr. Abzu said.

"Do you have enough fuel, food, and water?", the King asked.

"Yes, your highness. We are using atomic fuel for the ships. We are taking extra fuel just for emergency. As for the food and water, we have already prepared for the 6-8-month long travel, so we are taking more than what we have.", Mr. Abzu responded.

"Father, we have a lot of extra room in the saucers. Please come with us. We would like for you to join us in this journey and start anew in a new planet!", Prince Assur cried desperately.

The King looked solemnly at his son and said, "Please do not force us to go with you. I have already explained to you why we needed to stay. I know it's going to be hell here, but this is our fate. Your mother and I will stay here with our people. All that we wish right now is for you to arrive safely. And once you have arrived and established yourselves there, please make Assyria great on Earth!"

We have 3-6 months the planet Nibiru is about to smash into planet Tiamat. Time is ticking and doomsday is getting nearer each day. In the next couple of months, Tiamat will go through a great Tribulation period, where there will be heavenly war on the planet between the religious and anti-religious groups. Millions of people will be killed, slaughtered through murderous beliefs. Suicide is going to be their best solution to avoid the end of days, jumping off from a high building just to kill themselves. May families will burn themselves with their children. They don't want to die or vanish in heat of the two planets during the collision. The world's climate will change drastically, causing numerous natural disasters everywhere.

The last two to three weeks before the collision, there will be a lot of destruction and changes. First, the weather will start to change drastically—heavy rain or snow will be all over the planet. The heat will rise so high that humans cannot withstand it. The snow in the north and south poles will melt completely. Oceans will rise over one meter. Tornados and hurricanes will violently whirl columns of air like funnel-shaped clouds that usually will destroy everything in its narrow paths. Earthquakes and volcano eruptions will be activated by Nibiru's gravitational interaction of the heat from the incoming planet. The ten days for back-up, the planet Tiamat's rotation will slow down drastically and this will trigger the planet to destabilize from its orbit; and when this happens, any loose object or not fasted material will start flying on air towards planet Nibiru, like the cars, humans, buses, trees, and anything else. The ocean waves will rise up to 30-40 feet. High and the coastlines will be swept away. By then, Tiamat is totally destabilized of its orbit and violently pulled by planet Nibiru at the speed of 50 miles per second and the heat between the two planets before collision will rise to a very high degree as the planet Nibiru will rush closer to the planet Tiamat. The time and the impact will increase and the gravity between the two planetary objects will attract each other. The closing speed would be twice the speed of Tiamat's orbital speed. The velocity will be 60 kilometers per second, with just a few hours before the impact. Then a joint Sonomy will travel across the seas and oceans and that immediately will create deadly storm systems and strong lightning, and tornados will turn into hurricanes that will probably be off the category scale.

Since the planets are getting closer in each hour to the impact, there will be serious eruptions of volcanos throughout the whole planet. People who are specifically near the point of impact will be vaporized by the raw energy being released by the incoming planet. On the last minute before the impact, most of the population will die. During the collision, Tiamat will be liquified and every living thing will be vanished forever. This impact will be really bad to the Assyrian nation but good to the solar system.

Within the next few days, Tiamat's orbit will be weakened, causing it to stray from its path and eventually, take the direction of Nibiru's path—finally causing the collision.

A: SOLAR SYSTEM

The planet Tiamat was called the "God of Oceans." When the collision happened, most of the oceans in the planet will be vaporized from the heat of the impact then the vapor will rise up in space, stick together and create a solid, frozen ice that is 2-3 miles in diameter. A thin piece of ice landed on Mars when it was still a moon of Tiamat. So when this piece of ice landed on Mars, in an area the astronomers now call as "Valles Mariners", and when the ice melted, it created an extensive canyon system near Mars' equator. It is 4,200 kilometers long, 7 kilometers deep. This valley has water only one time but the water may still be underground. Planet Mars was white like our moon but the red color comes from the salty water of Tiamat's ocean. Eventually, the water evaporated all over Mars and its surface material contains lots of iron oxide, the same compound that gives blood and rust when exposed to the ocean's salty vapor. This color came to Mars after Tiamat's collision.

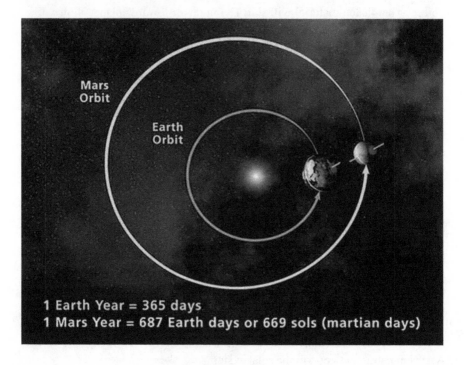

1 Earth Year = 365 days
1 Mars Year = 687 Earth days or 669 sols (martian days)

B: WHAT ARE THE BENEFITS OF PLANET EARTH

8,000 years ago, ¾ of the world was frozen. It was called the "Ice Age." When Nibiru collided with Tiamat, hundreds of large pieces of debris followed it during and after the impact and most of those meteoroids crashed on planet Earth—in the oceans of North Africa, China, Europe, Russia, and the northern part of the United States of America. This created a lot of fire all over the continents, which caused forests to be burned completely. This created a rise in heat and the smoke and carbon dioxide surrounded the affected continents. This changed the global temperature drastically and melted the glaciers in Europe, North America and parts of Russia.

Most of the climate researchers are still looking for answers and some scientists are blaming the "Fresh water diluted the salt water" and "some changes in the earth's rotation and orbit". It is a joke to see scientists make such strong suggestions like they do not want to admit the truth.

C: ASTEROID BELT

It was created by the impact caused by the collision of the planets Tiamat and Nibiru. Millions of pieces of Tiamat are still circling between the orbits of the planets Mars and Jupiter.

D. When the US Army sent astronauts to planet Mars, they will find some Assyrian artifacts to prove humanity.

**The word "Nibiru" in ancient Assyrian language means "crossing". It crossed our Solar System over the other planets; it pushed Mercury away from Venus even before it became a planet. It then collided with planet Tiamat and destroyed it. Then Mars became a planet. The Assyrian Annunakis wrote on thousands of tablets, which was found in the Assyrian capital "Nineveh," about their trip and how they escaped the collision. But unfortunately, the British, French, and Germans have been hiding the secret tablets in museum basements, far away from the reach of scientists.*

It was a bright, Sunday morning, and the King and queen were scheduled to visit the temple. While they were still in bed, the palace's chief of security, Mr. Baryoom, called the private line and spoke to the prince.

Mr. Baryoom said, "Your highness. We found out small pieces from a meteoroid has fallen to Mat-Assur, causing fire and chaos. I am calling to warn and inform you about this. Please relay this information to the king as well."

"Thank you for this information, Mr. Baryoon. I will certainly let the king know of this matter.", the prince said. Immediately after he hung up the phone, another call came in; this time, from Mr. Assur Ram.

"Oh, your highness. I am glad that you have answered. There is currently a situation at Mat-Assur. Very dreadful! Pieces from a meteoroid has landed on the city and it's causing fire and destruction! I believe you all should know and please make sure the king knows about this." Assur Ram said,

"I appreciate you for making us aware of the situation. I will let the king know about this. Please have Mr. Abzu call me.", the prince replied. As soon as he finished that sentence, another call came in and this time, it was from Mr. Abzu.

"Good morning, your highness. We have a problem and the situation is already dire. I have already contacted all the Annunakis and we need you, Atalia, Bonita, and Meeha to all come to the Air Force base at 10am. We now need to fly and leave.", Mr. Abzu hurriedly said.

"This is acknowledged. I will gather up everyone here and will be at the site before that time. Thank you, Mr. Abzu.", the prince replied.

After the call ended, prince Assur ran to his parents' bedroom. "Father, father, wake up! I received a call from our chief of security, as well as from Mr. Ram and Mr. Abzu. Pieces from a meteoroid have fallen and landed at Mat-Assur. There's fire and chaos everywhere. They are expecting the situation to worsen later today. That is why Mr. Abzu has called upon all Annunakis so we can fly out before more pieces will fall and he does not want to get any of the flying saucers to get hit by it; therefore, we all need to leave immediately.", the prince explained to his father in a worried tone. Six genies entered the king's bedroom when they sensed that the situation is dire.

The king replied. "I never thought it would happen sooner. Very well, go and wake your sister. Tell her that we will not be coming with you and make her understand." He looked at his son with a sad face and nodded to the direction of Atalia's bedroom.

Prince Assur then went to his sister's bedroom. "Wake up, Atalia. We need to hurry. We are now needed at the Air Force base. Go and prepare. We need to pick up Bonita then head straight to see Mr. Abzu at the base."

Atalia looked surprised and said, "Why, Assur? What is happening?" She quickly got up and ran to her mother's room. She was more surprised to see 6 genies standing at the door. It was then she knew that something is very wrong, so she went next to her father's room. It was the same—six genies guarding the door. She passed them and saw the king. "Father, what is happening? I can see the genies standing guard outside mother's door. I need to know what's wrong.", she cried.

The king said, "Honey, I want you to calm down. There were some pieces of rock from a meteoroid that have fallen from the sky and it landed in the city. There has been a lot of damage and we need to take precautions."

The queen entered the king's bedroom as well, and when she saw Atalia, she ran to her and hugged her. Then she spoke to the king. "Why are there genies outside of my room?" "Don't worry, honey. It's for security purposes.", the king replied. "What for? What's going on?" So the king explained to her again about the current situation, adding that there were people who died. "Honey, we already knew that this would happen but I didn't expect it to happen so soon!"

"Father, mother, let us go now. It seems that Nibiru's effect has come. The collision is happening very soon. Please come with us to Earth." Atalia begged.

With a sad face, the queen replied. "Honey, I understand how you're feeling right now. But you must go with your brother. Your father and I, we'll be staying here with our people. It's not that we don't want to be with you, but it is our duty to be strong for our nation. That's why we need you and Assur to leave and start anew on Earth. And I wish you a safe trip, honey. Always remember that your father and I love you both."

"No! No! I am not leaving you both here!" Atalia cried out loud. It was then prince Assur entered the bedroom. Seeing the situation before him, he approached his sister and held her by the shoulders, guiding her away from their parents.

"Stop it. Leave me alone! I am not leaving without mother and father. Don't you understand that?", she cried again. This time, the king stood up and hugged her. She cried on her father's shoulders when he spoke, "Honey, you know that we love and Assur, more than you can ever image. However, what about the innocent Assyrians that will be left here? Who's going to be with them? Our God Assur has given us the knowledge to create the flying saucers so we have the instrument to save our people. That's you and your brother and the other Annunakis. We do not have enough for everyone so we're staying here to survive whatever comes our way. Honey, again we love you and we want you to go to Earth and start a new life there. Build a great Assyrian empire just like what we have here."

"You are strong. Your mother and I are confident that you and your brother will survive the journey and create a new life in the new planet. Also honey, I like Mr. Abzu for you. He will take very good care of you and I trust him." With that, he kissed Atalia and hugged her tight. She continued crying until the genies went inside the room and motioned for her and Assur to go out. Her mother would not release her and she held on tight to her. However, the genies were persistent and she was immediately put inside the vehicle that would take them to the Air Force base.

Atalia started crying without stopping, especially when she hugged her mom and would not release her. Atalia was so upset because she did not want to go.

Her brother the prince had to go to pick up his future wife (Bonita), he kissed his mother and father goodbye. he took 3 genies with him in case of an emergency. The prince asked his father to send Atalia with 3 genies ASAP, and he left.

As the king wanted to talk to his daughter the phone rang, it was "Maha" the Egyptian King's daughter calling from Egypt. "Hi, Maha "Atalia said, "how are you ". Maha said "we are fine but we have a lot of fire & a lot of rocks falling on our country, I am going now to the base to fly to another planet, are you going?

Atalia: yes, my brother left to pick up Bonita, I am going very soon, however I can't leave my parents.

Maha: Me too, but we have no choice! my father wants to speak to your dad.

King Narmar: Good morning your Honor, I would like to thank you for this beautiful gift to our country. I told all my crew about the Assyrian hospitality.

this gift will give us hope to establisj a new nation on planet Earth, I'd like to thank you from the bottom of my heart.

Assyrian King: you are a great friend, I hope they arrive safe to planet Earth, that is all we need, it's a very long distance, anyway please give my best wished to your wife "Amasis"

King Narmar: same to you, your honor, regards to the Queen. We love you, make sure Atalia goes with her brother.

The king called 3 genies immediately and asked them to escort Atalia to the base without any delay. King ordered the genies: I do not want any harm to come to her. The weather situation was getting worse by the hour. Atalia was already late for than an hour, and the prince kept calling and sending her messages by phone asking her to rush, because they were leaving.

On the way there was a meteorite hit very close to their vehicle. Fortunately, Atalia did not get hurt but their car was badly damaged. So in order not to waste time one of the genies picked up Atalia to the base, but part of the Building in the base was on fire from the rocks that were falling by incoming Planet Nibiru, but while Atalia was in the air in the arm of the genie, she noticed some of the saucers have already left, she can see the smoke coming out of their engines, however saucer #10 was still on the runway but was ready to take off, because the situation was so critical,while he was trying to take off the genies immediately they dive on the fuselage of the aircraft where the pilot is sitting .

When the pilot saw Atalia he immediately stopped the aircraft and requested his staff to open the emergency exit for her and the 3 genies took off back to the palace. he immediately called the prince who had already taken off, to inform him that his sister is safe with him, the prince told Aweya she was to wear her custom made space suite before the take off. They also informed her fiancée Captain Abzu-bit—Anu, he was thrilled about it. Then her brother and his fiancé spoke to Atalia and they were all thrilled and emotionally excited especially her fiancé Abzu-bit- Anu since he never thought that he will see her again.

Captain Awiya: your honor, you must wear your space suite before you take off.

So she wore the suite and she was given a special seat, she placed her seat belt and then the pilot gave the word to take off.

The pilot, Captain Awiya, turned to speak with the princess. "Your highness, will you be afraid of our take off?" To which she replied no, and told him that as long as he's getting them safe out of her, then she is good.

"If you ever feel scared, just close your eyes and take deep breaths. Hold on to tight to your seat as well.", the pilot added. Then he nodded to the rest of the crew and announced "We are now taking off. Everyone, please hang on."

He continued to speak. "Our saucer needs to catch up with the others. They are 500 miles ahead of us. Please be patient as we try to reach them."

Mr. Abzu contacted him and said, "That was a really good take off. When we are already deep in space, we need to do an orbital maneuver to bring two space crafts close together. This will require a precise match of the orbital velocities and the position vectors of each ship, allowing both to remain a constant distance through the orbital station. We need to create a physical contact and maintain the link. Once we have established that, I will then take Atalia to my ship."

The pilot acknowledged this. "I will inform the princess about this. She has been asking when they will be transferred to your ship. I will let her know of your plan."

"Thank you so much. Please tell her as well that I miss her and that I will be with her soon." Mr. Abzu said. "Right now, I will need you to catch up with us. I can see you are 450 miles away. We are flying at 10,000 miles per hour. To reach us, you need to speed up and do 12,000 to 15,000 miles per hour."

"Yes sir. We are now speeding at 12,000 miles. We'll be seeing you very soon.", the pilot said. He then ended the communication and went to Atalia. "Princess, I have spoken with Mr. Abzu. We are on our way to catching up with his space craft. Once we have reached him, we will rendezvous with the saucer and once a link has been maintained, you will then be transferred to his ship."

Atalia nodded and asked, "Is it possible to be transferred from one ship to another while in space?"

"Yes, your highness. As long as you're wearing your space suit and the special helmet, you will be guided with the transfer from this ship to Mr. Abzu's.", the pilot replied. "He also said that he misses you a lot and that he'll be seeing you soon." With that, the pilot bowed and went back to his place at the cockpit.

They were flying steadily at 12,000 miles per hour. After two and a half hours, they finally caught up with Mr. Abzu's space craft. He then established communication and said "We're right behind you, sir."

Mr. Abzu responded. "Yes, I can see on my screen. Please lower your speed and stay with the group. How is Atalia doing?"

"She has fallen asleep.", Captain Awiya said. "Please let her sleep some more and let me know once she wakes up.", Mr. Abzu told him.

"That is noted. Are we now at the safe zone?", the captain inquired.

Mr. Abzu replied. "I believe we are. We are exactly 18,000 miles from Tiamat. We have an estimate of 2-3 hours from the collision and by then, we should be 35,000 miles away from the planet."

Then he made contact with the captain of saucer #60. "Prince Assur, how are you holding up?"

To which the prince replied, "It was not bad. We had a really smooth flight. How is Atalia?"

"I spoke with Captain Awiya and he said that she is still asleep. I told him not to wake her up yet and he will let me know once she does. How is Bonita?" Mr. Abzu asked.

"Bonita is doing fine, although a bit quiet. I wish Atalia was here so they can talk.", the prince responded.

Mr. Abzu said, "I'll take her on my ship first, then if she wants to travel with you, I'll make sure it will happen."

"Thank you, Mr. Abzu. I will talk to you soon. Let us know if you have already transferred Atalia to your ship." Then the prince cut off the communication.

It was then Mr. Abzu sat back and thought to himself: The impending apocalypse is getting near. I am scared to think of what will happen to Tiamat, of all the people left there, of the King and queen of Assyria. A planet will be wiped out of the solar system. I hope people will remember and cherish the memory of our dear planet.

He was still deep in his thoughts when suddenly, his ship's instruments started to buzz and made noises. It was then he knew that Nibiru has reached Tiamat and finally collided with it. He can feel the shockwave from the impact and his and the other space crafts were shaken from it. He immediately made contact with Prince Assur, who answered in a sad and quivering voice. "Is it real? Did that happen? Oh God Assur, my parents!"

"I am sorry, your highness. The inevitable has happened. Right now, we just have to move forward and start on our journey to planet Earth.", Mr. Abzu responded in a somber tone.

The prince responded. "I appreciate your sympathy, Mr. Abzu. As of now, please do not tell my sister about what happened. I will tell her at the right moment. Right now, please inform the other captains and their crew about the current situation."

"I will do that, your highness.", Mr. Abzu said. He then sent out a broadcast message to all the space crafts. It said: As you all know; the planet Tiamat has been destroyed when Nibiru finally collided with it. Everyone living there has vanished, as we predicted. The prince, princess, and Bonita send their condolences to everyone whose family and friends were left behind. Right now, we need to be strong, be brave; we need to look forward to a new life on planet Earth. As our great king Assur-Adamu I said: I want you to go without fear. Use your Assyrian strength and knowledge to create a new empire under god Assur's name."

He ended the broadcast. He turned quiet when suddenly, he felt a push and their space craft wavered. He looked around as his crew held on tight to their seats. Those who were standing ran to their seats and fastened themselves to avoid the shaking. At the same time, the captains from the different saucers have felt the same thing. Everyone started calling each other via their space communication and they asked Mr. Abzu about what happened.

ESCAPE FROM TIAMAT

He cleared his screen to take a look at what's happening outside and he saw that the space was on fire. He could see fire balls everywhere, remnants of the collision that happened between Tiamat and Nibiru.

"Ladies and gentlemen, I hope you are all alright. I can see that the impact resulted to a mighty force that radiated from the collision site. This force was what we felt a few minutes ago. Also, the fire balls we're seeing in space are remnants from the impact. This will continue to drift off into space and some would possibly hit us and the neighboring planets. Let's all hope that does not happen. Right now, we need to be vigilant. Captains, please make sure to keep an open eye on any approaching debris to avoid getting more damage to your space crafts.", Mr. Abzu announced to everyone.

They continued to travel at high speed, constantly dodging any flying rocks they came across. This went on for about an hour until they got to a part in space where the debris cannot reach them anymore. At that moment, all the space craft went idle and listened to the sound of silence around them. They waited for a few more minutes until they were satisfied that the ordeal was over.

Mr. Abzu then contacted prince Assur. "Your highness, how are you? How is everybody doing?" To which, the prince replied. "We are doing well. Bonita is a bit scared, but who wouldn't be? That was really unexpected and we are just glad that we all survived. My saucer has taken some damage but it is not detrimental to our journey. How about you? Is my sister okay?"

"I am glad to know that you are all okay. I will call Atalia right now and make sure she is doing fine.", Mr. Abzu said. He then called up the captain from Atalia's ship and asked to speak with her. After a minute, she answered the call. "Hello honey, I'm so scared! Are you okay? We are doing fine here but everyone's a bit shaken, including me. The space craft has been hit a few times but it's not that damaging."

"I am so happy to hear your voice and that you are doing well. I know that was a tough time to be but that is all over now. Your brother has been asking about you. Please contact him after we talk so he'll stop worrying about you. I'll talk to you and see you soon. I love you.", Mr. Abzu replied happily.

They continued their journey to Earth. There was no contact from each of the captains as they focused on their flights. Mr. Abzu was thinking about how soon he could get Atalia on his ship to pacify the feeling of constant worry that has been nagging him since they left Tiamat. He wished he could have brought her with him instead. He was deep in his thoughts when he received a call from the prince.

"Your highness. How have you been? Is there anything I can do for you?" He asked.

"I was just checking up on you and how you're all doing. Everyone here is always sleeping, including Bonita. Do you know why?", the prince inquired.

Mr. Abzu replied, "That's the effect of weightlessness as an effect of the microgravity environment. This is what happens in space as it impacts the body three ways: loss of proprioception, changes in fluid distribution, and deterioration of the muscular system. I have explained this to you in the past months during training."

"I see. I'm sorry. My mind is overwhelmed from what's happened. I cannot think straight and never imagined that kind of excitement in space. Our flight simulations were simple and I wasn't prepared for what we went through. Anyway, what can we expect in the next months of our journey?", the prince said.

"I understand your highness. I know how you must be feeling right now. Well, humans perform very badly in extreme environments, including the feeling of isolation and boredom; thinking that Earth is still very far away. A lot would go through the minds of each person here, there, and the other crews. I am worried about everyone's mental state; however, I am confident that no one will go deep down the dark recesses of their minds as these Annunakis were selected by our top psychologists prior to their acceptance in the program." Mr. Abzu explained.

He continued. "But I believe a few of the members are already suffering from depression, and this worries me a lot. I understand that they were thinking of the family members they left behind, who all died during Tiamat's apocalyptic end. I don't believe that we are sailing smoothly in rough seas, but our space crafts have windows. We need to make sure that everyone gets to see what is outside and revel in the beauty of the universe. I will call the other captains so they can check their crew members and help them with the feeling of isolation from this long journey."

Prince Assur agreed to this, and said, "Thank you, Mr. Abzu. I really appreciate your concern for everyone's wellness. I will leave you to it and please, please have Atalia contact me. I need to speak with her, and Bonita does as well." With that, he ended the call.

In a few seconds, Mr. Abzu's line rang again. This time, the call was from Captain Awiya. He answered immediately. "Hello captain. How are you? Is everything alright? Is Atalia there?"

"Yes captain. That's actually the reason why I'm calling. She has already awoken and has insisted to speak with you in private. She slept for 10 straight hours. She's currently in the canteen to eat and the crew here is treating her like a queen." Captain Awiya informed him.

"Well, she is queen. The prince would very much like to speak with her as well. Once she has finished eating, please call me right away. We'll also talk about how we can work on getting her transferred to my space craft." Mr. Abzu replied.

After their conversation, he immediately contacted the captains from the other saucers. He asked how they were doing and informed them to check on their crew members. One of the pilots, Captain Dinka, asked how long until they reach Earth. He responded, "We may arrive in 7 and a half months. This is because we are using nuclear energy packets. Also, we will consider the fact that Tiamat was 56 million light years from Earth and we are travelling at approximately 30,000 mph. We have also taken into consideration of the Earth's revolution around the sun. So in about 110 days, we can pinpoint where its exact location is in the solar system and we'll head straight there."

Captain Dinka appreciated the explanation. "Heads up. We need to rendezvous tomorrow morning. I need to create a strong link with Captain Awiya's ship. Princess Atalia is currently in that space craft and I need to get her to mine. I want you to oversee the process and help us out as well." Mr. Abzu continued.

Captain Dinka said, "Do not worry, Captain. We will make sure to be at the rendezvous spot. Just be careful though. We do not want to lose you."

"Thank you. And do not worry. I will call you tomorrow morning." With that, the conversation ended. But his series of call did not end there. As soon as he hung up, he received another call—this time, from Captain Awiya.

"Captain, I have the princess on the line. She wants to speak with you right now." With that, he handed over the communication device to Atalia. She then spoke to Mr. Abzu, "Honey, how are you? I really miss you." To which Mr. Abzu replied, "I miss you too, honey. It's so good to hear your voice again. I called you a lot of times but you were always sleeping. Did you have a good rest?"

"Yes. I slept for 10 hours. Have you heard from my brother and Bonita?"

"Yes. I have been in constant contact with your brother ever since the incident. I have not spoken with Bonita since she was always sleeping as well. Honey, I need you to prepare your space suit. Tomorrow morning, we will do your transfer to my space craft. You need to wear this as it is specially designed for outer space and will allow you to breathe while outside. Please prepare your belongings but you do not have to bring them along with you. The mission specialists would take care of that and bring them to us." Mr. Abzu said.

The princess agreed and was looking forward to the transfer, when she will be finally reunited with her beloved.

The next morning, Atalia woke up early. Then she prepared herself for the transfer. She wore the space suit that was given to her. After that, she was checked by the specialists to see if the suit was working properly on her, giving her the oxygen she will need while out in space. When everything was ready, Captain Awiya called Mr. Abzu, who then moved his space craft closer to theirs. The hatches for both space crafts were opened and Mr. Abzu waited on his end.

Atalia was then tied by a rope on her waist, while the other end was secured by his crew.

TRANSFER SHIP TO SHIP

He called out to Atalia and told her that everything is going to be alright. "Honey, just walk straight to me. It would feel weird at first to be floating but you need not worry as you are secured with that rope around your waist. I will reach for you when you are close."

Atalia nodded. She started walking or floating slowly. When she was halfway, she looked around and saw the infinite space around her. She had the time to look below and froze. Mr. Abzu called her attention and told her to continue but she would not budge. It was as if her fear had completely taken over her and she could not move. Alarmed, Mr.Abzu motioned for a specialist that they will rescue her. They tied themselves with rope and stepped out of the hatch. Mr. Abzu constantly called for Atalia's attention, saying that she needs to look at him and focus on him only. The specialist reached her first, with him following closely. He was then told by the specialist to just head back as she will bring Atalia to him. He then retreated and waited for them at the hatch. When they finally arrived, he immediately reached out to his beloved and hugged her close to him. He could feel that she was shaking and he assured her that everything is fine now. She removed her helmet then hugged and kissed her boyfriend. They were happy to be finally in each other's arms.

As they were busy catching up, a few specialists have been carrying Atalia's things to the space craft. Once they're done, Mr. Abzu thanked them and closed the hatch. He called Captain Awiya and thanked him for taking care of the princess on his behalf.

He helped the princess settle on his quarters then contacted the prince. "Your highness, we have completed the transfer. Your sister is now here with me. She wants to talk to you." He then handed the communication device to Atalia, who excitedly spoke to the prince. "Brother! I'm so glad to hear from you. I missed you so much. Are you and Bonita alright?"

"Yes, we are fine. How was the spacewalk? We saw you on the screen as it was streamed live for the other space crafts to see. I wanted to see you do it. Tell me about how you feel." Prince Assur asked.

Atalia cried out. "Oh brother, it was really scary! I couldn't move when I saw the space around me. Luckily, Mr. Abzu and a specialist helped and rescued me from where I was standing. or rather, floating."

The prince laughed. "Well, I would feel the same if I was in your shoes. Sister, Bonita wants to speak with you." He handed over the device to his fiancée who then spoke to Atalia. "How are you? I hope you're alright. I miss you. We saw you do the spacewalk and I wondered how you felt."

"As I told my brother, I was scared and I froze. But everything is alright now and I'm already in Mr. Abzu's space craft. Please call me if you're bored, okay? We have a lot of catching to do before reaching Earth." Atalia said.

The six space crafts from the now-extinct Tiamat continued their journey through space. They were restless and everyone was looking forward to reach their destination. Some had doubts that they will arrive on Earth successfully. They tried to busy themselves by remembering the great Assyrian nation by listening to pre-recorded songs and watching clips from the Virtual Space Station that were installed in each space craft. However, this is the only interaction they can get and the loneliness started to slowly creep in to some of the crew. They were trained together as a team but they do not wish to share the psychological difficulties of their experiences.

6-7 months in space was a long time to spend in space for the Annunakis. They were not prepared for such a long journey as it was very different from what they had in training. They also were not prepared for the effect being in space does to their bodies. The blood would rush first to their heads, causing lightheadedness. They would not be able to completely stand up as they were weightless, with the body producing only less blood. Then their muscles grew weaker as an effect of being on zero gravity. It's something they would not notice while still in space; however, the full impact would be felt once they reach land. The most lasting effect would be the brittleness of bones and issues with their eyesight. It would take years for them to recover from the changes in their bodies and it would greatly affect how they would function once they have arrived on Earth.

The human body never evolved to cope with zero gravity conditions. For the entire history of Tiamat and Earth, all living things were used to having gravity, which kept them literally grounded at all times.

Meanwhile, Mr. Abzu ordered all the Annunakis to exercise at least once a day. This will help regulate their blood and minimize the effects of bone brittleness. This would also get their bodies to produce serotonin, which could help them with their possible depression. At the same time, it helps keep their bodies in shape and healthy to be able to walk on Earth. "We do not know what type of humans we are going to face on Earth. As far as we know, they are dark-skinned. I wonder though if they are good or bad people. So we need to prepare ourselves for whatever happens. We need to stay strong and healthy. We have the prince and princess with us and our king's last request was to make sure that we start a new Assyrian empire; to spread our genes and knowledge throughout the planet Earth."

They were already in their second month of the journey and still a long way from Earth. Mr. Abzu kept himself busy with coordinating with the captains. He was happy to know that everyone was feeling better due to the activities and exercise he commanded them to do. However, he sometimes forgot about Atalia. One day, she visited him on his station and surprised him by hugging him from the back, whispering, "Honey, I miss you."

Mr. Abzu was indeed surprised yet happy to see his beloved. He kissed her and hugged her back. "I'm sorry, honey, if I rarely have time for you. I need to make sure that everyone is in shape, both physically and mentally. I also need to check how the other space crafts are as we are still far off from Earth."

"I understand. I know you have a very big responsibility. That is why I visited you here today." Atalia responded. She looked around and was amazed to see the controls. "Honey, I love it here. I wonder how you managed to memorize all these buttons, the controls."

"Well, there are different controls for specific tasks." He replied.

Atalia asked again. "How far are we from Earth?"

"Let me explain. Now focus on the screen. You see, Tiamat is 56 million light years from Earth. While we're traveling at approximately 25,000 to 30,000 mph, we can expect the journey to be completed in 120 days. However, we need to consider the fact that the planet Earth revolves around the sun. Therefore, we need to check its exact location in the solar system so we'll know where we are heading. What I'm saying is, we could possibly reach Earth in around 4 months." Mr. Abzu explained.

"Oh, I see. Thank you for the explanation, honey. But when exactly are we going to see Earth?" She inquired more.

"Probably in another month, I hope. Honey, can you fix me some tea? I am dying for the taste of hot tea." Mr. Abzu requested.

Atalia replied, "Honey, remember that you cannot have tea in the space craft, especially in this weightless environment." She frowned at the thought.

Mr. Abzu chuckled and told her that he was only joking. Now, please do exercise. I want you healthy and strong before we land on Earth. We do not know what to expect from the people there, alright? I love you." With that he kissed his beloved and waved her off to the exercise room.

On the third month, the Annunakis have slowed down their activities. They gave in to the weightlessness and were not spending most of their time sleeping. Mr. Abzu was enraged to know about this and he contacted the other captains and commanded that they need to have their crew up and active. "I want you all to understand that we do not know where we are landing. We need to be in full strength so we can prepare for whatever conditions we might be facing. Please do your job as leaders and force your crew to exercise."

ARRIVING TO NEW PLANT

They were fast approaching Earth and everyone was excited. However, Mr. Abzu has grown weary. He had a lot of things to think about—where they'll be landing, what to look for—these questions have been bugging him and he could not shake them off. He was busy with his thoughts that he did not notice Atalia come in. She tapped him on the shoulder and he was surprised. Then smiled when he saw her.

"Honey, are you okay? You were staring blankly and I'm worried." Atalia asked.

Mr. Abzu responded. "I am fine, honey. I was just thinking about you. I'm always thinking about you and our future together on Earth. Also, we should be able to finally see it today. I am glad you are here so you can be the first to take a glimpse of it." He hugged her while telling her this information.

"Oh, I am so excited! Thank you, honey. I never thought we'd come to the day when we could finally see Earth." She said in an excited tone.

Mr. Abzu said. "I am glad too. I was also thinking about what we need to look for when we arrive. I am worried of running blind in a completely new environment."

"Well, you need to look for a good land that is surrounded by water. The weather should not be too hot or too cold so it would be good for planting and irrigation. Most importantly, you need to look for a place where there's gas, oil, and fuel. I'm pretty sure you have the instruments ready for this, to help detect where to get these natural resources that are essential to living." Atalia suggested.

Mr. Abzu was shocked and warmth spread over him. "Honey, you are not only beautiful but you are a genius as well. I have never thought of that. I am so lucky to have you." With that, he kissed her deeply and the nagging thoughts have quickly dissipated.

"Now, show me the planet Earth, honey. You promised." Atalia told him.

He told her to take a seat in front of the screen. He pushed some buttons and there, right in the middle of it, was Earth. Atalia could not believe her eyes and was in awe of what was before her. She stared at it then felt tears fall from her eyes.

"Honey, it's so wonderful. It's blue and white. I never expected it to be so beautiful! I love you." She cried. "Have you told my brother about this?"

Mr. Abzu replied. "No honey. I want you to be the first to see Earth. If you want, you can call your brother now. You see that button? Press that and you should be able to see each other while on call." Atalia pressed the control and in a few seconds, she was happy to see her brother on the screen.

"Hello, sister. You look good today. How are you? Why are you in the cockpit and where is Captain Abzu?", the prince asked her.

"I am doing fine, brother. He showed me planet Earth. It's so beautiful. Have you seen it yet?" She told the prince. It was then she saw Bonita on the screen.

"Hello, Atalia. We are doing fine here, although a bit sleepy at most times. Your brother is really strong and he's doing his best to command the crew. And I am so happy to know you were able to see Earth first. I'm sure we can look at it later. I'll have to wait for your brother's signal to do so." Bonita said.

"I am sure you will love it when you see it. Anyway, Mr. Abzu is back and I will call you later. I miss you. Please hug my brother for me, okay?" With that, Atalia ended the call.

In a few minutes, Mr. Abzu entered the cockpit and asked her, "Honey, did you tell everyone that they can see the planet Earth on my screen?"

"Why yes, honey. I thought they should know." She responded quickly.

Mr. Abzu laughed and told her, "Well, I told everyone to return to their stations. I will be sending them a picture of it so they won't crowd the command center. I'll be sending the image as well to the other captains. But I'm thankful you told them because you got them all excited. It's been a boring three months and we still have another one to go before we reach Earth."

Atalia got into deep thought and said, "If that's the case, then you should prepare everyone for our arrival. Refresh them on how and where to land. Once we are near, you need to find the right spot on Earth for us to settle."

"You're right, honey. I have been thinking about that as well. It would be hard for me to explain about the landing procedures, so I will write and send it to everyone to flash on their screens. We have 3 more weeks and we have plenty of time to study about Earth's environment while we get near it."

Right after he said that, he received a call from the prince. "Captain Abzu, I heard that you have already seen Earth."

"Yes, your highness. It looks lovely. You can see it now too. I will send you to coordinates and show it to Bonita and your crew." Mr. Abzu replied.

"Thank you, captain. Please inform the other captains as well so they can take a look at it. And we'll see you all soon on planet Earth!" The prince happily said.

Mr. Abzu then sent a message to all the captains with the coordinates to Earth and how they can view it from their screens.

ASSUR SPACE TRANSPORTATION SYSTEM

Mr. Abzu proceeded to work on writing the landing procedure, which he'll be disseminating to the other captains. It included instructions on how to land the flying saucers in a new environment, although he was confident of his fellow captains' skills as they were trained hard for this.

He also included a brief explanation on how their space craft works.

The flying saucer has two, powerful atomic engines. Total thrust of both engines is 10,000 million pounds of thrust. It can fly and land vertically. It can fly in reverse as the engines can be directed at any direction. If the commander wants to turn left, he can simply close the right shutter, and vice versa. The shutter is located at the end of the engines. This releases the pressure in the rocket per speed as set by the commanders.

LANDING PROCEDURE ON THE NEW PLANET

"First, we have to be very careful when landing on Earth. After traveling for several months in space, our bodies are not accustomed to the new environment. When we arrive, we must first close all cabinet doors and put everything in its place. Second, when we are 10,000 miles from Earth, we must slow down our speed to 5,000 mph. This will give us 20 minutes of flight time from its atmosphere to our landing spot. At this point, our flight computers can fly the space craft. It will make a series of banking turns and slow the descent speed as it nears the landing area.

However, the commanders must take control of the space craft to safely land it to the ground. The speed must be slowed down for the descent. Next, the landing gears must be deployed as it gets ready for touchdown.

Once we have landed, we must stay vigilant and follow all commands. All space crafts must be within 1km from each other. We must land vertically if there is no flat land.

Please study this. Take time to practice and exercise. We must have our strength as we embrace the new planet, its environment, and its inhabitants." He reviewed what we have written then sent it out to all the captains.

Three weeks have passed and they were all excited as they are approaching Earth. They

were even amazed when they saw the moon. It was such a majestic sight that Atalia wasteary-eyed when she saw it. Moreover, everyone was working hard and were busy preparing for their arrival. Mr. Abzu was busy scanning Earth for the best possible place to land. He needed the perfect spot where it was surrounded by water and that there should be fuel, gas, uranium and oil. After hours of scanning, he found several locations. He took some photos of it and showed it to the prince. He then asked him to choose. Prince Assur chose the land that was near to a lot of water and large quantities of underground oil and fossil fuel. He agreed to the prince's decision.

He then sent the coordinates of the location to the other captains. When they were received the message, they were all happy. They were thankful to both Mr. Abzu and Prince Assur for bringing them all here. It was at that time that Atalia went inside the cockpit and hugged him.

"Honey, it's good that you're here. We have finally found a good landing spot. Your brother approved of it. It is the perfect place with all the resources nearby. We will start our descent at 10am tomorrow." He informed her.

Atalia was elated at the news. "That's really good. Oh praise, god Assur! Please guide us as we land safely to our new home."

Mr. Azbu told her, "Please get a good night's sleep. Tomorrow will be a long day. Everyone is going to be busy. Once my co-pilot comes in, I will take some rest, too. I need all the energy for tomorrow's landing and it will take some strength in me to command all space crafts at once, and giving the instructions once we have safely landed." He then kissed Atalia goodnight.

As soon as the princess stepped out, he quickly wrote another instruction to the captains. It said:

Please take lots of rest tonight. We have a long day tomorrow. We need all the energy and strength for the landing and to prepare ourselves for what's on Earth. I have sent you the coordinates to our landing spot and we will synchronize during the descent to make sure we land smoothly and safely.

Just in case a space craft would get lost or come across an unforeseen problem, please still follow the coordinates and inform me and the prince right away.

Morning came quick and excitement was in the air. Today, they will finally land on Earth. Mr. Abzu commanded all the pilots to gather around him and follow him closely, with a distance of 1km from each space craft. As they started their descent, they followed and headed towards Earth in an orderly manner. They passed by the moon and Atalia was still in awe.

They sat and admired the moon when a call came from the prince. "Your highness, we will now start our descent. It will take us some time to pass through the Earth's atmosphere. Once we're inside it, we must slow down. The atmosphere is around 100km above the planet and the air grows thicker once we're near the surface." Mr. Abzu informed the prince.

The prince looked at his screen and expressed his concerns to Mr. Abzu. "Why is the northern part of Earth white? And there's a lot of white cloud over it, like smoke from fire."

To which the head captain replied, "It appears that the northern part of Earth is frozen. They must be in their Ice Age era. As for the white clouds, they're large, fiery big rocks that passed us a couple of months ago. They crashed on earth which probably caused fire on some of the places."

After that, Mr. Abzu reported to the other captains that they will be starting their descent. The excitement was palpable in all the space crafts. Their flight path was programmed by the space transportation system. The plan was that the 6 space crafts would come from the west to east; descending at from 100,000 feet above the Arabian sea. They will then continue north at 1,600km from the Persian Gulf. The ground they have chosen should be in that location at the end of the gulf. The river will then go wide and they saw thousands of date palm trees around it. When they reached that area, heavy rain started to fall. He was a bit worried that it might create issues with their landing; however, he persisted and instructed the other space crafts to follow him. It was becoming hard to find the exact spot as the rain grew heavier and it was harder to see. After a few minutes, he landed on a flat ground 300km from the gulf. He requested the others to follow suit and still keep the 1km distance from each other.

They stayed in their space crafts while they waited for the rain to subside, which became torrential as the hours passed. They slept overnight and when morning came, they noticed that it was sunny outside. Mr. Abzu requested all Annunakis to bring some weapons with them as they disembarked from their space crafts. Once they were all on the ground, he called to gather everyone near his ship so they can inaugurate their new king. He waited for the prince to arrive and when he did, everyone started singing the Assyrian national song. The prince was astounded. Mr. Abzu then asked him, "Your highness, we would like to be the king of the new Assyrian nation. God Assur bless you!"

LANDED ON EARTH

The Annunakis clapped their hands in agreement and sang more of their national song. Bonita stood by King Assur's side while Atalia cried from joy.

The new king then addressed his constituents:

"I am grateful for god Assur for bringing us safely to this planet. I would also like to thank you all for your efforts and dedication to the great Assyrian nation. While we are heartbroken with what transpired in our old home, we are now able to start anew. I promise you this—we will build an empire far stronger than what we previously had in Tiamat. We will create a new world and we will call it Mat-Assur—the land of Assur."

Once the prince accepted to be the Assyrian king, all Annunakis started singing Assyrian National Anthem. The King was at the top of the stairs, once the Assyrian Anthem ended.

Both the Prince and Bonita run down the Spacecraft stairs, at first the prince grabbed "Atalia" and started kissing her and wouldn't let her for few minutes. he was so happy to see his sister and Bonita too, she hugged her and then they both cried, it was a happy reunion. Remembering their parents, then the prince hug Captain Abzu and shook hands with all the Annunakis one by one.

Once the celebration of safe arrival to the new planet ended, Captain Abzu requested one of the crew to put one of the most famous Assyrian Music called "Sheikhani" once the music started, everybody 300 of them started dancing, there were all very happy and they enjoyed their new home, at the same time the weather was good and sun was shiny, but unfortunately until then, there was not any sign of any earth people. It was completely silent even though the landing of six spacecraft with 2 rocket engines but there was no sign at all. so the prince ordered the Annunakis to start bringing things down, one they were all busy. Suddenly in 300 feet away from their spacecraft 200 earth people standing away and looking directly on them, but they were all bowing to them trying to worship the new comers. And their hand was up and down. They believe that the new comers are God's from heaven, after looking at them for few minutes, the prince and Mr. Abzu-bet-Anu with few Annunakis with their weapons, they started walking towards the people, the closer they got, the, the prince found out that they are all barbarians, the way they were dressed up, filthy clothes, barefoot all of them, some started going back there were very scared when they got closer, but some kept bowing down. They came 50 ft away, the prince raised his right hand. Some started backing up, but most of them remained.

Finally, the prince and Mr. Abzu tried to talk to them, but there was no response from the earth people. So the prince and Mr. Abzu moved closer to them, some ran away and only few did not move, finally the prince waved his hand to greet them. Only one barbarian touched the prince hand, but he was very scared. But the prince bowed his head to the gentleman. They became good friends, the earth man looked around him, he could not see any of his friends, and they were all gone because they were scared. The prince tried to bring him in to join and see his people and to have good feeling, but the earth man refused because he was scared.

So Mr. Abzu and the prince went back. They were happy because they met the earth humans, now they were white not black. The prince and Abzu were surprised.

Abzu: where are the black that we saw in the Rover lander?

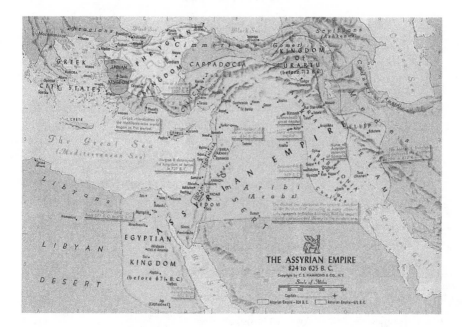

This reminds me of scripture: Genesis 6:1-4

Now it came about when men began to multiply on the face of the land and daughters were born to them that the sons of God saw that the daughters of men were beautiful, and they took wives for themselves, whoever they chose. Then the Lord said, "My spirit shall not strive with man forever because he also is flesh; nevertheless, his days shall be one hundred and twenty years." Annunaki were on the earth in those days and also afterward when the sons of God came into the daughters of men and they bore children to the them. Those were the mighty men who were of old, men of renown."

DEFINITIONS

1. Nibiru: The Planet of Crossing "The Brilliant in the heaven the most of Tiamat keep crossing" Nibiru in Assyrian language means Crossing.

2. Annunaki: "Those whom descended from heaven" "Those who from heaven come" the word only mentioned in Assyrian history "Anu" means sky, "KI" means earth

3. Planet Tiamat: third planet in our Solar System. 7000 years ago, when Mars was the moon of planet Tiamat, it was only mentioned in "Epic of Creation". "Goddess of the Salt Seas"

4. Chaldean: Ancient Astronomers

5. Mesopotamia: Land between two rivers

6. Assur: Assyrian Heavenly god

7. Kuyunjek: Ancient Nineveh

8. Thoth: Egyptian god of knowledge

9. Epic of Gilgamesh: An ancient Assyrian poem that required as the earliest surviving great work literature. Was discovered in library of Assyrian King Ashurpanipal

10. VA/243:   Assyrian Cylinder Seal in Berlin Museum, it shows our Solar System as it was 10,000 BC before Nibiru collided with Planet Tiamat and shows Mars was the moon and Mercury was the moon of Venus.

11. Epic of Creation: the original story of God's creation of the world "Assyrian Genesis "was written 3,500 BC. The Bible story was copied and revised by Jewish writers.

INDEX

BIO

Johnson D. Karam was Born in Baghdad, Iraq. He was a student at the academy of aeronautic in New York, Major in aeronautic design technology. Johnson then moved to beautiful sunny California where he worked at the International Firm Ralph M. Parson as a Civil engineer. In his spare time, he started reading books on Ancient Assyrians history. He traveled all around the globe visiting museums like the Louvre in Paris and the Pergamon museum in berlin. In 2019 the British museum had on display the Great king Asurbanipal Library that was stored in the basement unseen for 180 years. Here I found that my people were not from this planet, so I started investigating the final consequence of sequence of events and in the book show the old and new solar system of the alinement of the plants.

THE FIRST ROCKET
BUILD IN IRAQ IN 1958

BY JOHNSON DAVID KARAM

I was born in Baghdad (Iraq) on 11-11-40 son of David Karam and my mother Nanajan Issac Karam. My father and mother was born in Ormia Iran, my father was from Dizatacha village and my mother from Javilan village. I had one brother and four sisters, I was second youngest in the family.

When I was young, my parents sent me to Christian school up the 9th grade, and the last three years I went to the government school, I graduated in 1960 as a science student in a school called Jafaria high school in Baghdad. All my school life I was an average (B+) student, I never failed in class, but I was unable to be first class student because my mind was in inventing, and making things that I was more interested in. Especially building machines, like cars, airplanes, model buildings, kites. When I was 17 years old, I built a telescope with a tube four feet long with a ten-inch diameter, I used a ten-inch mirror with one side curved and the other end I made a lens with a 45-degree simple mirror that I could see the reflection view from the far distance. I use to look at the moon and stars in heaven, especially in Baghdad at night you can feel the stars, it was so bright and clear at midnight, you can see all the details of cratered on the surface of the moon.

In 1960 after I graduated from high school, I registered in American institute to learn the English language, I studied two semesters because I was planning to study in the U.S. Because my parents wanted me to study in America, especially my father he told American ambassador that "I hate this country I want my son to go to USA and never to come back" I had a lot of time after my high school graduation to spare. And with my spare time, in 1958, I started seriously to design and build a rocket, I knew very little about rocketry and rocket engines.

I started looking for books about rockets and how to make one. It was very hard to find scientific books in Baghdad, I asked my teacher in the American institute, he referred me to the American library in Baghdad very close to the U.S. Embassy. I became a member of the U.S. Library and I was excepted because I was a student of the American Institute. At some time, I was very good in ink drafting, as a matter-of-fact, I started working in the British engineering company called "Binnie, Deacon and Gourley." They were consulting engineers for Dokan Dam in North of Iraq. One of the highest dam in middle east located on Grader River Zab.

246

In the library I found one books that I could hardly understand because of my undeveloped English language. Rocket engineering is not easy. It involves a knowhow of chemical engineering with mechanical processes – to produce such machine, in Iraq was very hard. Especially 1960 Iraq was in revolution, and cannot find any chemicals.

I had my own knowledge of how jet engine and flying bomb of Germany works, and I find this was very easy machine to draw and to build, especially in home, so I decided to considerate to build "Ram Jet Engine" because Ram engine did not have any moving parts in the engine. The ram engine is in between a jet engine and a rocket engine. Ram jet engine uses aircraft fuel not chemicals.

It took me 6 months to build the rocket. I had my own two rooms on the side of our house, none of my parents knew what I was doing, and they did not care because I was always building or doing something ever since I was ten years old. But I kept it secret from all my friends only my cousin his name "Yoush" he was a car electrician he had a car repair shop half an hour away from my home by car. He was very helpful to introduce me to those who can make aluminum body, nose and fins (steering mechanisms of the rocket), I use to give him plans with all the measurements to make sure that all the parts can fit together. Be correctly adjusted or adapted, be of the right size. The rocket engine was very hard to build, and it was very important that we can built it to the specification or per my design. My cousin Yoush had welding machine in his shop, we built it together. It took a few weeks, because we had to find all the special metal, which was not easy to melt in hot temperature in the degree of the heat that will create in the rocket engine. Then we built a fuel tank, 8" diameter and 2'-6" long, which we used a very light metal, then we found very small battery and strong electrical pump that can work to motorize the pump and 2 fire plugs in the engine compartment, the pump and the battery was installed in the middle of the rocket between the engine and fuel compartment. And I had installed a barrier between the engine and battery to keep heat out in the upper compartment. I used aluminum plumbing from the fuel tank to the pump but from the pump to the engine I used copper piping and in the middle of the copper pipe between the engine and pump I installed back flow preventer, to prevent the pressure from damaging the pump motor.

Rocket needed carrier, a vertical support to take the rocket from one place to another. I built it with two tires that I can pull it by our cars, we had an Oldsmobile American car 1955, I was the only driver in the house at the time.

All the time that I was working to build the rocket, I was preparing my college papers, I had sent my final baccalaureate degree to the university of Arizona to study Aeronautical Engineering, and I was accepted. I had a letter from the university to present it to the U.S. Embassy, to get student visa.

One day, I was working on the rocket, and same time I was preparing it for engine test. Every think was ready, the rocket was ready, all the component was tested on the ground. I have asked my uncle David Isacc, of my intention to take the rocket in the car and test the engine at his area, my uncle was living on the outskirts of Baghdad. His house was very far from other houses, and beyond their house there was no other houses, it was new subdivision, so, I thought no one can hear the engine rumbling and heavy rolling sound, during testing the rocket engine. My uncle accepted to test the engine experiment, but he did not know the consequences, I was hesitant too, because I was afraid. The time was very dangerous for a Christian student at the age of 18 to build a rocket and not tell or ask the government especially in revolution time. That was the reason I kept it a secret.

While I was thinking about testing the engine, I thought about my uncle and his family if the military government caught us we will be all in deep trouble nor only my uncle's family, but my family as well. One day I was so busy working in my shop a gentleman came upstairs to see me. This gentleman was a Minister of Public work in Baghdad. His name was Kamal he was Kurdish his wife was Assyrian, she was my sister friend, she uses to make all her dresses by my sister. My sister was very famous dress maker in Baghdad, she knew a lot of rich families in the city. One day Mr. Kamal came with his wife to pick up her dress, but Mr. Kamal had to wait for fifteen minutes for his wife to check the dress one more time. Mr. Kamal use to come to our house with his wife regularly, he uses to like to chat with me whenever he comes with his wife, but I never told him about the rocket. While waiting for his wife to finish, he asked "where is Johnson." my sister without thinking she told Kamal that I was upstairs in my room working on the rocket.

Mr. Kamal, Minister of Public workers was shocked, and surprised. He asked my sister, what rocket? My sister told him "I do not know, go and see yourself what he is building, he is up satire." Mr. Kamal came upstairs to see me with anger in his face especially when he saw a six-foot rocket standing straight up in the middle of the room. "What are you doing, are you crazy, do you know if the military establishment and the government finds out about this rocket you and your family will be in a lot of trouble, even I cannot help you." As he shouted with a loud cry. At this point he calls my father and sister to come upstairs, and he told them that this must be destroyed immediately, without delay. He asked me if anyone knew about the rocket, and I told him, no. He told me that tomorrow at 2pm you will go and see a friend of mine, he is the head of the Iraq Atomic Energy agency, you will take all the plans and all the pictures that you have about this rocket, after your meeting with these two scientist they will report to me immediately. Then I will let you know his opinion about this rocket.

Next day at two o'clock, I arrived and IAE agency as he told me the minister (Kamal) I took all the plans of the rocket and pictures that I had. I arrived at the building and went upstairs to the office on the second floor. I entered at the address as Mr. Kamal gave it to me. The office was very clean and I can see a lot of shelves full of scientific books, the sign on the door says "Iraq Atomic Energy Agency." When I entered, I met a man secretary, he asked me who I was, and I told him my name, and that Mr. Kamal sent me. He replied "Yes, I know, they are expecting you." He took me to a large meeting room. After waiting five-minute two gentleman, well dressed came to the meeting room, they introduced themselves, and they ask me first, "how do I know Mr. Kamal?" I told him he is a family friend. Than they asked me my religion. I told them that I am Christian, Assyrian. Then he asked me, "did you bring all the documents and pictures," and I said "yes" and gave him all plans and pictures. They opened the drawings and started looking at all the plans and details. There were three drawings, 24 x 36, and about fifteen black and white pictures related to the rocket design. After looking at the plans, he asked me if I drew them. I told him yes I did, and he said they are fine drawings and very good in detail. I told them I am a draftsman, and it is what I do, and that I work with British Engineering Company. Again he told me they are very nice drawings, and that I do good work. Both gentleman looked at the pictures and drawings, I could tell they were surprised about all the plans and pictures, they were not expecting that 18-year-old can build such a perfect rocket in Iraq. At last, one of these scientists asked me, "Do you believe this machine will work?" I told them "Yes, I believe it will work." Then he asked me, "Did you test the engine?" and I told him that I did not. Then he said "Wait here, we will be back," and they took all the plans and pictures with them and left the meeting room.

They came back in fifteen minutes and told me they just spoke to Mr. Kamal, and we advise him strongly to tell your family and we are telling you too. "You are Christian Assyrian; we do not want you to be caught by Iraqi Secret Service or military. You are lucky that Mr. Kamal is your friend. We care for you and your family. We advise you to go home and destroy these plans and pictures for your security," and then they wished me good luck and I left the office.

Same day, when I arrived home, I immediately started dismantling the rocket and destroy all the parts, except the extra plans and pictures, which I kept in a safe place. Ten days after Iraqi IAE-interview, when I came home at 4pm, my sister told me that American Library called at home asking for you. She handed me the telephone number to call back. I immediately called back, the secretary of the library answered, I told her my name, she immediately recognized me. She asked, "did you build a rocket?" I did not know what to say, I was afraid I waited for second, then I said yes, and she asked me, "can you bring drawings or pictures?" I asked why, and she said "The library manager will like to see you and the pictures." I said when, and she said "now, he is here" the library was a few blocks from my house, I took everything with me and I went.

I arrived at the library and met the secretary. She asked me to wait, she went inside to let her supervisor know, then she came back and took me to her supervisor. An American that looked like a CIA agent, very educated and knowledgeable, he had very big office and a lot of books all over his office. When I entered the room, he immediately knew my name, he got out of his chair and shook my hand. He asked me to sit down, and asked the secretary to leave and close the door.

He asked me, "can I see what you have?" I handed him all the plans and pictures of the rocket. He started looking at plans, He was very surprise about the details of plans, he asked me, did you do this plans, I told him yes, he said, they are very good plans and details are very clear. Then he asked me "did you finish your high school," and I said yes. He asked if I had the rocket at home, and I told him I did not. He asked why, and I said the government wanted me to destroy it, otherwise I will be in deep trouble with the Iraqi government, so I had no choice only to destroy it. He shook his head, he asked me, "did you build this from the books," and I said "no, I have no book of rocket," he said "but your drawings are very good. The detail is well done and pictures of the rocket looks like the plans, who drew these plans?" I told him that I did, "I work as a draftsman for a British company." "I wonder..." he replied.

"Johnson, you are a very bright young man, the government should care for you and send you to the best university because very few students have the gift that you have, building a rocket in this country they should encourage you, give you help and be proud of you, but not destroy the invention, they have to invest in you!

Now, he paused for a few seconds, then he looked at me and asked, "are you going to continue your education?" I replied "yes, I am going to study in America." He said "very good, I am very happy for you, you will do good, and you will have a successful career in America," he opened the drawer and he gave me his card, he told me if you have any problems in the U.S. Embassy, just give them this card, and then he gave me two books of rocketing. He got up, he shook my hand, and told me "Good luck." But most interesting was before I left the room. the American told me, ever since I came to this country I started reading about the history of this country (Iraq) the Assyrian civilization was one of the most advance culture 5000 years ago and they had dramatic growth in science astronomy and mathematics. This can be in part explained by the Assyrian obsession with universe, stares and Gods. I wonder if this civilization is from this world or came from a different world. You are Assyrian and you have the same blood. That shows you have the knowledge of your ancestors.

Anyway the card that he gave me to show it to the American Embassy, it did work, and help me to expedite my visa.

Johnson D Karam

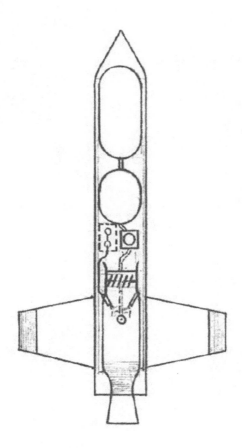

CPSIA information can be obtained
at www.ICGtesting.com
Printed in the USA
LVHW050737031120
670551LV00001B/72